THE DARK CAVALIER

Virginia Rath

THE DARK CAVALIER

VIRGINIA RATH

COACHWHIP PUBLICATIONS
Greenville, Ohio

The Dark Cavalier, by Virginia Rath
© 2019 Coachwhip Publications

Published 1938
No claims made on public domain material.

Coachwhipbooks.com

ISBN 1-61646-478-X
ISBN-13 978-1-61646-478-3

THE DARK CAVALIER

CHAPTER ONE
CURTAIN-RAISER

There was another of the letters under the door this morning. Valerie picked it up, using only the tips of her fingers, handling the thing like some dead insect she was forced to dispose of.

There was never any name on the cheap envelopes or any doubt for whom the message inside was meant. Valerie released the latch and softly closed the front door of their apartment. Geneva had a way of coming up behind you before you knew she was there—and no scruples about reading over your shoulder. If she read this, she would insist that Valerie's mother should be "told." For the letter:

EVEN IF YOU DO HATE HER AND WOULD LIKE TO GET RID OF HER YOUD BETTER KEEP AN EYE ON YOUR STEPDAUGHTER IF YOU CAN SPARE THE TIME FROM PAINTING YOUR FACE TO CATCH ANOTHER MAN, was without question intended for Patricia Farley.

"Crude," Valerie murmured. "If Mother saw this it would mean hysterics and explanations. And after that, Heaven knows what."

The letters were always like this one: stamped in purplish ink on half sheets of slick, thin paper, enclosed in unsealed white envelopes and slipped under the front door. In three months there had been perhaps six altogether.

Valerie realized suddenly that she was not alone in the hall. The new tenant—the slight, dark man whose name was Michael Dundas—had come down the stairs and within a few feet of her before she heard him. She stooped hastily to pick up the folded morning paper, somehow dropped the letter and, grabbing at it frantically, only managed to kick it away with the toe of her green slipper.

"May I?"

He held the letter out to her but he had moved so quickly she couldn't be certain he had not had time to read it. She said: "Thank you," resenting his glance that was impersonal to the point of insolence. And, being feminine, noted the white triangle in his black hair just over one eyebrow and that his eyes were unexpectedly and deeply blue. Then he was gone with only a quick nod for her "Thank you."

Valerie muttered: "Polite! I'm glad Tommy doesn't—doesn't slink," and went back into the apartment and the bedroom she shared with Maxine.

Maxine was sitting up, yawning and running her fingers through her mop of red-gold hair. Even at eight o'clock in the morning she was as extravagantly pretty as a girl on a magazine cover. She said:

"I've got to get my hair done today. And if Mathilde charges me extra for curls, I'll quit her. Why are you up so early?"

"I couldn't sleep. I met our new tenant in the hall," Valerie said, wondering if she could slip the letter from her pocket to a bureau drawer without Maxine seeing it.

"And you in your most becoming house coat. That's luck for you."

"I doubt it, even if I'd been wanting to meet Mr. Dundas. He looked at me like something a not-too-particular cat had laid at his feet."

"I wonder if he's one of these rich Italians. There's plenty of 'em in San Francisco. I saw his furniture: not so much of it, but good. And that top floor back has a view, which means they soak him plenty for it."

"I think Dundas is a Scotch name. And his eyes are blue even if he is very dark."

"I noticed that. I— What's the matter? Another love letter under the door?"

"Y-yes. For Mother this time."

"U-mm." Maxine's green-gray eyes became all gray: cold and shrewd. "I wonder how long they'll risk it."

"This makes about six in three months."

"Unless there's been some you haven't told me about."

"No. I was wondering—"

"If I'd been hiding out some on you? No. But I'll tell you something," Maxine said. "We aren't the only ones who get them."

"Oh—how did you know?"

"Then you know that too?"

"Miss Julian—" Valerie stopped, biting her lip. "I promised not to tell. But she did show me one. Asked me to tear it up and I did. But then I got it out of the wastepaper basket because I thought— Geneva—"

"Damned good idea," Maxine said. "Dear Cousin Geneva would rather go through wastepaper baskets than eat. 'Just to be sure nothing important will be thrown away.' Funny that the Julian should be so confiding. No one else has been."

"But she is confiding. And lately she often looks as if she'd been crying."

"More than usual? She's always crying on account of Brother Charlie's about as easy to live with as a wildcat."

Maxine yawned and lay back on the pillow. Valerie sat down before the dressing table and began to brush her hair.

"We've got too many old maids in this house," Maxine went on. "It's usually some dame suffering from sex repression that writes letters like these—I've heard. Well, there's our own Geneva and the Julian and Sara Putnam—"

"I wouldn't call Sara repressed," Valerie objected. "Not with that to-hell-with-it manner."

"Maybe. But I could tell you something funny about Sara. And her grandmother is crazy as a bat. Nice people!"

"The Callendars are a perfectly normal young married couple."

"I suppose. But they've had at least one letter. I saw one under their door."

"Oh. Was that why you got up early for two or three mornings?"

"Not like me, was it? I'm interested in this business," Maxine said coolly. "We always get the letters in the morning and the Callendars had one. Not that that means anything. The Julians were already up, I think, so they may already have taken their special mail in."

Valerie did not say: "And you read that letter?" Because of course Maxine had. And, though there was no real affection between them, by adhering to an unspoken agreement that each should go her own way and ask no questions of the other, they had managed to avoid friction for four years.

"Of course it has to be someone in this house," Maxine said. "An outsider wouldn't know enough to write the letters and couldn't deliver them."

"Unless it was someone who comes here constantly."

"Who is there among anyone's friends—as long as the Julians and Callendars get letters too—that fits the picture? Who'd know all about all of us?"

Valerie began combing the curling gold-tipped ends of her brown hair over her finger. "You seem to have given the matter a great deal of thought," she said.

"Why not? Of course," Maxine said maliciously, "Tommy is always underfoot and at all hours. But there was that letter to your mother, saying he'd make hay of your money."

"Do you believe that?"

"I think it's a good thing one of you has money and that he hasn't any real objection to it being you. I've always said that. Not that he isn't crazy about you. I've got nothing against Tommy but his so-called sense of humor. He thinks any gal should be grateful when a big, handsome man notices her."

"He teases everyone: not just you. If you wouldn't fire up and make nasty cracks about my money—that I don't get until I'm twenty-one—"

"That's only 'six months to wait. But I was going to say: everyone in this house knows you're engaged to Tommy, and when you get your father's money. Except for the Ortons, who else anywhere near here knows that? It's got to be someone in this house writing those letters. They know I've slipped out at night after I'm supposed to be in bed."

Under the terms of their gentleman's agreement Valerie could not ask: "Why do you? Where do you go?" She remarked instead: "It isn't blackmail. A blackmailer would have evidence and demand money."

"Yes, a blackmailer goes about things in a businesslike way. I think the letter-writer just likes to see people squirm. And I'm almost certain—"

Maxine stopped as Valerie shook her head warningly. Geneva, tall and compactly fleshy, appeared in the doorway with the God's-in-his-heaven-all's-right-with-the-world smile that was particularly hard to endure before breakfast.

"*Good* morning. My, such lazy girlies. And what would they like for breakfast this morning?"

"Orange juice and coffee: same as for the last four years," Maxine said.

"My goodness, did we get up on the wrong side of the bed this morning? Or didn't we get up at all?" Geneva laughed—alone. "Well, you just hop right up and I'll beat up a few muffins and you'll find this isn't a bad old world, after all."

"You should be conducting a Wake-Up-Alone-and-Like-It organization," Maxine said insolently. "Or do you like it?"

"Muffins would be nice," Valerie said hastily. "Mother likes them."

"Dear Mother isn't feeling so well this morning. I'd run right in and see her. And I'll have breakfast ready in just a jiffy—for anyone who wants it."

Geneva withdrew, her substantial corsets creaking resentfully. Maxine said:

"The way she snoops around— Still, if she'd seen any letters we'd have heard about it and— Oh, don't look like that, Val! You know Geneva gets you down too. What does that hair of hers date back to?"

"About 1923, I guess, or whenever it was that the covered-wagon effect went out of style."

"Imagine wearing a rat and back-combing your hair for fourteen years. That rat gets on my nerves, peeping out from her own hair. Someday," Maxine said viciously, "I'm going to yank the thing out. I suppose she thinks I don't know she wouldn't like to strangle me if she could get away with it."

"There are times when I'd like to slap you."

"I guess you would at that." Maxine got out of bed, opened the closet door and looked disparagingly at the clothes inside. "Except for my black and green I'm in rags. If I had your money— I tried on the most gorgeous mink at Liebes' yesterday. If they don't sell it soon I'll buy it. And not on time, either."

She disappeared into the bathroom. Valerie put away her nail file and went down the hall to her mother's room. Patricia Farley was lying back against a mound of silk-and-lace pillows, studying her tiny-featured, pink-and-white face in a small hand mirror.

"Oh—Valerie. I had the most terrible night. I lay awake for simply hours. My nerves. I thought I would sc-*ream*. But I wouldn't disturb anyone."

Valerie sat down, only half listening to the petulant, childish voice. But when it stopped she said automatically:

"I'm sorry, Mother. I hope you feel better now."

"Ye-es. But I'll have a tray, just this once. I'm not hungry but I don't want to risk a headache."

Valerie moved restlessly. The air was heavy with the thick scent of powders, creams and perfumes and the windows were up only a cautious half-foot.

"I do wish you wouldn't fidget, Valerie. You never listen to me. Don't you think a party would be nice?"

"What kind of party?"

"Oh—something informal. Tonight, maybe. We could ask the new man who moved in yesterday. That would be a friendly gesture."

Valerie got up and went to the window, looking down at the slope of the back garden. Patricia's parties were inexpressibly painful. Herself, Valerie and Maxine—and young or youngish men invited by the two girls. Besides Geneva, so openly effacing herself when she wasn't carrying around trays of food. And the men were bored—as John Dozier had been—or slightly bewildered, or simply thought Patricia was funny.

And she couldn't understand why the "nice young men" didn't accept her invitations to drop in to tea "just any afternoon." The ones who did come back usually turned out to be "not at all nice." Well, at least Patricia was too indolent to go out to hotels, night clubs—wherever women like her did go looking for unattached men.

"I'm afraid it's too short notice," Valerie said. "And I promised to stay all night with Lucie Orton. Tommy and I are going to a show tonight with her and Herbert."

"Oh, so it's Lucie and Herbert now, is it? What can he see in a pasty-faced little stenographer? If you hadn't treated Herbert so badly—"

"I treated Herbert just as he wanted to be treated, Mother. He was never in love with me."

"Nonsense. Men don't know who they're in love with. And Herbert is such a promising young lawyer and he has connections and a private income. But no! You have to throw yourself away on a penniless young nobody!"

Valerie looked at the dressing table and a silver-framed photograph of her father. She saw in the pictured face her own wide-spaced hazel eyes, broad forehead and generous, full-lipped mouth. She had not been too young when he died to forget the sunny tolerance of his smile. And, turning to glance at another photograph, this one of Wayne Farley, handsome, unimpressive in mouth and chin, she said lightly:

"Well, Mother, you married twice for love. Why not let me do the same—once?"

"I'd hate to think you'd marry anyone you didn't love. But Tommy Howard isn't dependable. For once I agree with Maxine. Even if she—" Patricia's eyes narrowed; she lowered her voice. "Valerie, was she at home all night last night?"

"You know I sleep very soundly, Mother."

"Really, Valerie, I can't understand you. Maxine's not even your own sister and I'm your mother.

If you know anything, it's your duty to tell me. I'm not satisfied she's behaving herself and why should I have her on my hands if she isn't even grateful enough to—"

"Here's Geneva with your breakfast." Valerie got up to open the door and slipped out of the room before Geneva had done cooing:

"And how are we feeling now? Here's something to make a poor, sick lady feel just lots better."

CHAPTER TWO
GENEVA DOES HER DUTY

Valerie picked up the morning paper, let herself into the apartment and walked quietly down the hall to the kitchen. Geneva, pouring cream into two small painted pitchers, looked up in surprise.

"My goodness, I didn't expect you so early. Not after you and Lucie talked secrets all night."

"We didn't talk very long. We didn't get home until after eleven," Valerie said. "Why are double bills?"

"Oh, I think they're nice. You get twice as much for your money."

"Quantity, not quality." Valerie sat down and threw her hat on the kitchen table. "Lucie works Saturday mornings so I ate breakfast with her and came home. Mother wants me to change those stockings I got for her yesterday. She doesn't like the shade."

"Poor Mother was so lonely last night," Geneva said reproachfully. "She was saying Herbert Ellison never comes here anymore. How is dear Herbert?"

"Dear Herbert is as painfully pompous as ever." Valerie unfolded the newspaper. "He knows our new tenant. He told him there was a vacancy here."

"Well, isn't that interesting? What does Mr. Dundas do? Did Herbert say?"

"N-no."

What Herbert had said was: "Michael has money but I don't know where he gets it. He's clever but—uh—a little—unscrupulous, I'm afraid. Oh, he's a—a gentleman. I don't mean that—"

"Oh. Well," Geneva said, "where did Herbert meet him?"

"He didn't say."

"He probably met Herbert professionally then. If Mr. Dundas is well-to-do he— By the way, after you'd left last night, Mr. Julian and his sister had the awfulest quarrel."

"Did they have it in the hall?" Valerie said sharply.

"My goodness, Valerie, I'm afraid late hours don't agree with our little girl. When people have their doors open when I'm talking to a nice young man selling magazines, I can't help hearing. Neither could the young man. Miss Julian was crying and Mr. Julian said: 'Well, I guess I have a right to know where my money goes.'

"And she was all choked up, poor thing, so all I heard was something about 'cruel' and 'must have some pleasure.' I wish you'd seen how he glared at me when he came downstairs. So I suppose her housekeeping money didn't last again. You know, I do wonder where she goes every Friday night. She let it slip she'd been out on Haight Street. And you know parts of Haight are not at all nice."

"According to the newspaper, the police are still under fire in the graft investigation."

"Well, no wonder," Geneva said comfortably, taking a pan of biscuits from the oven. Neither she nor Patricia cared for the morning paper, which circumstance Valerie had lately considered fortunate. Because, though she rose early, Geneva didn't bother to bring in the newspaper and so had missed being first to see the envelopes under the door. "Orange or pineapple juice, dear?"

"I don't care."

"There's grapefruit juice if you'd rather have that."

"Geneva, I—don't—care!"

"Well, my goodness, Valerie! The grapefruit juice is open but it will only take a minute to squeeze oranges. You might ask Mother—and wake Maxine. Oh, and there's the doorbell! Now, who do you suppose that could—"

"I'll go," Valerie said quickly.

She expected, as she opened the door, to see some boy with an armload of cheap tablecloths and crockery, inducement to subscribe to the *Call-Bulletin* "for just one month to help me out." Instead, she faced a tall man with a brown, long-chinned face and high, bumpy cheekbones. He hesitated momentarily; then:

"Does a Miss Maxine Farley live here?" he asked.

"Why—yes. I'm afraid she isn't awake. If you—"

"Don't bother." He took something from his pocket and held it out for Valerie's inspection. "Is this hers?"

"This" was a round black kid purse. "Why—it looks like Maxine's," Valerie said. "Do you want her to identify—"

"There are some cards and bills in it. I'm sorry, miss, but there's a woman been shot in the park over here. A girl with red hair— Here, don't do that!"

For an instant Valerie leaned against the substantial gray-clad arm that shot out to steady her. "I'm—I'm sorry," she said. "I thought Maxine was in her room. I wasn't home last night so I didn't know."

"Well, I'm sorry to break it to you like this, Miss— Miss—"

"Sheridan. Mrs. Farley is my mother: not Maxine's."

"I see. My name is Sullivan. Homicide Squad. Can I come in? I'll have to talk to you. Just a minute—"

Sullivan went back to the front door, opened it and called to someone outside: "Stick around, boys. Now, Miss Sheridan—"

Inside the apartment Valerie hesitated. "Would you—would you mind coming to the kitchen? My mother isn't—isn't well and I'm afraid she'll— She might—"

"Get hysterical? I'm used to that," Sullivan said. "But I'd like to talk to you first."

"And my cousin, Miss Nolan—" Valerie stopped, as Geneva emerged from the kitchen, carrying Patricia's breakfast tray. "Geneva, this is Mr. Sullivan. He— Will you tell her? I'll—come back in just an instant."

In the bathroom she dashed cold water on her face; let it run over her wrists. Unreasonable or not, she could bear whatever Sullivan had to tell but not, for a moment, Geneva's avid curiosity. Give Sullivan a little time to satisfy it and Geneva opportunity to utter the motheaten platitudes she reserved for death.

Geneva was leaning against the sink when Valerie came back to the kitchen, her large, fair face expressive at once of melancholy and pleasurable excitement. She moved starchily toward Valerie.

"Do you feel better, girlie? The inspector tells me she died almost instantly and that is a comfort, isn't it? And that she looks quite peaceful."

Valerie moved away from the comforting arm; sat down by the kitchen table. "I don't imagine that's what he came here to talk to us about."

Sullivan's noncommittal murmur was smothered by Geneva's: "He understands we want to know those things. Even if we didn't always approve of her we did love Maxine."

"I didn't—really," Valerie said. "And I'm quite sure you didn't. That doesn't mean I'm not sorry."

"Of course you are: just terribly sorry. She was so young. Poor Maxine! But I must admit she—she did—queer things."

Sullivan pounced on this statement. "Did she? What?"

"Well, she slipped out at night, late. This proves it. I just looked in her room, Valerie, and her bed wasn't slept in. You weren't home so she didn't need to try to fool you. She went to bed way after eleven. She was still reading in the living room when I went to bed."

"Eleven, hunh? The doctor's guessing she was killed about midnight. We'll see." Sullivan turned to Valerie. "Did you know she slipped out at night?"

"We had twin beds and I'm not easily wakened. But she—she admitted she did, yesterday morning. I didn't ask questions. My mother married Mr. Farley four years ago and he died a year later.

So I've only known Maxine those four years. We got along by respecting each other's privacy. We knew some of the same people; anyone who visited us here. But she had friends I never met."

"She certainly never told any more than she had to," Geneva said. "She'd go out without one word to say where she was going and come back when she wanted to. She was of age—twenty-two—but she owed Mrs. Farley something for giving her a home. She didn't have enough money of her own to live on."

"What did she do yesterday?"

"She had her hair done after lunch and then went shopping. At least she brought home some pajamas. But she was home by four," Geneva said. "Then we had dinner at seven and Valerie went out and Maxine stayed in. But I don't know what she was doing between four and seven because I was busy in here."

"I was downtown until five," Valerie said. "Maxine wasn't in the apartment when I got back. She came in about six-thirty and said she'd been sitting in the back yard."

"Was she friendly with anyone in this building?"

"N-no." Let someone else tell him Maxine had been more friendly with Grant Callendar than Winona Callendar liked. "But we all know each

other here. There are only five apartments, you
see. Just this one on the first floor because it has
six rooms and— Well, that's not important. But
we've been here six years and everyone else at least
two, except for Mr. Dundas."

"Hunh? Michael Dundas? Well, it is a small
world after all," Sullivan said reflectively.

"Oh, you know him? We are rather curious
about Mr. Dundas," Geneva said archly. "Don't
tell me he isn't—isn't—"

"Michael's all right. When did he move in?
Thursday? Well, that seems to let him out but I'll
talk to him along with everyone else here."

"But, Inspector, even if Maxine was in the park
at a very late hour it's very dark over there and
there are men wandering around. Women," Geneva said, "are always being killed by maniacs in
Golden Gate Park."

Sullivan shook his head. "I don't think it's that
kind of case, Miss Nolan. We aren't certain yet but
we're pretty sure she wasn't attacked. She didn't
fight and her clothes weren't disarranged. There
wasn't one sign of struggle. And why was she in
the park at that hour of night if she didn't go
there to meet someone?"

"I can tell you the names of some of her
friends," Valerie said slowly. "But only people we

both knew." She added: "I didn't think the police ever told people things."

"Oh, we all have our own ways of working. I don't know how well you know this park."

"Very well. I play tennis there, for one thing."

"Well, this street—Gough—is its eastern boundary. There's Laguna on the west, Sacramento and Washington south and north. And you know there's lots of paths running through it. You're so near Washington you probably use the steps up to one path—right here at the corner of Gough and Washington."

"Of course. I always do, and cut through the park when I'm going over to Laguna. It saves time."

"It's dark in there at night," Sullivan said. "Trees and bushes along the paths. Well, I won't draw a diagram for you but we found Miss Farley in a place like that. A good place to meet anyone secretly because it is so dark and deserted at night. Right near another little flight of steps. Her purse had rolled away so we didn't know who she was at first. I gave the newspaper boys the slip but they'll pick up the trail and you'd better be prepared for them. Now, if you'll—"

"Inspector," Geneva had been, for her, strangely silent for several minutes, "I think I should— Valerie, wouldn't you like to take poor Mother's breakfast in to her?"

"If she were awake she would have called. And I want to hear what you're going to say."

"I only wanted to spare you. But I feel it's my duty to tell the inspector that Tommy and Maxine were quarreling last night while he was waiting for you."

"Tommy and— Good heavens! Tommy and Maxine always quarrel. You know that as well as I do."

"And who is Tommy?"

"Thomas Howard, Inspector. I suppose you'd say he is 'that way' about our Valerie. Nothing at all serious—"

"Mr. Howard and I are engaged," Valerie said quietly.

"It hasn't been announced, dear, and your mother wouldn't want it to be. We wouldn't want the newspapers to know about it, Inspector. And while they did quarrel there was something very unusual about this quarrel," Geneva went on. "I heard Maxine say: 'You can't treat me like this.' She was speaking quite loudly. Tommy wasn't, but after a while I heard him say: 'I thought we agreed to call it quits.'"

"Well? I can think of a dozen explanations for that."

"So can I, Miss Sheridan. Still—was that all, Miss Nolan?" Sullivan asked.

"My goodness, no! The next I heard was Tommy saying something about the park and 'meeting you.' I'm just as sorry as I can be to have to tell this, Valerie, but—"

"Are you finished?"

"Oh no, dear. Maxine said: 'And you won't tell.' Then I didn't hear anything for quite a while until Tommy said: 'We'll be late getting home.'"

"We were," Valerie said. "Late getting home from the theater because I wasn't dressed when Tommy got here. Tommy and Maxine were never together without squabbling. He teased her and she resented it. She's often said to me: 'Your boy friend can't treat me like that.'"

"Yes, dear, I know. But Maxine has known Tommy as long as you have and she may have liked him better than you know. And I do wonder why he spoke of meeting her in the park."

"He may have seen her there if she made a habit of going there," Sullivan said. "Where does he live?"

"On Laguna," Geneva said and gave the number. "And of course he cuts through the park going home after he's been here. Now, Valerie dear, we mustn't be foolish. We must co-operate and—"

Valerie got up, white-lipped. "I'll leave the inspector to your co-operation then. You can tell him as much about Maxine's friends as I can. Besides," as Patricia's voice was heard fretfully calling Geneva, "someone had better go to Mother. I will . . ."

CHAPTER THREE
"ENOUGH TO HOLD HIM ON"

But instead of going to Patricia, Valerie slipped into her own room and took the little hoard of anonymous letters from the secret drawer of her desk. Then, very carefully, she raised a window, sat on its sill and dropped lightly to the narrow strip of pavement that separated this building from its neighbor.

Looking around the corner of the house she saw there was a car parked in front of it but with its back to her. A uniformed policeman was standing beside it, talking to someone inside, not looking her way.

Valerie drew a long breath, stepped into the street and walked slowly toward Sacramento, fighting the impulse to break into a run. But no one stopped her or called to her and she turned off Gough and up Sacramento.

Although she had liked Sullivan and even briefly felt at ease with him, Valerie had the average,

law-abiding citizen's fear of the police. Not the
police as represented by stoutish men who leni-
ently enforced traffic signals on Market Street but
the members of the mysterious Homicide Squad
who arrested people "on suspicion", "grilled" them
"intensively"—

She desperately regretted her own ignorance of
law and police procedure. But it didn't matter if
they did arrest her for coming over here to warn
Tommy. She had to do that, and he had no private
telephone. Had Sullivan taken Geneva's story seriously? Surely he must see she didn't like Tommy.
And what would he do when he discovered Valerie
was gone?

She reached Laguna; began to run, nearing
Tommy's rooming house—a vast wooden structure
badly broken out with cornices and cupolas. The
front door with its red-paned fanlight was open.
Valerie slipped through the hall and up the stairs,
glad that for once Mrs. O'Dea was not in the front
part of the house taking an unrelenting interest in
her roomers' visitors or telephone calls.

A sleepy voice said: "'At you, Bill? C'mon in."

"It's not me, Bill. It's me, Valerie," she said
and walked into the room. Tommy raised a tousled and startled head from his pillow. She had
guessed that since he did not work on Saturdays
he would probably still be in bed. To combine

breakfast and lunch whenever possible was one of his economies.

"Tommy, I have to talk to you and there's no time to waste so please don't gape at me like that."

"All right," Tommy said amiably. "I was dreaming about angels. Toss me my bathrobe, baby. I've only got half my pajamas on. And look out the window or something."

"But— Oh, very well."

Valerie threw the bathrobe toward the bed and looked impatiently toward a window. Men were funny. Tommy swam in trunks designed for a better display of an impressive physique—which he possessed. But just because this was a bedroom—

She turned as he said: "O.K. What's it all about?" and found it wasn't so easy, after all, to tell him. He brushed his tawny hair out of his eyes and pulled her into his arms. "Come on, tell me. You look like it was serious."

"It is. It's— Maxine has been killed, Tommy. They found her this morning in the park."

Tommy said: "My good gosh!" And then: "Well, why didn't you phone? I'd have come right over and— Look: what are the police doing?"

"That's the trouble. They—Tommy, Geneva says . . ."

He was scowling when she had finished. He let her go, walked over to the bed and sat down, his big-knuckled hands dangling between his knees.

"The old battle-ax! But I can explain it, Val. I just kidded Maxine about her hair. Asked if she'd been dyeing it because it did look redder than usual."

"It had just been washed. Oh, Tommy, why would you tease her?"

"You don't mind and neither do most girls. But she got mad: said I couldn't talk to her like that. Then I said I thought we'd agreed not to fight because it worried you. And then," Tommy said, flushing, "she made a nasty crack about money. That made me sore and I asked why she was wandering around that park late at night last week."

"Then you did see her!"

"Sure. It was Thursday when I went over to see Bill Jackson. He was coming by this morning if he didn't have to go to Merced. Well, his folks live on Pacific and Franklin so coming home I took the usual short cut through the park. Before I got to it, coming up Washington, I saw Maxine come running down those steps. She crossed the street so we didn't meet. I didn't know if she saw me so I kept still till I got sore at her last night. Then she just said I'd better not tell anyone. I said I wouldn't if she'd lay off the wisecracks. Then I said you and I were going to be late getting home from the show. Changing the subject, you see."

"But that's so reasonable to anyone who knows you two."

"I think so," Tommy said with a wry grin; "but will the police? Anyway, I just happened to think. I didn't get in till after twelve. I took a walk after I left you at Lucie's. I— Oh hell! all the love scenes in that picture and God knows when we can get married on what I make. And old Herb the successful lawyer and I'm just not fitted for office work."

"Tommy, what does it matter which one of us has money?"

"It does—and sometimes it gets me down, so I just walked around for a while. And old lady O'Dea knows when I got in because she wanted her room rent and waited up for me in the hall downstairs. She remarked on the time."

"You mean—she'll tell?"

"You're darn tootin' she'll tell. She's got it in for me. And I suppose she'd tell anyway."

"If I hadn't stayed all night with Lucie so that she knows what time you left us—"

"Hunh? Forget that—quick! You're going to keep out of this and not try to fake any alibis for me. Anyway, Herb knows what time we left you and Lucie. He wanted to drive me home but I said I'd rather walk. And I didn't meet anyone.

No, we'll have to tell the truth," Tommy said. "Do it before the O'Dea gets in her licks and make a good impression. Look, baby, what was it Geneva said about me liking Maxine?"

"She said she wondered if Maxine didn't like you better than I suspected."

"She certainly hid it damn well, then. She was looking for a guy with money. You don't believe that I—well, that I—"

"Tommy!" Valerie stooped and kissed him. He put his arm about her waist, leaning his head against her. "There was nothing to keep you from marrying Maxine, was there? If you'd met her first and been attracted by her, then met me and it had been love at first sight and damn the consequences with us. But it wasn't. We all three met at the same time and had plenty of time to make our choice. And how anyone who knows you could imagine you shooting anyone—"

"Shooting? Was she shot?"

"Didn't I tell you? Does it matter?"

"How do I know?" Tommy got up, went over to the heavy fumed-oak bureau and began yanking drawers open. "I've got a gun. Maybe it isn't the right kind, but I had a permit and they'll find out about that. Where the hell is it?"

"But they have ways of telling if a particular gun has been used in a murder, haven't they? So— Tommy! What's the matter?"

"I can't find the thing. I thought it was in one of these top drawers. But my things are always in a mess and they get shifted around. But where— Try the table drawers."

"No," Valerie said, standing still with her hands full of bills, old letters and football programs, "it isn't here."

"Maybe it doesn't matter. They'll know what kind of gun Maxine was killed with. Only mine's a fairly popular make. There's the closet: maybe I didn't take it out."

He stopped, listening; shook his head at Valerie as she started to speak. "Shh-h! That's O'Dea coming upstairs."

Mrs. O'Dea's voice was rather more acid than usual. "Mr. Howard, there's a policeman wants to see you. Will you come down or will he come up and get you?"

"Hunh? A policeman? Why, wait till I get my pants on," Tommy said craftily. The doorknob that had been turning suddenly became stationary. "You tell him I'll be right down but he can come up if he wants to."

The slip-slap of Mrs. O'Dea's heelless slippers died away down the hall. "They can't see you from downstairs," Tommy whispered urgently. "Go to the back and get down the fire escape. The window on it's open. If you're not scared—"

"No, but—" Valerie tightened her arms about his neck. "Darling, don't worry. There's more to this than you know."

"Val, for Christ's sake get going!" He kissed her roughly. "This don't amount to anything. Don't worry."

Herbert Ellison telephoned late that afternoon. "Valerie? Valerie, this is Herbert. I'm awfully sorry but—"

"They've arrested Tommy—"

"Now keep cool, Valerie. They're just holding him for questioning," Herbert said soothingly. "And they finally let him call me. He showed his good sense there. That was when he saw they weren't going to let him go tonight."

"But why, Herbert? How can they hold him?"

"They do it. And his gun was the same caliber as the one that was used to kill Maxine. And he can't find his so he can't prove the bullets weren't fired from it. So of course the police say he threw it away so it wouldn't be traced to him. And then he took a walk just to be walking and right by the park and there's what Geneva told them.

"It's not a strong case," Herbert added quickly. "But enough to hold him on. Don't you worry. I could get a writ of habeas corpus but then they'd be sure to clap a charge on him. We think since tomorrow's Sunday we won't force their hand too soon. I know Sullivan would rather not act till he's more certain he has the right man."

"While he tries to make Tommy confess and uses rubber hoses and things!"

"Now, Valerie. If they do put him through a mild third degree just asking him questions, he can stand that. He's tough and he hasn't any nerves. The whole thing is ridiculous, of course. We can produce dozens of character witnesses—"

Valerie moistened her dry lips. "If he comes to trial, you mean?"

"We-el, yes. We might as well be prepared for all contingencies, you know. And while Sullivan is all right I don't care so much for this Hunt who's working with him. And if he does come to trial you'll want somebody with experience in criminal cases, which I haven't had. There are two or three I'd recommend but they come high."

"I'll see to that," Valerie said.

"Well, if you think you can. Probably you won't have to. Don't talk to any reporters and don't try to see Tommy," Herbert warned. "Not yet. I'll be over to talk to you tonight."

Patricia was demanding as she had been for the last five minutes: "Valerie, who is that? Is it Herbert? What does he say?"

Valerie went slowly into her mother's bedroom. Patricia had progressed to the chaise longue, a pink negligee and an imported lace handkerchief. The last two items, Valerie guessed, were props for the pictures the cameramen had taken. She said:

"They've arrested Tommy: that's all."

"Well, I'm not surprised. Of course Mother sympathizes with her baby girl but it's best you should find out now."

"They can't hold him! If this is the way the police work I don't want any part of them!"

"Oh, Valerie—pl-*ease!*" Patricia raised the lace handkerchief to her eyes. "Not after what I've been through. I'm sure Mr. Sullivan is very charming. He told me about Maxine in the nicest way and when we found you were gone he didn't lose his temper. He was more thoughtful than you, I'm sure. Because someone had to go down to the— where Maxine is and identify her. It seems it's a law or something. While Geneva isn't related to Maxine, neither am I, really, and of course I couldn't stand an ordeal of that kind. So Geneva went and you know I was alone until you came back. My nerves—"

"Mother," Valerie's voice trembled in spite of her effort to keep it steady, "I do think, for once, other things are more important than your nerves. Tommy may need a good lawyer. I want you to loan me enough money for that. I'll pay you back, with interest."

"Are you crazy?" Patricia said shrilly. "Getting yourself mixed up in this any more than you are! Tommy got himself into it: let him get himself out. Besides, I haven't any money to spare. It takes every cent to keep this place going. Well, maybe I'm 'stravagant and too gen'rous. But that's just the way I am and—"

"I don't think you're generous, Mother," Valerie said quietly.

She looked about the room: at its fragile, expensive furniture; the dozens of tiny pillows on the chaise longue, silver and crystal on the bureau, the shoes and hatboxes spilling out of a crowded closet. She stared, last of all, at the painted simper on the face of a leggy french doll sprawled on the floor at the end of the bed.

"I don't believe you're even really extravagant. You spend money only for what you want. You want this apartment. Geneva is an unpaid servant. And you're allowed a certain sum for taking care of me. I never have asked what you do with it even when you wanted me to leave college. Because you wanted me at home you said. You could help me if you wanted to and if you won't, I'll get whatever money I need, somehow."

"Valerie!" Patricia's face was mottled pink and white now. "I forbid you—" She burst into tears, her small hands fluttering pathetically. "When I'm dead you'll wish you'd died too before you ever spoke to me like this! O-ohh!" She buried her face in a not-too-clean pillow. "My baby girl doesn't love her muzzer."

"I've loved you enough that I've been pretty spineless just because I dread scenes. But this is important," Valerie said. "I'm going to stick by Tommy—"

Patricia sat up, her face a deeper pink. She hurled the smelling salts she had been sniffing to the floor.

"You do what I tell you, young lady, or you can just get out and stay out! I won't have you throwing yourself away on a man who's gotten himself arrested for murder. You're just like your fool of a father. I won't—"

She looked at her daughter's unmoved face and fell back against the pillows. "W-water," she said feebly. "I—I feel ill. My heart—"

"I think your heart will stand almost any strain, Mother," Valerie said, moving toward the door. "I'll call Geneva."

Geneva, entering hastily without being called, gasped: "Valerie, my goodness, what is it? There, there! Don't cry so hard, dear. Valerie, how could you—"

"Don't you start too," Valerie said briefly and left the room.

She took coat and hat from her closet; looked in her purse to see that she had money and the letters she had taken from her desk that morning. Patricia's noisy crying and smothered moans beat like blows against her temples. She put on her hat, flung her coat over one arm and ran from the apartment.

Closing the door, she leaned against it, forcing herself to take deep and even breaths. Even here she could still hear Patricia but, comparatively speaking, the hall was quiet. What now? She could go to Lucie: she would take her in gladly. But Mrs. Orton and Lucie would be curious and they didn't like Patricia. No fault of theirs that they didn't. Still—

A hotel, then. She would have to pay in advance without luggage and the clerk and bellboys would stare at her, but it was easier to face strangers than friends. She opened her purse again to count her money; took out the half-sheets of paper, fingering them indecisively.

What was she going to do with these? They might save Tommy, suggesting as they did another motive for Maxine's death. But she could not show all of them to the police for at least two might add to their case against him.

And an investigation would involve everyone here. Too bad to have these letters printed in the newspapers—as they probably would be. To have Geneva's and Miss Julian's and Patricia's peculiarities or small meannesses everyone's property.

A soft voice said: "Can't you make up your mind what to do with them, Miss Sheridan?"

CHAPTER FOUR
DEFINITION OF A GENTLEMAN

For an instant Valerie stared at Michael Dundas, standing so quietly just inside the front door. She said childishly:

"I hate people who walk like—like cats." And then: "Besides, how do you know what these are? I suppose you managed to read the one you picked up for me yesterday. Chivalry! Well, it's still none of your business."

"But you see I can so easily make it my business. And I think I will. If I walk like a cat perhaps I'm as curious as one. Shall we talk in your apartment or mine?"

"Nowhere! I'm going—"

Valerie stopped. Where was she going? A lump in her throat grew to uncomfortable proportions and refused to go away. She stared blindly at her own hands, clutching the letters as if she expected them to be snatched from her.

"Exactly," said Michael Dundas. "Where are you going? You'd better come with me before you drench the hall with tears."

"I'm not—going to—cry. I never—do."

"I believe you. I imagine you can very safely leave that to your mother. Oh, I'm not deaf. And you don't like that, do you? But why are you—"

From down the street came a stentorian voice uttering sounds uncouth and indecipherable. "It appears that the extras are coming this way. Have you been interviewed by the press?"

"No. Will I be?" Valerie asked.

"Unless you are able to disappear at will in a puff of smoke. You can't evade them forever and it would be bad policy to try to. But just now—"

"Just now," Valerie whispered, "someone is on the doorstep, ringing our bell. I can hear it in our hall. I—I simply can't—"

"Then don't be an idiot." Michael Dundas caught her arm and propelled her toward the stairs. "That might be a reporter. My thanks to the Fourth Estate. Because I intend to talk to you—"

"But you would rather not have to threaten me!"

"Oh no, there is nothing I like better than to browbeat helpless females," Michael said blandly. "But not here for the benefit of our fellow tenants." He unlocked his own front door. "Straight ahead. Not that chair: it's a leftover from the Spanish

Inquisition. The one on your right is comfortable. Sit down. Brandy or scotch?"

"Neither one. I don't drink."

"'And lo! Abou Ben Adhem's name led all the rest!' The woman who doesn't drink. But this is in the nature of a prescription," Michael said, pouring brandy into a round-bellied amber glass.

"Why," Valerie said combatively, "shouldn't women drink if men do?"

"No reason. Except that women in public always make a great deal of noise. Given two drinks they make a great deal more. Let's not go into that."

He sat down, expressionless under her deliberate and troubled scrutiny of his face. His profile, she decided, was definitely ugly: chin broad and square, nose blunt like a bit of carelessly done sculpture. His eyelashes were ridiculous. If he were a woman you'd be certain they were pasted on.

She wondered if he were sorry for her but dismissed that idea instantly. He did not look as if sympathy entered into his scheme of things. His mouth was too thin, too straight and unsmiling . . .

"You don't look to me like a particularly curious person," she said. "Why should I trust you? Sullivan knows you, so you must know him. Of course Herbert Ellison did say you are a gentleman."

"What do you think?"

"I suppose you are if a gentleman is a person who never insults anyone—unintentionally."

Unexpectedly he laughed. "There is another definition. A gentleman is a man who bathes and has never been in jail. I've been in jail. Did Herbert tell you that?"

"No. He is very discreet. Did he get you out?"

"He did not. I got out on bail. And discovered who really stole the lady's jools. That involved a little matter of illegal entry to confirm my own suspicions. Herbert was properly horrified. But, I think, secretly rather impressed."

"I suppose he might be. He is so very cautious."

"Cautious! Herbert would bet on War Admiral—to show."

"But why," Valerie said, "did they think you stole the—the jewels?"

"Because the communicating door between my room and the lady's happened to be unlocked. It was one of these hotel robberies. An assistant manager was the thief. In a smaller way he'd been at it for some time. Is there anything else you would care to know?"

"Why shouldn't I ask questions? Am I supposed to trust you when I don't know anything about you?"

Michael smiled provokingly. "Were you thinking of trusting me? But why not? I don't eat little girls like you. Only would you mind removing
that God-awful hat? It looks like a candle snuffer
and it's all wrong with a nose like yours."

Valerie snatched off the candle snuffer and
smoothed back her hair. "My nose may be turned
up a little but it's not—not just half done!"

"'Behold, behold the nose that traitorously destroyed the beauty of its master!' Must you be so
quarrelsome? I was going to say it was Sullivan
who arrested me. He was on the burglary detail
then. I don't dislike him: quite the contrary. But
I wouldn't mind proving him wrong again. Also,
there is such a thing as purely intellectual curiosity."

"Just how much do you know? You did read
that letter I dropped yesterday morning?"

"Of course. And I saw just now that you have
others like it. Do you find them under the doors?"

"Yes. In the mornings. It's been going on for
about three months."

"And you can't think of any reason why it started just when it did? The janitor told me all of you
have been here for some time."

"Yes, even the Callendars have been here two
years. I've wondered why it happened so suddenly," Valerie said. "We've been here nearly six

years and the Putnams and Julians about five. As
I told Inspector Sullivan we know each other better than most people in apartment houses do. But
why weren't these letters written before? Maxine
said she thought such things were usually written
by—well, old maids, she said, and that there are
too many of that type in this building."

"What do you think?"

"How can I know what people's thoughts and
feelings are? It's true neither Geneva nor Miss
Julian is married. As to Sara Putnam, she's not
thirty and may have a perfectly satisfactory private life—except for her grandmother. She likes
sports and teaches them afternoons in some private school. But if I had to choose the person I
thought most likely to have written those letters
it would be old Mrs. Putnam."

"Why?"

"I suppose because she's the most loathsome
person, not to have sores, that I've ever seen. Not
that anyone very often does see her. She lives in
her bedroom and has it filled with plants."

"How would she get her information?"

"That's the sticking point," Valerie said. "Not
from Sara, I'm sure. And Mrs. Putnam doesn't visit anyone here. Of course she does know Geneva
and Miss Julian and they go up to see her now
and then but she doesn't seem to appreciate their
visits."

"Who had this apartment before I did?" Michael said.

"Why—Winona Callendar's uncle, John Dozier. But I don't believe he left because he was receiving his share of these notes. I believe he moved to Los Angeles for business reasons. That was six weeks ago. He didn't impress me as a man who'd run away from anything unpleasant. Especially as he'd be leaving Winona in the same predicament and he seemed very fond of her."

"Do you know that Mrs. Callendar has received any letters?"

"Maxine said so. What Maxine said to me Friday morning is really the crux of the whole thing. . . ."

Valerie repeated their conversation. She had given it so much thought since early morning that she believed she had finally recalled every word Maxine had said.

"She was shrewd and fearless—and pretty unscrupulous, I imagine," she added. "She hadn't very much money and she wanted a great deal. I think she was going to say she had an idea who was writing those letters but Geneva interrupted us. Then, after Geneva left, she said there was a mink coat at Liebes she hoped to buy—and not on time."

"Why mink—with her coloring? Well, as you two agreed, those letters can't be called blackmail. But if one found out who their writer is that would be material for blackmail. And since she admitted she had been investigating—"

"Yes, and even if she wasn't sure then, we don't know what she was doing all Friday afternoon. She had time to approach someone if she was ready to turn blackmailer."

"There's another possibility," Michael said. "You think she would have read any letters she might have happened to find before the persons they were meant for took them in. Well, if she did, in them she might have found some information that was basis for blackmail of perfectly innocent parties. Innocent of letter writing, that is."

"Oh. Yes, it might have happened that way. But she could only have gotten a lead from the letters because there has been nothing in any we've received that would be basis for blackmail. They aren't pleasant: not the kind of thing you'd like to have made public."

"I haven't seen them, you know."

"No—" Valerie hesitated; then held the letters out to him. "We didn't show Mother and Geneva the ones we knew were meant for them. The pieces pasted on another sheet of paper are the one Miss Julian showed me."

Michael read: "WHY NOT TRY ARSENIC ON CHARLIE THEN YOUD BE SURE OF HIS MONEY   BETTER WATCH OUT HE DONT MARRY YET HA-HA. I believe that 'ha-ha' is very typical. You might explain this."

"Well— Oh, it seems so—so low to tell."

"Do you want to be charitable or do you want to prove your fiancé didn't kill your stepsister? Please make up your mind—for good. Unless you're trying to fool yourself when you say these letters must have something to do with her death."

"I am not! All right: Miss Julian is dependent on her brother and he is rather short-tempered. He's generous enough, I imagine, but she is forever running short on her housekeeping allowance. When they begin having too many stews and hamburger steaks, I think Mr. Julian investigates and then blows up."

"And does Charlie show any signs of marrying?"

Valerie laughed. "When you see a turkey gobbler with a mustache, that's Charlie. Of course Miss Julian does worry that he might marry. I don't know why. His only diversion seems to be card playing with some old friends every Friday night."

Michael was reading the letters meant for Geneva. "H-mm. Comments on her appearance, her lack of success in the matrimonial sweepstakes, her hatred of your mother and Miss Farley."

"Geneva doesn't hate Mother," Valerie said quickly. "She—I don't think she would ever let herself realize she dislikes anyone. I think she really has made herself believe 'this is a pretty good old world, after all.'"

Michael grimaced. "Yes, it is pretty awful," Valerie said. "She is so good-hearted and full of good intentions—and curious and talkative. She gets on your nerves so! She always asks: 'What are you reading?' when a book, to her, is just something to be dusted."

"'Instead of the cross, the Albatross about my neck was hung—'"

Valerie giggled. "That's a good name for her. But she's led a blameless life, if she is a poor relation. As to my mother—"

She knew what he was reading now: the first letter meant for Patricia; the one that said: SO YOU CANT KEEP YOUR DAUGHTER AND HER MONEY UNDER YOUR CONTROL HOWARD WILL SEE TO SPENDING IT AND WONT YOU LIKE THAT ABOUT AS WELL AS BEING A GRANDMOTHER.

"I—I haven't any illusions about my mother."

"Good. That's one step toward becoming an adult."

Valerie looked at him quickly but his face was impassive whatever faint echo of bitterness she thought she had detected in his voice.

"But still she is my mother."

"A completely idiotic statement," Michael said pleasantly. "Young animals are grateful to their mothers because they feed and protect them. When they—presumably—become endowed with reason they love them because they're lovable or admire them because they're admirable. Not because of a simple biological fact—"

"Oh, I've heard all that! Let's not argue. I'll admit Mother is a selfish, spoiled child. But shrewd, as children are sometimes when it comes to getting what they want."

"And she doesn't want you to marry?"

"Well, you see Mother was more or less in society back in '14 and '15. She sent me to the same school the Helens—Wills and Jacobs—went to but that didn't improve my tennis. And I didn't go Kappa or Theta when I entered college. After two years Mother wanted me to stay home.

"She seems to think I've only to set my mind to it to be a spinster and Junior Leaguer and all the rest of it. She is too lazy to help even if any connections she still has weren't more or less imaginary. And I detest social climbers," Valerie said. "So I don't know where Mother expects me to pick up a rich, socially prominent husband. Perhaps she doesn't really. She takes a year or two from my age when she can and she *would* hate to be a grandmother. Of course Tommy is not what she would call a 'good match.' She dates herself so, the expressions she uses at times. But I can't show that letter to the police because it might only add to their suspicions against him. And there's something in one of the two letters for Maxine. Will you read them?"

The first letter was a single bleak question: CANT YOU LEAVE OTHER WOMENS HUSBANDS AND LOVERS ALONE. The second, beginning: SO YOURE STILL SNEAKING OUT NIGHTS YOU . . . then became entirely obscene.

"You don't need," Michael said, "to be afraid this will ever see print. I believe it's also typical." But he held the letters suddenly as if he were handling something filthy. "Were you engaged when that first letter was written?"

"I think we were—just. That was the first one. I wasn't certain whom it was meant for and showed it to Maxine. She accepted it as being meant for her."

"On account of Mr. Callendar, I suppose?"

"You're guessing but—yes. Grant and Winona have been married two years. They eloped. Grant's mother didn't want him to marry Winona. Probably she thinks no one would be good enough for him, though I think he's about as exciting as lemon jello."

"I believe I saw them early this afternoon. A soft blonde with a dimple in his chin and a very pretty, dark woman."

"That would be the Callendars. They were probably leaving for the week end."

"Their apartment is like this one, isn't it? Three rooms, so they have no servant?"

"None of us but Mrs. Putnam have. She has a Negro cook by the day. What made you ask?" Valerie said. "About the servants, I mean."

"If there were servants they'd have to be taken into account," Michael said unsatisfactorily. "Tell me about Miss Farley and Callendar."

"Maxine made it a point to be friendly with him. As she would have with you because she thought you might be a rich Italian," Valerie said maliciously. "You aren't, are you?"

"Italian? No, nor rich. Go on."

Valerie flushed and counted ten. She didn't enjoy being snubbed but she supposed she deserved it. She said:

"Sometimes he and Maxine used to talk out in the back garden and Winona didn't like it. But Maxine was even more friendly with Mr. Dozier. He's not more than forty-five, I imagine, and very good-looking."

"Does Mr. Howard know all these people?"

"Not Mrs. Putnam, of course, but the Callendars and Sara Putnam and the Julians. Not the
Julians so well because they're older. Why do you
ask that?"

CHAPTER FIVE
ILLEGAL ENTRY

When he did not answer Valerie looked curiously about the long room. Maxine, who had spent countless hours "just looking" in the city's best stores, had known the furniture was good. By which she had undoubtedly meant expensive. To Valerie it was simply interesting, mainly because it was confined to no one style or period. Their own living room had recently become a modernistic confection in black, white and chromium which she detested.

But in this room a heavy red-and-gold Chinese chest, a demure love seat, a mahogany secretary, Persian rugs and a variety of tray and coffee tables managed, somehow, to hobnob in the friendliest way. The hearth set before the fireplace was hand-made: she had seen its twin in a small shop on Sutter. And the exquisitely colored figures on the long mantel, a medieval and an Elizabethan court

lady and two Napoleonic soldiers, were probably
from A. Schmidt and Son's.

She thought: he may deny being rich but he
certainly has money. Enough for expensive trifles.

"I'm reading this one letter I suppose was meant
for you," Michael said.

"Nice, wasn't it? DOES YOUR MOTHER KNOW
WHAT TIME YOU SNEAKED HOME SATURDAY MORN-
ING. That's proof enough someone here wrote
those letters," Valerie said. "What outsider would
know I got in at four that Saturday morning? A
friend of Tommy's loaned him an old wreck of a
car that broke down. Not that it matters. What
can we do about these things? What would the
police do?"

"Look for fingerprints. Check up on purchases
of rubber stamps. However, you can buy them in
all sizes and at all prices. This seems a rather large
one which would rule out Woolworth's. That still
leaves a good many stores but we could try to find
out for ourselves if any clerks remember any such
purchase about three months ago."

"Could we? I wouldn't like to try."

"It could be done. But not until Monday. I take
it you don't want to confide in Mr. Sullivan just
now?"

"N-no. It would be so easy to scare Poison Pen.
And I haven't much faith in Mr. Sullivan."

"He's no fool," Michael said. "An honest cop."

"Is there such a thing?"

"I said an honest *cop*. Jim is practical; he probably thinks that since graft is always going to be paid some of it might as well be paid to him. Don't take that seriously. The police do well enough with the ordinary murder case and no one could buy Jim off when he's dealing with murder. I do agree he might frighten the bird away. Or at least into throwing those stamps away."

"Oh. Yes, it would be proof if we found them. But what then? Would that help Tommy?"

Michael shrugged. "If you could prove there was at least a possibility Miss Farley knew who the letter writer is and had threatened to expose him. It would certainly introduce an element of doubt into the case against Howard."

"I hate to think of those letters being made public. I think newspapers are indecent. In spite of that I'll throw everyone to the wolves if I have to. That's not so nice, is it?"

"I think," Michael said, "that you are probably hungry."

He got up and pulled heavy curtains over the windows that made up the back wall of the room. Outside, an orange-pink light lingered in the sky but the streets that climbed steeply toward Nob Hill were shadowed. Toy cable cars crept up them or slowly down to Van Ness where the electric signs along Automobile Row were pale flashes in the dusk.

"Come into the kitchen," he said. "We'll see what there is to eat. I'm afraid the icebox runs mainly to bacon and eggs."

"I wouldn't want anything better," Valerie said, turning up her sleeves. "I tried to eat lunch but Geneva talked and talked. So I went to my room and waited until Herbert called. You see— Have you an egg beater? Thank you. You see, I went over to warn Tommy and the police came before we had done talking so I had to go down the back fire escape."

"And you went—without feminine squeals or argument?"

"What's a fire escape? Tommy didn't think it would look well for me to be caught there."

"And Tommy was right. But I once tried to shove a lady down a fire escape—"

"Maybe," Valerie said innocently, "she thought her husband was the lesser of two evils."

"You never saw her husband. I've read the evening papers but there are gaps. Why did you think you had to warn Howard?"

"Didn't they give Geneva any publicity? She started it," Valerie said and told him how as she scrambled eggs and laid crisp strips of bacon across them. Michael drew out a chair for her and sat down opposite at the dinette table.

"So the Albatross jumped the gun? When did your mother marry Farley?"

"Four years ago. He was one of her most unfortunate investments. However, he died before she really regretted him—except as a widow."

"What became of his money?"

"What money? He didn't get through quite all Maxine's mother left him but what little was left went to Maxine. So none of us gains financially by her death. Mother didn't like her and neither did Geneva. That doesn't mean either of them killed her. Anyway, why do it in Lafayette Square and not here?"

"Why not?" Michael said. "It would be wiser to do it there than here. We should consider all possibilities or we might make the mistake of being too clever. How old was Miss Farley when you first met her?"

"Not quite eighteen. She was in a convent in San Rafael when Mother met Wayne. The poor sisters finally asked him to take her away. There wasn't anything in her life before I knew her that would explain her death—I'm almost certain."

"And Mr. Howard? I know you're going to marry him but try to look at him as a mere man might."

Valerie frowned at her plate, realizing how nearly impossible it was for her to consider Tommy impersonally. Impossible to think of him at all without remembering his one-sided grin, the way his hair fell into his eyes, his manner of moving like a leggy colt. You were always expecting him to bump into things and surprised when he never did. She smiled apologetically.

"I'll give you facts. His parents are dead. He has relatives in Washington he doesn't care much about. He worked his way through Stanford. At least—"

"You mean he did as much honest labor as any potential All-American tackle is ever required to do. The newspapers mentioned his late athletic prowess."

"Well, he graduated three years ago. He's twenty-six. He got the usual job selling bonds only he didn't. Didn't sell them, I mean. Or insurance, either. He works for the Pacific Oil Company now. He's a glorified office-boy and he'd really be happier driving a truck. I'd have thought," Valerie added bitterly, "that he's led a sufficiently blameless existence."

"In the eyes of the police, so have most murderers before they turn to murder. There's nothing much you can do about that—directly."

Valerie wondered, not for the first time, why she had talked so freely to this man. He couldn't have forced her to talk. He wouldn't have made good his implied threat to tell Sullivan about those letters. Well, perhaps he would have. She doubted if he had much use or liking for chivalric gestures. But it had been so necessary for her to talk to someone . . .

"And why not me?" Michael said. "I wondered how soon you would begin to regret having been so confiding."

"I don't regret it. Which is very odd. But you won't tell, will you?"

"Only to keep out of jail."

"To keep— What are you planning to do that might get you in jail?"

"Aren't we both suppressing evidence?"

"That isn't what you're thinking of," Valerie said positively. "Could you be remembering I said the Callenders are probably away and have no servants?"

"What do you think?"

"You wouldn't be so idiotic. But then—you might. Only you can't get into their apartment."

"That's what you think. Suppose you forget all about it."

"I won't be treated like a child! If you're going so am I." Valerie settled herself more solidly in her chair. "You can't keep me from it. I don't think even you will drag me screaming, by the heels, from your apartment." She smiled at him sweetly. "Well?"

"You're quite pleased with yourself, aren't you?"

"Yes. When do we go? And how are you going to get in? The janitor is nearsighted. I might be able to steal his passkey."

"That won't be necessary." Michael left the bedroom: came back with a bunch of queer, thin keys, a flashlight and a pair of gloves. "Just in case," he said, indicating the latter. "I hope the Callenders will never know their apartment has been entered."

"If they do they'll probably think it's just a professional burglar that got in. There was quite an epidemic of burglaries over on Sutter Street not long ago. What funny keys. Where did you get them?"

"You'll never know. I suppose you'll be useful as a lookout. If you begin hearing things and scream I'll throttle you. And you'd better be prepared to take to the fire escape again."

"I still don't know why we have to do this," Valerie said.

"The letter writer may still have his equipment: stamps and ink pads. Or some or all of these people may have kept letters they've received."

"And that would help us find out what Maxine might have discovered if she read other people's letters? But if she meant to use them she would have kept them," Valerie said. "I don't see how she could have hidden anything in our room. And if Inspector Sullivan had found any on her or in her purse surely he would have mentioned that. Of course the person who killed her might have taken them even if it was Poison Pen she was blackmailing and not someone else. How long must we wait?"

"No longer. It's dark. Of course it would be safer to wait until about two o'clock but you won't have it that way."

"I never said—"

"You have to be deposited somewhere for the night," Michael said. "You most certainly are not going to stay here. You go out first and down to the second floor. Loiter until I come down. If there is anyone around I won't stop."

It was very quiet on the second floor. No reason, of course, why it should not be, with the Callendars away, attending someone else's party instead of giving one of their own. Inside the Julians' front four-room apartment a nasal voice droned faintly:

"My foot's in the stirrup, My reins are in my hand. Good-by, old Paint, I'm a-leavin' Chey-ey-enne—"

Which meant Mr. Julian was peacefully listening to the radio and would not stir until Billy's Bronco-Busters had finished their broadcast.
And Sara, on the third floor, was forced to stay
with her grandmother after Lily Washington had
cooked dinner and gone home.

"All quiet?" Michael said. "Watch the stairs until I get this door open." After a few minutes,
in which the metallic scrape of key against lock
sounded phenomenally loud in Valerie's ears, he
turned and beckoned to her. "All right; get inside."

The Callendars' living room wanted only a sign:
Seven Piece Early California Suite. Inquire Inside
for Our Easy Budget Terms."

"I don't think," Michael muttered, "that I could
find a hiding place here for anything I really wanted to keep hidden."

"It's ridiculous to think Winona might have
written those letters. You don't know her."

"What are your favorite hiding places?"

"I have a secret drawer in my desk. At least I
hope Geneva doesn't know how to open it. She
rolls money up in her spare stockings. Do we—do
we have to discuss things like that here?" Valerie
said nervously. "Why didn't we—"

Michael gave her an unflattering look and
walked toward the bedroom. "There's nothing to

prevent your leaving. If you're going to stay keep an eye on the front door."

Valerie sat down on the extreme edge of the chesterfield; got up hastily and patted the cushions back into shape. The Callendars had friends in Marin County: they were probably weekending there and wouldn't be back until late tomorrow night. And there was no reason why Gus, the janitor, should come into the apartment. He might, of course, to see if everything was all right but he was the only one who could get in.

For an instant, as she heard the murmur of voices outside the door, Valerie stood perfectly still. She thought with desperate humor: I hope they give me a cell near Tommy's. Then she tiptoed with careful haste toward the bedroom, groped for the door and found it. Strong fingers slid down her arm and tightened about her wrist.

"I've opened the window. Get up the fire escape."

The cool, unexcited whisper was reassuring. Valerie said. "Up?"

"Yes. My bedroom window is open so you can get in."

"Aren't you coming?"

"Not just yet."

"Then I'm not either."

Michael pushed her toward the window. He said, not piously: "*Válgame Dios!* You little fool!"

"Sh-h! They're inside. Why, it's the Callendars. What do you suppose—"

Michael's hand shifted quickly from her wrist to her mouth. "*Cállese!*" he hissed. "Shut up—and listen."

It was at once evident the Callendars were quarreling and had been for some time. Grant's buttery tenor suggested it might have been he who had just slammed the door. He said:

"That's right: jump all over me. How could I find my door key with you yelling at me?"

"I never yell: I leave that to my great big he-man." Winona's voice was exasperatingly well bred. "Take off your shoes and make yourself comfortable, dear. Shall I get your pipe and slippers? This was your idea. It was you who didn't like the party."

"I still say it was crummy. Bunch of half-wits. And when you go off in corners with Jack and that fellow Ward am I supposed to like it? Or sit and twiddle my thumbs or talk to some nice old lady?"

"Like the one who offered to show you her panties?"

"Can't you let up on that? I told you she was tight. All I did was admire the color of her dress. She's the host's sister. I've got to be polite, haven't

I? It's different with a man. Can I help it if she says: 'I've got panties to match my dress. Want to see?' Can I?"

"I suppose you can't help your fatal fascination for middle-aged women," Winona conceded. "Or some not so old."

"I tell you there was absolutely nothing between me and that Farley girl! Do you expect me never to look at any woman but you?"

"You expect me never to look at another man. What's sauce for the goose, lovey."

"I don't know what's wrong with you lately, Nona. You used to be a pretty good sport. Lately you've been jumpy as a flea."

"What about yourself?"

"I have things at the bank to worry about," Mr. Callendar said unconvincingly. "Since we heard about Max—the Farley girl, there's been no living with you."

"You didn't take it so calmly."

"I don't like the police barking questions at me. Asking what she said to me yesterday when I talked to her a minute in the hall. She didn't say anything. But Sullivan acted like I was holding out on him. Why don't he question old Julian? He was always goggling after her."

"Why not Miss Julian?" Winona said. "She hated Maxine or I miss my guess. Well, you and

I alibied each other for last night. Not that it
means anything with twin beds. And it takes an
earthquake to wake you and I take sleeping tablets. But, my lad, you may be lucky they picked
poor Tommy Howard for the goat. If they hadn't
it might have been you or I. Jealous wife, philandering husband—"

"Oh—philandering? Look here, Nona, that's
putting it pretty strong. Have you anything to go
on? Have you"—Grant's voice suddenly sounded
less like that of a sulky boy—"have you gotten
any anonymous letters? Because I had one about—
well, that time you stayed over in San Rafael with
Fay. I—well, I took Maxine to the theater. I just
happened to mention it to her and somehow, before I realized it—"

"All right, darling. Mother understands. Only
you didn't tell me about it and I had a nasty, gloat-
ing letter—I threw it away. But how did you get
yours?"

"Why—in the mailbox. I always look in it when
I go to work."

"Oh. I hadn't thought of that. Then Mr. Julian
probably gets his that way—if he gets any."

"I'd like to know," Grant said. "Only you can't
ask or do anything. Tell the police and there 'd be
a lot of publicity."

"So what? You can't chase people in the dark and catch them delivering letters. Why not let the police do the dirty work?"

"I just told you why not. We'd be spread all over the newspapers and a man in my position can't afford scandal. No one can, Mother always says. Anyway, it's not serious. But how did you get your letter?"

"Under the door. You know I always get the paper while you're dressing. Oh, I'm glad you told me! Only don't you try it again. You leave red-heads alone."

Valerie moved cautiously, envying Michael his ability to stand perfectly still at the same time relaxed and alert. He whispered:

"Reconciliation. We'd better get out of here."

Valerie nodded, tiptoed across the narrow shaft of light streaming in from the living room and then stopped, one hand on the windowsill, as the doorbell rang.

CHAPTER SIX
"WHY'S HE COMING?"

Grant Callendar said fervently: "Damn! Can't a guy kiss his wife in peace? I'll get it, pet. But who knows we're home?"

An adolescent bass said: "Telegram, Mr. Callendar. Sign here. Thank you, sir. Good night."

"Well, now what— It's for you, Nona," Grant said. "Here: open it up. Who do you suppose—"

"It's from John. 'Will take evening plane. Meet me at airport seven Sunday night.'"

"Well?"

"Well—what? That's all," Winona said.

"I mean: why's he coming? You know he doesn't like to fly. What's his hurry? Has he had time to hear about Maxine? Would it be in the Los Angeles papers so soon?"

"How could it? It wasn't in our morning papers."

"He could hear it over the radio, though. It's funny," Grant said stubbornly. "Look: did he get any of those letters? Does he know you did?"

"Do you think I'd show it to him and let him know you'd stepped out with Maxine? He wouldn't have liked that—for more than one reason."

"Because he had a yen for her himself?"

"Yes—and on my account."

"That's none of his business," Grant said. "He's always criticizing me to you."

"No more than your mother is always running me down when she gets you alone. I don't know why he's coming. It must be important business and he wants to see us too. And I'll be glad to see him. He's always been very good to me. To us. He's generous, and if it wasn't for him we'd be broke all the time instead of just most of it. And don't scowl at me like that. I'm going to bed."

Michael said: "Alley-oop!" and joined Valerie on the fire escape. He stopped to pull down the window, shutting off Grant's: "You know I don't care how much he comes to see us. Just the same, he was pretty thick with Maxine."

Light flashed out from Winona Callendar's bedroom as Valerie scrambled across the windowsill into Michael's. She stood erect, shook herself experimentally and stared at her face in the mirror.

"Gosh! Is my hair still the same color? I thought I'd acquired a white streak like yours. If you go in for stunts like this I should think it would be white all over."

"'My hair is gray, but not with years,'" Michael drawled. "'Nor grew it white in a single night.' You would go along."

"You might at least say: 'I'm sorry I let you in for that.' What do you think?"

"Of the Callendars at home? I don't know—now."

"Well, did you have time to find anything?"

"Time not to find anything."

"Oh. Well, I'm sure Winona's had more than one letter," Valerie said. "Because she implied the one about Grant's taking Maxine to the theater came before Mr. Dozier left. And Maxine said she saw one under their door. If she saw it Winona may never have seen it at all."

"Have you decided where you're going to spend the night?"

"I'm not going to be sensible and go home. It might do Mother good to worry about me. Only whatever friend's home Geneva chooses to place me in, Mother will probably be convinced there I must be. I suppose one of those family hotels on Sutter will be the best place. Could you give me an overnight bag? It would look better to have luggage."

"I can give you a small Gladstone bag. And a toothbrush with cellophane unbroken and pajamas— I knew," Michael said, "that sooner or later this would begin to be a movie. Lovely young girl in out of fog, rain or what have you. Takes refuge in bachelor's apartment; dons host's pajamas which are inevitably too large. However, considering our relative heights, mine won't be—much. Yellow or dark red?"

Valerie giggled. "Have you nothing more subdued?"

"Yes, but not for you. Why is a person of your coloring fool enough to wear brown?"

"I don't know. I suppose I'm not much interested in clothes. Mother says brown is my color."

"Then Mother doesn't know what she's talking about." Michael closed the bag and stood erect. "Have you plenty of money? Well, then, let's go."

Valerie retrieved her hat from a chair in the living room. "You don't have to do this. In fact, I'm surprised that you do. It's quite safe for me to walk over to Sutter alone."

"Yes. Charge it up to the defects of education. I was taught always to pick up a lady's handkerchief when she drops it."

"And to yell at her in Spanish when she won't do what you say?"

"Spanish?" Some slight change in Michael's voice, if not his face, made Valerie think he might be somewhat annoyed. "Another defect of education," he said and held the door open. "If you're ready?"

"Oh, I'm going. I wouldn't think of compromising you," Valerie said sweetly, stepping into the hall. "Because— Oh! G-good evening."

"Is it?" Sara Putnam said. "I wouldn't know. I came out for some fresh air after getting the old lady to bed. That room of hers—" She put her fingers expressively to her thin nose. "I didn't know you and Mr. Dundas knew each other."

"Didn't you?" Michael said. Somehow the Gladstone bag had disappeared. He leaned against the wall, hands in his pockets. "We have a mutal friend. Herbert Ellison—you know Herbert?"

"I know him and I just saw him. He came out of your place, Valerie, all hot and bothered because you weren't home."

"I forgot about Herbert," Valerie said guiltily. "You see, I—that is, we—"

"Don't tell me: let me guess. You and Mamma had a row. I thought you would. I'm sorry about them arresting Tommy," Sara said, sounding not at all sorry. "Well, as they say about our relatives, thank God we can choose our friends. Going back and eat humble pie now?"

"No!"

"Which? Neither? Well, I can take you in if you don't mind sleeping on a couch," Sara said ungraciously. "And if you'll be quiet so the old lady don't wake up and want to know what it's all about."

"How charmingly you speak of your grandmother," Michael murmured.

"Did you ever see my grandmother? Well, save your comments till you do. Then you can probably think of two or three better terms for her. Well, what about it? Don't bother to be polite. It's wasted on me," Sara said truthfully. "If you'd rather crawl into a hole by yourself, say so."

Valerie did have just that desire but she realized suddenly that she was very tired. Only to think of walking six or seven blocks to some hotel had a weakening effect on her knees. She looked questioningly at Michael.

"I can get the car out," he said. "But it might be wise for you to stay here. If it was discovered you'd spent the night at a hotel the newspapers would want to know why. 'Rift Between Suspect's Fiancé and Mother . . .'"

"That's ambiguous," Valerie said wearily. "But I suppose newspapers are. I'll stay, Sara, thank you. Good night—Michael."

That was all she could say with Sara standing there.

But his blue eyes were suddenly amused as if he knew exactly what she was thinking: that she did not intend in any way to take advantage of Sara's hospitality.

"Good night. Don't worry. As Herbert would say, we must let events take their course," he said. "I'll see you tomorrow."

In her small bedroom Sara removed a tennis racket, three golf clubs, a racing form and a hockey stick from the couch.

"You take the bed. Go ahead, it's more comfortable even if it is a single. And the sheets are clean. I've got to make this up and you're all in. I could see that: like you'd just finished a hard game of basketball. Excitement doesn't keep you going forever. Sorry I can't give you any cold cream."

"Soap and water will do," Valerie said, laughing. "It usually does."

"Another hope gone. I like to kid myself that if I took care of it my skin 'd look like something besides leather."

"Oh, but it—"

"Save it," Sara said, grinning. "What else does a big wholesome out-of-doors girl like me expect? Here's some pajamas. You get into bed."

Meekly Valerie obeyed while Sara spread sheets and blankets on the couch, pulled three hairpins from her yellowish-brown hair and brushed it vigorously. She was not, Valerie thought drowsily, half so unattractive as she believed. Or perhaps her frankness regarding her own shortcomings was only a protective pose. If you admitted the worst about yourself that usually kept others from making disparaging remarks.

If Sara was, secretly, sensitive, she'd been forced to learn to hide the fact. You couldn't coach sports at an exclusive private school and be a shrinking violet.

Valerie yawned and closed her eyes as Sara put out the light. She was right: you couldn't keep going forever on excitement or anger. Even fear must be, sometimes, replaced by something approaching apathy, when it came to you that what you thought couldn't be endured, must be.

And there was no use painting pathetic pictures of Tommy lying awake in his cell, thinking wistfully of her. Because—Valerie smiled into her pillow—Tommy, if she knew him, would sleep as soundly on a prison bed as on his own. As Herbert had said, Tommy had no nerves and he was superbly healthy.

What was he going to think of Michael Dundas? Though normally he appeared trusting as a puppy, he might very well ask: "What's Dundas getting out of it?" And naturally, why Valerie had trusted him. Well, why had she? Simply because he did not loudly protest his good intentions? Or because his cold scrutiny of facts helped restore one's sense of proportion?

"If Dundas makes his money playing the ponies," Sara said suddenly, "I'd like to know his system."

"His—what?"

"I've seen him at Bay Meadows. Once he was sitting two rows in front of me and I happened to see he had fifty on Tall Oak to win. Well, Tall Oak paid about sixty-eight for two—"

"Dollars, you mean?"

"What else? The man must have ice water in his veins; he never even blinked an eye."

"I can believe that," Valerie murmured. "Do you bet?"

"Do you think I go to look at the horses?"

"I've heard of people who like horses and like to see them run."

"Oh, I do. But you always end by backing your judgment. That's what you call it if you're optimistic. Why not? Have you any idea what kind of salaries they pay teachers at ritzy private schools? And my honored grandparent is rolling," Sara said. "Also, she gets tighter every year. Keeps telling me what my father cost her."

"But—but don't mothers expect to spend some money on their children?"

"You didn't know my father. Grandma paid plenty to keep him out of trouble. She was plain foolish over him. You see, she got him back when my mother died. Then we trotted all over the world, up to five years ago. That's how we met Geneva, you know. She was companioning that foul Kelsey woman who was a pal of Grandma's once and we ran into them in Italy. Funny how Americans traveling do run into each other. But Dad died and sometimes I think Grandma's never been just right since then."

"I'd forgotten that. I mean: that you did meet Geneva before you moved here."

"Oh yes, she greeted me like a long-lost pal when we happened to run into each other down on Market," Sara said. "She recommended this place when she found out I was looking for an apartment. She's a great little recommender. When we first got back from Europe Grandma had an idea she wanted to live by the sea: where she could see it, you know. She picked a dump called White Sands down near Santa Cruz. I came up here and thought I was going to be on my own. It didn't work out. She got mad at the hotel management because they had to do the place over and sent for me. Said she needed my loving care and she's been getting it ever since."

The couch springs creaked violently as she changed position. "I've been wondering—I suppose the police wanted to know who Maxine's friends were and you mentioned Gregory Lutz?"

"Gregory Lutz?" The name finally brought back to Valerie a hazy remembrance of a thin man badly in need of a haircut, who had stared at her for some minutes, muttered: "Good bones," and walked away. "Isn't he a painter?"

"Yes. I met him at your place. Maxine had invited him. She met him at art school. I like him," Sara said. "I don't know why. He thinks Seabiscuit is something sailors eat. But I— Well, I was wondering if you'd told the police about him."

"I didn't and I don't believe Geneva would remember him. We only saw him once and Maxine never spoke of him."

"She saw him more than once though. I've been in his studio: he wanted a woman athlete for some work he was doing. There are about four heads of Maxine in his place."

"Oh. But—but are you telling just me this?" Valerie said. "Or may I—"

"You can tell Dundas if you want to. You obviously weren't talking to him about the weather. Well, I have an idea he'd be a damned good friend and a bad enemy. Anyway, I suppose the police will discover Gregory for themselves. There's nothing I can do about that.

"Anyway, he doesn't really know I exist," Sara added stoically. "Oh, he doesn't mind having me around. He likes the way I cook spaghetti and I'm fool enough to go up to his studio sometimes. It's just—funny. Me and the artistic set."

"But Maxine was probably just a face to him."

"Maybe—and maybe not. If I see him, I'll warn him. I don't think he reads anything but the art section in the newspapers. Sorry I kept you awake. Good night. . . ."

In a few minutes, to judge by her breathing, she was asleep. To Valerie, suddenly wakeful, the slight sound was annoying. She wished Sara hadn't spoken to Gregory Lutz. He and any other men Maxine might have known were a complication she and Michael couldn't deal with.

Of course the police could and would. Sullivan would find out, if he didn't already know, about Maxine's spasmodic attendance at the California School of Fine Arts. There would be people there to tell him Maxine had known Gregory. And when Sullivan discovered Sara knew him too he wouldn't be apt to overlook the "woman-scorned" angle.

On that thought Valerie fell asleep. When she woke it was to that unnatural quiet that comes so briefly to a city. No sound of automobiles on the streets; not even the faint jingle of the bell on the Washington Street cable car. Too early for milk-men or garbage collectors, too late for more than a stray home-going pedestrian or motorist.

Valerie sighed rebelliously. She had dreamed: a pleasant, vague dream of racing hand in hand with

Tommy along the edge of the curling surf on the white wet sand at Carmel. And someone had been watching them: someone whose features remained a dim blur. Was it Maxine or Michael?—or Inspector Sullivan? Why hadn't she finished that dream?

Because someone was watching her now. Fat hunched shoulders were dark against the pale light from the open window. The face, in that light, was a featureless blob of white that moved tremulously from side to side. Toward the bureau, the door and the couch where Sara should have been.

Valerie closed her eyes tightly. It was only old Mrs. Putnam and if she pretended to be asleep she would go away. But feet padded softly across the carpet toward the bed and hands fumbled over the covers. Too vividly Valerie remembered those mottled hands with their long, dirty nails— She would scream if they touched her.

She opened her eyes and looked into Mrs. Putnam's face, trying to smile. The old woman smiled back: a toothless, repulsive smile that Valerie still guessed was meant to be reassuring. She whispered:

"Are you ill? Shall I call Sara?"

"No! Sara says I'm sick because she wants me to sleep. You can't sleep well when you get old. I get nervous too. I think I smell smoke and there's a fire. Of course I don't, but I'm afraid of fire."

"I'm sorry you can't sleep."

The eyes looking into hers were perfectly sane. They must even have been beautiful before they were blurred with age. She had never noticed that before or, the few times she had seen her, looked at Mrs. Putnam too closely. She didn't want to now; pity could overcome fear but not repulsion. Mrs. Putnam's thick whisper continued:

"Sara had to tell me your sister is dead. She doesn't like to tell me things. But they don't upset me so she might as well. Do you get letters?"

"What—what kind of letters?"

"One said I was crazy. Sara hides them but I saw this one. As if I'd care. People always say you're crazy if you don't act like they do. I'm sane enough to hold onto money and make more. Sara will get plenty—if she behaves."

"Does Lily Washington see the letters?" Valerie said.

"She doesn't get here early enough and she can't read. You know, Mr. Dozier called me crazy once. But I know something about crazy people. You can't always tell. That cousin of yours and Emma Julian—they come up here with their long faces, pitying me. They needn't. What have they ever had out of life? Emma was in love once. Her family didn't approve. Gave her a trip to Europe."

"Grandma"—Sara's voice was low and controlled but her hand on the old lady's shoulder was peremptory— "Valerie is tired and you shouldn't be up. Come back to bed."

Mrs. Putnam turned obediently. "All right. But where were you, Sara?"

"Where do you suppose? Come on." Returning in a few minutes Sara said: "I'm sorry, but I warned you. Don't pay any attention to anything she said. She takes streaks when she wants to talk. Good night."

CHAPTER SEVEN
"DEATH COMES AT LAST—"

"Oh, sure, the police was here," Mathilde said. "And I had to admit I've did your hair and Miss Farley's three years, includin' the day she was killed. But believe me I told that Mick where to head in when he begun asking was you friendly with Miss Farley did I know. The idea!"

"Well, Mathilde, you do say that women tell beauty operators what they wouldn't tell their best friends as a secret."

"That's so. But I didn't tell Sullivan so or that I do Mrs. Callendar and Miss Julian that lives in your place and once in a while Miss Putnam."

"Do you think Inspector Sullivan would suspect them?"

"How would I know?" Mathilde, who had been born Martha, put down her nail file and regarded herself resignedly in a mirror. "Never get a chance to do my own hair," she mourned, vainly attempting to smooth down her yellow-white bush of stringy curls. "I'm a swell ad for a beauty shop."

She got up, tugging at the starched apron that rode high over her substantial bosom. "My slip still show? Oh well, the strap's broke. Mind if I get on with my work?"

"I didn't think of you until this morning," Valerie said. "Then I came right over. I knew you cleaned the place Sunday mornings. Mathilde, was Maxine the same as usual Friday?"

"Fussy about her hair, like always. I asked was she getting ready for a heavy date and she said: maybe. Laughing. She did seem kind of excited," Mathilde remembered, pausing in her sweeping. "We was talking about money and she says: 'I'm going to get money. And then—you watch my smoke.'"

"Was that all?"

"I asked what 'd she spend money for. Fool question. She says: 'Oh, you'd be surprised. You can get anything you want with money.' So I said: 'You got a job?' just keeping the conversation going, the way we do. She laughed and says: 'Not a job. Just nerve.' Then I put her under the dryer so that was all."

"You didn't tell Inspector Sullivan what she said?"

"He come right when I was busiest, doing a permanent on long hair with a dame that had nerves. Honest, she acted like a six-year-old. Well, I've always liked you, dearie, and it's tough, them arresting your boyfriend. I'm not one of these fool women wants their picture in the paper and I got my customers to think of."

"You mean Mrs. Callendar and Miss Julian?"

"Um-hum. They didn't like Miss Farley very well."

"I know Mrs. Callendar didn't."

"On account of her husband? The things women tell me about their husbands it ain't hardly decent. Mrs. Callendar never come right out and said he was too friendly with Miss Farley but she might as well have. And they just barely spoke when they'd happen to meet in here."

Valerie silently gave thanks for the scorn of the police that caused Mathilde's loquacity to be directed toward her and not Inspector Sullivan. Mathilde, absently using a buffer on her broad nails, went on:

"One day Miss Farley was in the booth and Miss Putnam out here—only Miss Farley didn't know it. We was talking about athaletics and how they put bulges in legs and Miss Farley says: look at Miss Putnam's. Well, Miss Putnam's got nice legs, seems to me like. But then Miss Farley says: 'These athaletic women are all just sweet sixteen at heart. When they fall in love they're weird.' She laughed real nasty too. But when she came out here and seen Miss Putnam she never turned a hair. But the way Miss Putnam looked at her!

"Well, she's not a talker. Miss Julian's just the other way. She worries a lot about that brother of hers marrying."

Valerie laughed. "Did you ever see Mr. Julian?"

"Dearie, I don't care what he looks like, a man with a bank roll can get somebody. I wouldn't mind marrying again." Mathilde said candidly. "I wouldn't expect the guy to look like Robert Taylor. But evert guys like Julian want something for their money. If he got him a young wife—or any kind—where 'd Miss Julian be?"

"She took care of the mother who was bedrid for years. Says she was a saint but old people got a right to die and it ain't right to want to keep 'em alive forever. Why, for all she's been dead six years, Miss Julian still worries would her mamma want her to touch up her hair. What I tell her: gray hair is faded hair and you wouldn't wear a faded dress, would you?"

"But surely Miss Julian didn't think Maxine would marry Mr. Julian—if he wanted her to."

"She called Miss Farley a hussy, which is strong language for her. Said she'd flirt with anything that wore pants. Well, if there's a bank roll in the pocket of the pants— But I told your sister once: with her looks she'd ought to do well for herself.

She said: 'Oh—looks! What chance have I to meet the right kind of man in my own home?' She says some things about your mamma horning in on parties that I won't repeat.

"But then she said: the trouble is girls like you ain't in society but you got a certain position. Too respectable, was the way she put it. And so, first thing you know you fall for some fellow that's got nothing—and there you are."

"I suppose she had me in mind."

"I wouldn't wonder. She never talked about you though, except to say she wished she had your money. But your mamma come here once—"

"Go on."

"Well, maybe I shouldn't tell you." Mathilde stacked ancient movie magazines in a neat pile. "She said she didn't like Mr. Howard. Said he was rude to her."

"Oh, he isn't! It's just—he isn't very—deferential or gallant and Mother—"

"I guess your mamma's kind of flirtatious," Mathilde said. Valerie winced. "Not very maternal. The wrong women gets the babies, seems to me like. I should 've had about six but me 'n Jellick never had no luck. It wasn't for want of trying. Well, I got to get togged up to go out for dinner, and take my clippers and scissors along," Mathilde said cynically, "because someone's going to want a free haircut after dinner. Honest, the crust of some people. Well, dearie, good luck to you."

Valerie thought, walking the four blocks back to the apartment house, not of what she would say to her mother but of early morning in the Putnam apartment and of what Mathilde had just told her. She produced her latchkey mechanically, went into her bedroom and took off coat and hat.

But the room seemed, all at once, horribly empty. Maxine had always dominated it, flinging her clothes untidily on bed and chairs, smearing the top of the dressing table with lipstick and powder. She never closed a powder jar: it was open now with the puff lying beside it.

Valerie put the lid back on the jar and a comb in its brush; went into the living room and raised the blinds. She was sitting there on the chesterfield when Geneva tiptoed in, with her look of a good Samaritan in a house of sorrow.

"Well! My goodness, Valerie, how could you? I had to call a doctor for poor Mother."

"The good-looking young one?"

"Oh, if you're going to be like that! Doctor Sanford understands your mother's case perfectly."

"I never doubted that."

"Well—you did give us a scare, Valerie, but I see there's no use talking to you. Where did you stay?"

"With Sara Putnam."

"Oh. Did Mrs. Putnam ask you or did Sara? Why did they do it, do you suppose? Did you see Mrs. Putnam or did Sara say how she was?"

"The same as usual, I suppose."

"She's a sick woman," Geneva said solemnly. "And Sara isn't at all sympathetic. I'd like to know Mrs. Putnam is getting good care. Oh, Herbert came last night and he was very upset when you weren't here. He says Tommy is bearing up very well and he dosen't want you to come to the jail to see him."

"Why not? I think I've been very—very discreet and patient, waiting this long and I'm not—"

"Now, dear, let's not get excited. I must say Tommy is being surprisingly thoughtful. Though Herbert did hint that if you admit your little understanding it might make the case against him stronger."

"Make me the 'other woman'? I thought Maxine was that."

"Now you mustn't be bitter. We're all so sorry for you. Well, now, what have I said?" Geneva inquired plaintively. "But Herbert did say to wait and see and surely one day doesn't matter? Because of course you'd be seen and they'd probably take your picture. There were reporters here again last night and it was very hard to know what to tell them."

"What did you tell them?" Valerie asked.

"That you were staying with friends. But I know it looked queer when your mother was prostrated. She's still asleep but I know as soon as she's awake you'll go right in and say you're sorry."

Valerie looked at her stonily. "Do you? Then you're an incurable optimist. Geneva, did Mother talk to Maxine Friday?"

"You know Patricia didn't feel well enough to get up for lunch. And Maxine left right afterward to have her hair done."

"But she didn't," Valerie said. "Her appointment was for two o'clock and I left here before she did. And from something Mother said that morning I think she was considering talking to Maxine."

"Well, you know I was in the kitchen after lunch so I wouldn't have heard if she had."

"Since when?" Valerie said rudely. "You mean: if you did hear them quarreling, you won't tell. Geneva, honestly, have you lived with us all this time with your eyes closed? Don't you know Mother pretty well by now? Why can't you be honest, just once?"

"Why, Valerie, I am! I just hate insincere people. But I have a way of always seeing the best in people and—"

"Oh, all right," Valerie said wearily. She got up, stooped to push back one of the three white leather cushions and saw the edge of a sheet of paper protruding from the space between the cushion and the side of the chesterfield.

With her back to Geneva she drew it out, glanced at it quickly. But it wasn't one of the anonymous letters. It was a pencil sketch of a man in the court costume of Charles I. Curling hair fell to the shoulders and the rosettes and ribbons at the knees of the breeches and the fanciful design on the skirts of the doublet were carefully done. But the face had been left blank.

It was Maxine's work, for at the bottom of the page she had printed in block letters: "Death comes at last like a dark cavalier." Below that in her own writing was the name "Valerie," its final "*e*" trailing off indecisively as if the pencil had faltered and then stopped.

Valerie turned quickly, one hand behind her back, as Geneva said: "What is it? Lose something? Those cushions just won't stay back."

"Where was Maxine sitting when she was reading Friday night?"

"Right there in that corner. She was drawing too, I thought. I asked her what she was doing but she didn't answer me. She was reading that circulating-library book on the table over there. I told Inspector Sullivan that and he looked through it. Did you you find something, Valerie? What is it? A letter?"

"Have you done anything to these cushions since then?"

"I haven't had time and no one sat in here yesterday."

"All right. I'm going out," Valerie said.

"But you just came in! And where—"

"I'll be upstairs talking to Mr. Dundas. Tell Herbert if he calls again."

Michael, opening the door, said ungraciously: "You? What now?"

"Well—good heavens! Didn't you expect to see me again? May I come in or are you going to close the door in my face?"

"Come in, of course. Certainly I expected to see you but not at this hour."

"What hour? It's after ten. You're up, aren't you?"

"Just," Michael said, sitting down and pouring coffee from the pot on a small table by his chair. "Will you have some? I have," he added morosely, "nothing but hatred for people who spring out of bed shouting: 'Isn't this a glorious morning?'"

"I don't," Valerie said indignantly. Then she giggled. "I'm sure no one will ever accuse you of that. And if you'd had the kind of night I had you probably wouldn't be up even at this late hour. Well, aren't you curious?"

"Not yet. I'm never curious in the morning: just at night. Or perhaps after three o'clock in the afternoon."

"Well, you don't need to go on with this, you know! I don't have to have your help."

"You remind me of a wire-haired terrier," Michael said. "They won't be snubbed, they're desperately loyal and they'll often tackle things too large for them. All right, unburden yourself."

He lay back in the chair and closed his eyes. When Valerie had finished talking he said exasperatingly: "Well?"

"You'd better go back to bed. Or would you like an aspirin?"

"Make it two aspirins." Michael poured a few last it drops from the coffeepot. "I had an idea or two after we parted, my child. And work to do while you slept."

"Slept! I told you—"

"Yes, yes. What your hairdresser told you may be very useful. It fits in nicely with the hints Miss Farley had already thrown out to you. Although— Well, file that conversation for future reference."

"But what do you think about Mrs. Putnam?"

"What do you?"

"I do wonder where Sara was," Valerie said. "Perhaps in the bathroom. Perhaps not. I don't know what to think. Was Sara out distributing notes and Mrs. Putnam trying to catch her at it or vice versa?"

"Sara knew you were there and Mrs. Putnam, presumably, didn't."

"I know I said I'd pick Mrs. Putnam as Poison Pen. But until last night I never really talked to her. And she did seem different than I'd expected. It worried me, not being able to decide if she wanted to talk to me for some special reason. If Sara wanted to keep her isolated from people I suppose she could, with Lily Washington's help. And does Mrs. Putnam think someone here is insane? How could she know—"

"But that, I thought, was one of the most interesting things you learned. I mean: that she appears to know something of Miss Julian's life. And that your cousin, Geneva, had come in contact with the Putnams before they came here."

"I could have told you that," Valerie said. "I don't see why it's important. Are those points against Mrs. Putnam?"

"Not necessarily. If Mrs. Putnam knew Miss Julian and Miss Nolan some years ago so did they know her. It works both ways."

"Oh. And what about Gregory Lutz?"

"Sullivan will discover him—and deal with him. I've met Lutz."

"You have? Did he ever mention Maxine? Have you been in his studio?"

"I said I'd met him, not that we are friends. I'd say Lutz is singularly harmless. When did Miss Farley first begin attending art classes?"

"Off and on for the past year. At least, she said she was attending some night classes and she must have gone sometimes because she introduced us to people she met at them. I thought she drew rather well but she wouldn't work at it."

"This isn't bad," Michael agreed, glancing at the drawing she had given him. "Do you think it's important?"

"Doesn't it show what direction her thoughts were taking that night? I think she knew she was in danger. If she'd ever confided in anyone she might have in me. I think she started to write to me and then decided not to. I don't think she meant the picture for a message at first. She often sketched aimlessly when she was reading."

"She did sometimes read poetry?"

"Yes. That quotation is from the beginning of a poem I know she read and liked."

"'I am the dark cavalier; I am the last lover.'* Well, I'll keep this and you keep still about it. It might be useful later on. Just now I'm very much interested in Mr. Dozier."

"But he may be coming here just on business. That explanation didn't satisfy Grant," Valerie ad-

* From Margaret Widdemer's poem, "The Dark Cavalier," and reprinted by permission of Farrar & Rinehart, Inc., publishers.

mitted, "and I don't think Winona really believed it. But he couldn't have killed Maxine. And where does he fit in as far as the letters are concerned?"

"I wish I knew. Would he talk to you?"

"He was always very pleasant. Mother," Valerie said with a wry smile, "issued several invitations but that didn't lead to friendship. To put it vulgarly, Mr. Dozier wasn't having any. But we're not supposed even to know he's coming here."

"I think," Michael said dreamily, "that I have a friend on the same plane Mr. Dozier is taking. Of course he may be unavoidably delayed but I shall meet him at the airport."

"May I go too? I can point Mr. Dozier out to you. But after that—"

"After that we must use our wits and . . ." Michael broke off, listening. "The silence was shattered by a strange and unusual sound," he drawled, getting up. "Shall we see what it is?"

CHAPTER EIGHT
CANCELED CHECK

Sara Putnam was leaning over the banisters, looking down at the second-floor hall. "The Wyoming cowboys have arrived," she said over her shoulder. "Brother Charlie in person."

Brother Charlie, catching sight of her, stopped in his rendition of the "Hills of Old Wyoming" and bellowed: "Hi, Babe! Climb down from your balcony, Juliet, and give a guy a break."

"Well, I'll be— First time anyone called me Juliet. Is he pie-eyed?" Sara said admiringly. "Wait till Emma sees him."

"But Mr. Julian never drinks," Valerie said, meeting Michael's quizzical look. "Honestly, I never saw him like this."

Mr. Julian had one foot on an imaginary rail and was singing loudly: "'The Rhine may be fine but a cold stein for mine, Down where the Wurzburger flows . . . Nora Bayes, God bless her! Set 'em up, barkeep. Will you join me, young feller? What 'll you have?"

"Make mine the same," Michael said gravely, starting down the stairs. Mr. Julian attempted to lean his elbow on a nonexistent bar and Michael was just in time to hoist him to his feet again.

"Damn funniest bar I ever saw," Mr. Julian confided. "You don' wanna trus' it. Don't stan' still! Hi, Emmie! Howsa girl? What 'll you have? This one's on me."

"He's sick!" Miss Julian gasped. "He's—he's delirious!"

"Never felt better in my life." Mr. Julian draped himself lovingly on Michael's shoulder. "Me 'n my ol' pal. What's your name, buddy? No memory for names but never forget a face. Dundas? Sure, I remember you."

"You've never even met him, Charlie. Oh, you are sick!"

Miss Julian clasped her hands agitatedly and a few wisps of ostrich feather floated away from the sleeves of her negligee. Miss Julian fell heir to the cast-off wardrobe of a sister in Portland and wore it, suitable or not. Beads and feathers were forever dropping from her clothes or they were decorated with dejected flounces and limp frills. Her brassy hair glittered mendaciously above a soft, ineffectual face that was puckered now as a prelude to tears.

"I'll—I'll get a doctor. It must be something he ate."

"He hasn't been eating," Michael said coolly. "He's tight."

"T-tight?"

"Cock-eyed, blotto, stinko, swacked, soused, tanked. Or, if you prefer, under the influence."

"Oh, but Charlie never— Except for a little prune wine. It was really breaking the law but Mother always— Perfectly harmless in case of sickness. Oh, what would Mother say?"

"Now, we mustn't take on," Geneva said firmly, swishing up the stairs. "We must be charitable. Brother probably wasn't feeling well and he took just a *litt*-le too much. Tomorrow he'll be so ashamed of himself and we'll forget all about it."

Michael looked at Valerie, his straight black brows lifted in wordless ejaculation. She smiled down at him, shoulders raised, hands outstretched in the traditional Hebraic gesture. He grinned at her suddenly; murmured: "'Why lookest thou so? With my crossbow I shot the Albatross.'"

Geneva, dealing firmly with the situation, went on: "He must go to bed. You come right along with me, Mr. Julian."

Mr. Julian looked at her like a curious turkey gobbler eyeing a doubtful worm. "Don' wanna," he decided. "It's like the Irishman says to Mrs. Murphy: 'I've got the time but not the inclination.'"

"Well, I—" Geneva's face was a full-blown scarlet peony. She caught Valerie's subdued snicker and Sara's deep snort of laughter, looked at them in sorrowing resentment and withdrew.

"Where," Michael wondered, "does she get all the starch?" and gave ear to Mr. Julian's confidences.

"Like 'em young, I do. Like to buy 'em pretty things. No use draping clothes on a bean pole, is there? Em's a bean pole. Other woman's too fat. Don' like her hair. Don' like Em's hair. She— S-hh!" Mr. Julian said loudly. "Em dyes her hair. Foolishness! Well, why don' we sing . . ."

He droned: "'The jushdge said: Stan' up, boy, An' dry up your tearsh. You' goin' to Nashville for twen'y-one yearsh . . .' Good song. You know a song? Oughta have a guitar."

"I have." Michael adjusted an imaginary guitar and began to strum it, steering Mr. Julian unobtrusively toward his own door. "Do you like this one? 'Mexican maidens strum guit-*ars* and sing, About young Billy, their boy-bandit king.'"

"Hi-de-oh-de-oh!" said Mr. Julian happily. "Y'know, I didn't see that guitar at first. Play s'more."

To the accompaniment of the wailing minor refrain they disappeared into the apartment while Miss Julian skittered aside like a frightened hen.

"Men—men know what to do. Oh, dear, whatever possessed— My palpitation— I feel so—so—"

"Give her a snort of prune juice," Sara advised. "I've got to get home before Grandma adds herself to the menagerie. Oh—hello."

"H-hello," Grant Callendar said uncertainly. "We heard— It's all right, Nona. Nothing, after all."

"Just Mr. Julian," Sara said. "He's been hoisting a few."

"Julian! Well, I'm damned. Thought he was a teetotaler," Grant said with his high abrupt laugh. "Hear that, Nona?"

"I heard. Don't take it too hard, Miss Julian," Winona said perfunctorily.

"Oh, but Charlie— The most awful fluttering feelings." Miss Julian clutched her heart in the manner of a movie villain receiving his death wound. "Bicarbonate! And Charlie hasn't ever—"

"You want to watch them at that age," Winona said. "He may have been drowning a sorrow or two. I'm going inside."

She slammed the door. Grant murmured embarrassedly: "She's kind of cross this morning. Maybe you'd like a drink yourself, Miss Julian. I've got some brandy: do you good."

"Oh, I couldn't! I never in my— Oh, dear; they're singing again!"

Valerie giggled as Michael's clear plaintive baritone blended with Mr. Julian's thick bass, announcing that the Martins and the Coys were reckless mountain boys.

"An opportunist at work," she murmured. "Give him time and they'll be playing cards together. You might as well come inside and sit down, Miss Julian."

"Well . . ." Miss Julian allowed herself to be led into the living room. Then: "Cards!" she said. "Oh, those dreadful cards! It worries me. And Charlie sneers at the finer things in life. Like Faith and Hope and the other world. And now this. After all, Mother . . . And if it comforts me . . . Oh, dear!"

The room was overcrowded with gaudily upholstered furniture, pictures from Woolworth's hanging a little crooked, and small inexpertly braided rugs scattered haphazardly over a floral carpet. Valerie removed a stack of newspapers, a sewing basket, three wrapped taffy chews and

a needle from the chesterfield and invited Miss
Julian again to sit down.

"Mr. Dundas is putting your brother to bed.
There! Can I get something for you?"

"Oh no. So nice of Mr. Dundas. Well, I
shouldn't, but this all-gone feeling— Just one little glass. Because prune wine couldn't hurt—not
the way Mother made it. In that decanter—"

Valerie looked dubiously at the muddy liquid
in the decanter but Miss Julian sipped it gratefully. "Has—has your brother been upset about
anything lately?" she asked.

"He was a little cross Friday but I don't— And
I must tell you you have our sincerest sympathy
though of course she wasn't really your sister but
Mr. Howard— You must forgive me, but did your
sister—of course I mean your stepsister—did she
ever mention my brother to you?"

"Not in the way I think you mean."

"Well, your sister was flirtatious and Charlie—
he admires pretty girls. So I thought— You remember, dear, I showed you a—a letter and I've
wondered if you've had—"

"Have you had other letters?"

"Oh yes. So disagreeable that I burned them.
This morning there was another." Miss Julian drew
a sheet of paper from her flat bosom. "You see—

WHERE WAS YOUR BROTHER FRIDAY NIGHT WHERE
WERE YOU. And Charlie said he was going to play
cards like he always does but this morning one of
the men phoned and asked why he hadn't turned
up. And I don't like to ask him to explain because— Well, and I went to bed early and don't
know what time he got in."

"I wouldn't worry," Valerie said. "Whoever
wrote that letter is probably asking the same question of everyone here."

Miss Julian brightened. "I hadn't thought of
that. And you know, dear, I'm afraid your sister
wasn't so well liked. Mrs. Callendar—well, there
was Mr. Callendar but there was Mr. Dozier too.
And he was very good to Mrs. Callendar and she
didn't like him being interested in your sister.
I'm sure your sister used to go to his apartment
and that wasn't—nice. But she's dead, poor thing,
so—"

She suddenly sat forward on the chesterfield,
lowering her voice until Valerie could hardly hear
her. "My dear, could you—could you lend me ten
dollars?"

Valerie, following the direction of Miss Julian's
eyes, realized that she had not put down her purse
in Michael's apartment and was holding it in her
lap.

"Why—of course," she said, opening it. "Is that enough?"

"Well, if you could—twenty? Oh, I do thank you! I'll pay you back the first of June when I get my housekeeping money. And I wouldn't ask you but I— Charlie is so cross," Miss Julian said, clutching the bills. "And I simply must know. Oh, dear, isn't he ever going to be quiet?"

"I think he's going to sleep now," Valerie said. "Mr. Dundas is crooning a final lullaby."

"You won't have any trouble with him for a while," Michael promised, coming into the room. "Have some good strong coffee for him when he wakes. If he feels too badly I'll mix him a little concoction that might reduce the size of his head."

"His—his head? The size—"

"It will probably feel like a balloon inflated to the bursting point when he does wake up."

"Oh. You see, I don't understand about— Thank you so much, Mr. Dundas. And you really have a lovely voice," Miss Julian said gratefully. "You should be in radio."

"That," Michael said, "is a doubtful compliment. I've been in radio. Are you ready, Valerie?"

"Whenever you are," Valerie said dutifully. But in the hall she complained: "I sound like a browbeaten wife. And this sudden excess of chivalry toward a helpless maiden lady—"

"I was under the impression I heard you pumping her very skillfully. But perhaps that was two other people?"

Valerie flushed. "Well—I did. And you listened. But I don't think you heard her borrow twenty dollars from me."

"Has she ever done that before?"

"She's never borrowed from me. I wonder if she has from anyone else? And if she wanted this for some real emergency or just because she finds herself short in her housekeeping accounts again?"

"She must be a superlatively bad manager if she is twenty dollars short with the first of the month more than two weeks away." Michael opened his front door. "Here is something interesting for you to look at. Does it mean anything to you?"

"A canceled check. Why, it's made out to Maxine! One hundred and fifty dollars—Charles Julian." She turned the check over, staring at Maxine's name and a further stamped endorsement. "'Gisele'—so that's where she got the money!"

"For what?"

"A matching dress and light coat and hat. She bought it last month and I wondered how she could afford it. Because Gisele's is a very exclusive shop in Maiden Lane and they don't sell anything cheap. But I wouldn't have supposed Mr. Julian would be foolish enough to give her a check or that he would at least have made it out to cash."

Michael shrugged. "He isn't married and his money is his own. Are there any other items in Miss Farley's wardrobe not warranted by her income?"

"A coat she bought last winter, perhaps. I thought when she told me what it cost that she had found a wonderful bargain. But I know so little about clothes. I'll look through her closet."

"We aren't getting anywhere," Michael said discontentedly. "We're discovering some facts about our fellow tenants."

"But what good is it doing us? Well, what else can we do? It does seem that the more we know about everyone the nearer we should be to knowing who wrote those letters. But it's maddening to go so slowly with Tommy still in jail."

"The mere fact of being in jail won't hurt him," Michael said unsympathetically. "It's a very restful place."

"But if he's brought to trial that won't be restful!"

"You don't look far enough ahead. Suppose he's freed simply because the case against him is not quite strong enough? In a way, that would be simply a bastard verdict and while it might satisfy you I doubt if it would him."

"And it won't me! Why don't we prove something? Do something?"

Michael sighed and sank deeper into his chair. "Last night we broke and entered and I have just picked a man's pocket."

"Oh, is that how you got that check?"

"No, I hung his coat in the closet and an envelope with his bank statement fell out of an inside pocket."

"Did it?" Valerie said doubtfully. "Fall, I mean?"

"What do you think? That's my story and I'll stick to it. He was also carrying three letters I thought it unwise to appropriate. One asked pleasantly if he were fool enough to suppose any woman was interested in anything but his money. The second warned him to beware of his sister since his death will make her a rich woman. And the third wanted to know if his sister did not find Miss Farley's death somewhat convenient. Ending with the classic query: 'Where were you when the lights went out?'"

"Oh, Michael—not really?"

"No," Michael said wearily. "Literally, if you insist: WHERE WERE YOU FRIDAY NIGHT WHERE WAS YOUR SISTER."

"If Grant got his letters in the mailbox, I should think Mr. Julian would too. But this is Sunday."

"Have you never investigated your mailbox on Sundays?"

"Well—yes. I've put my fingers into the slot as I passed—automatically. And there are advertisements. I suppose that's what Mr. Julian did. Of course you know we have a very early delivery here. Often as early as eight-thirty, which is about the time Grant leaves the house. And Mr. Julian often takes a walk after breakfast. All of us know that. They always write letters to themselves, don't they? They don't dare not to."

"Yes, but if your letter writer wanted to be clever it might be a good stunt to omit sending herself any letters."

"Why? Oh—then she could argue: 'If I'd written them I wouldn't place myself under suspicion by *not* writing any to myself.' Oh—oh, gosh!"

"The Albatross must have taken in this morning's paper," Michael said.

"Because I wasn't home? Yes, it was gone from the hall when I finally got home. So if there was a letter she got that too. Maybe," Valerie said pessimistically as the doorbell rang, "that's her now. If it is you can try your hand at dealing with her. I'd like to see you."

But it was Herbert Ellison, tallish, plumpish, pinkish—in nothing would Herbert go to extremes—looking at them uneasily.

"Geneva said you were here, Valerie. She seemed to think it is rather indiscreet."

"Geneva just got insulted," Valerie said flippantly. "So don't mind her. Well?"

"Oh, Tommy's fine, Valerie. I saw him this morning and the first thing he asked was: 'What did DiMaggio do yesterday?' So—well—well, what is there about that—"

"There is no cataloging the things that make a woman cry," Michael said. "You know that tear jerker called 'Lay My Head Beneath a Rose?' I knew a woman who always wept ferociously from its first saccharine chord. Yet her heart would have made granite look like cream cheese. For that matter, there is an ex-pug who is now a bouncer in a joint on Howard Street who weeps like a little child over the 'Last Round-up.'"

"All right; you can stop talking," Valerie said. "I'm over it—only Tommy is such a—a kid."

"Well, he's kept his head and told a straight story," Herbert said. "And you must be patient and do what he asks. Wait until tomorrow to see him."

"Why tomorrow?"

"Well, I'm afraid they'll arraign him tomorrow. Now, Valerie, don't—"

"That doesn't make me cry: it makes me mad."

"Well, Tommy is hopeful and he wants to keep you out of this. Of course we can't if he comes to trial. That gun of his is the sticking point," Herbert said. "If we could find it, then the police would know it wasn't the right one."

"Unless, of course, it is," Michael said. "It didn't take wings and fly away."

"Anyone could get into his room by being a little careful to avoid the landlady. But if it was stolen that means someone planned ahead to kill Maxine and cast suspicion on Tommy by using his gun. As Sullivan says, whom are you going to suspect?"

"If I know Jim Sullivan, he didn't say 'whom'," Michael remarked. Herbert glanced at him in dignified displeasure and went on:

"You have to find someone who knew both Tommy and Maxine very well and there's no one who quite fits in. But we haven't time to talk about that now. I had a tip the reporters will be here soon to see you, Valerie, and it would be better for you to be at home."

Michael nodded as Valerie looked at him. "He's right. And you don't want them to get an ax out for you. But if there is a sob sister among those present and you begin to think what a kind motherly face she has or feel a perilous gratitude for

her sympathetic understanding, take a good look
at her eyes—and don't. I'll stop by for you some
time this afternoon."

"I wish," Herbert complained as they went
down the stairs, "that I knew what advice Michael
has been giving you. He's reckless and I'm afraid
you're impatient and I don't see why he should
bother unless— It's just possible that he—"

"Yes indeed," Valerie said absently. "Herbert,
doesn't anyone ever call him Mike? Not that he's
the type—"

"He doesn't like it. And when he doesn't like
something—or someone—no one is ever left in
any doubt of the fact," Herbert said. "Now, listen,
Valerie—you let me do the talking if the newspa-
permen show up. That is: be guided by me."

CHAPTER NINE
INSPECTOR SULLIVAN IS NOT SATISFIED

Jim Sullivan parked his car on Washington, just off Gough, and for a few minutes sat looking toward Lafayette Square. He could have drawn an accurate small-scale map of its network of paths and the trees and shrubbery that had hidden Maxine Farley's body until morning. They had been over every inch of that ground and the search had yielded them, except for her purse, exactly nothing.

That was the trouble with these park murders: fingerprints were nonexistent. That went for footprints too, when the soil was loose and dry and dozens of people had passed through that park during the day. Not, Sullivan reflected, that he'd ever had the pleasure of finding any of these perfect footprints that you made casts of and triumphantly produced in court.

The Washington Street cable car rumbled by, its little bell tinkling shrewishly. Too bad, Sullivan thought, that a cable hadn't been passing the park about midnight of Friday. The gripman or conductor might have noticed anything out of the way.

He was at once relieved and embarrassed by the scarcity of innocent and communicative bystanders in this case. But few people would cut through the park late at night and with it on one side of Washington and only three buildings with large courts and driveways facing it, that block was apt to be a very quiet one after ten or eleven o'clock.

Sullivan got out of his car and stretched enjoyably, approving the weather. Being by birth a San Franciscan he would not admit that the still, warm sunshine was "unusual." But he looked automatically toward the Marina and acknowledged the existence of the fog bank sleeping there with a philosophical: "Be a little colder tonight."

He didn't know why he was going to talk to Michael Dundas, who frequently annoyed him intensely, unless it was because he was tired of discussing the case with subordinates who slavishly agreed with him and a colleague who didn't. And he did respect Michael's intelligence though he would have been apt, had there been such a word in his vocabulary, to label it intuition.

To talk things over with Michael was stimulating even if he did have a not-too-flattering opinion of the mental processes of the average policeman. But Sullivan was not sensitive. He was healthily self-confident and his occasional complacency was justified by his record. One case out of a thousand, he thought, might be solved by an amateur where professionals had failed.

Not that it followed that the professional could not pick the amateur's brains to advantage. Either Michael was not in or was taking an infernally long time to answer his doorbell. Sullivan rang again, impatiently, and was turning away when the latch began to click.

Inside the house, Michael looked down at him from the third floor, frowned and then shrugged resignedly.

"Wouldn't anyone else let you in?" he said. "Oh, now that you're here you'd better sit down and rest. Three flights of stairs."

"Meaning I'm getting fat?" Sullivan sank rather breathlessly into a chair. "I don't seem to be using the same hole in my belt this year that I did last. That's a complaint you'll never suffer from," he added, eyeing Michael's slight wiry figure. "Sure, I'll have a drink. I dropped in to tell you we had to give you a clean bill of health."

"I suppose," Michael said indifferently, "that you worked on the assumption that I'd known Maxine Farley and moved here in order to kill her more conveniently?"

"People do dumber things than that. However, no one seems to have ever seen you with the girl in your usual haunts—or hers. The last dame you were seen with was at the Deauville. The one," Sullivan said maliciously, "that started making a scene and you planked down some money, walked out and left her flat."

"How you do get around, Mr. Sullivan. And did your operatives discover why I moved?"

"Cockroaches."

"Yes. They rattled when they walked and sat on the drainboard and sneered at me. And if you want the record complete, Ellison told me about this place and I took it because of the windows, which are not so easy to find."

The curtains were pulled back and sunlight flooded the room. The day was so clear, every line so sharply defined, that the tall apartment houses and hotels on Nob Hill were something cut from cardboard, propped up against a sky impossibly blue.

"It's a swell view," Sullivan conceded. "And like they say: man don't live by bread alone."

"I'll send you a pot of white hyacinths for your soul next Christmas, Inspector. Had I but two loaves of bread . . . Well, if I may ask, what were Miss Farley's favorite haunts?"

"There's one of these taverns on Larkin."

"How far down Larkin?"

"Not *that* far down," Sullivan said, grinning. "It's respectable enough though it's been closed several times and the cop on the beat don't think highly of it. It's called the Black Raven."

"Larkin and Bush?"

"I kind of thought you'd know it, because where you lived before you came here wasn't so far away."

"But you found, to your great regret, that I have never been in the Black Raven?"

"You certainly aren't one of the regulars," Sullivan said. "Neither was Miss Farley, really. But naturally, the bartender would remember her. She came in now and then and she'd talk to men if they were presentable and not stewed but she never picked anyone up there.

"But she did meet Howard there once: he says by accident. That he was passing, went in for a drink and pretty soon she came in. So he walked home with her and kept still about it, being kind of shocked to see her there alone. The bartender remembers they seemed to be quarreling. Miss Sheridan would say that was natural. Howard claims he gave her a few brotherly words of advice and she flared up. The barkeep can't remember seeing him there but the once."

"What do you think of Howard, Inspector?"

"Damn it, I like the kid. So does everybody. Oh, they admit where he works he's no great shakes at his job. Well, the best of character witnesses don't always keep a man from being hung. But I can't say I'm satisfied.

"That's a swell little girl he's engaged to," Sullivan added. "I'm damned glad she's in the clear. And she is, because this Miss Orton she stayed with swears they didn't get to sleep before one. The medical examiner puts the time of Miss Farley's death between eleven-thirty and twelve-thirty. Well, she was alive at eleven- thirty. Miss Nolan admits she was watching the clock to see when her light went out. I think the girl must 've got out the window or Miss Nolan would 've heard her.

"Well, the four of 'em got to the Ortons' at eleven-twenty. Then Ellison drove off and Howard started to walk home—he says. He could have sneaked home and got his gun before he met Miss Farley even if his landlady was waiting up for him. But if he did that, why let her see him come in at twelve-fifteen when he'd been able to avoid her at eleven-thirty?

"I admit that gun bothers me as much as it does him. Hunt gives the easiest explanation and maybe the right one: that Howard used his own gun and threw it away. He says guns aren't as easy to come by as some folks think.

"On the other hand," Sullivan said, "he may have mislaid the gun and it hasn't anything to do with the case. And it could easily have been stolen from his room. But who knew he had the gun? Not anyone that I can find, who also had a motive for killing the Farley girl."

Michael was slow in answering and then he said, carefully, Sullivan thought:

"As to motive, I don't know. But it's quite possible some of the people in this house knew he had the gun. He knows people here and those things come up in conversation."

"I know that. I'm not missing any angles," Sullivan said uneasily. "The girl was born to make trouble and she knew a lot of men. Nice young fellows with small salaries and also a different type altogether that she met at art classes.

"But while some of the first kind knew Howard too, they all have alibis, and anyway none of 'em seem to have been much involved with her. They all hint the same thing: that she was looking out for number one. One of them, who seems to have been pretty hard hit for a while, did suggest there was 'another man.'"

"Arguing there must have been if she remained impervious to his charms?"

"If you want to put it that way. Well, Hunt says Howard was the other man. But Howard hasn't a dime. Of course Hunt argues he wanted to marry a girl with money and if Maxine Farley stood in his way she had to go. Seems Howard has been kind of plunging on the horses— Say, who do you like in the second at Bay Meadows Tuesday?"

"Translucent."

"Listen, that horse has been running since I was in diapers."

"Then she's withstanding the ravages of time better than you are, Inspector. Make it a place bet and you won't lose."

"Well, maybe you're right. I'll risk two dollars."

"With Bookie Levy?" Michael said, grinning.

"Any time I do my betting in a cigar store that might be raided any minute!" Sullivan snorted indignantly. "Or over a tapped telephone wire? When you hear my name mentioned in a graft investigation you'll know I'm in my dotage. I can afford to gamble a little but did you ever know anyone who made money on the horses?"

"It can be done if you make up your mind to be satisfied with ten cents on a dollar."

"Show bets? That's slow work unless you've got quite a bit of capital. But I heard there was a guy took plenty out of Tanforan that way, about six years back. Where 'd you get your stake? Win on a long shot?"

"Yes. I also met a man who thought *he* could play blackjack," Michael said pensively.

"So that's how you got your start? I often wondered. When I first met you—"

"When you arrested me," Michael corrected gently.

"That was a mistake. No hard feelings," Sullivan said generously. "You showed me up. We found then that you knew some—well, call 'em queer people. Two or three shady pawnbrokers. Of course that's how you got your tip that that assistant hotel manager had gotten rid of one or two small pieces before he decided to make a big haul. Also, you knew old Hymie Rose, who knows all there is to know about locks and keys. However, you've never been mixed up in anything shady and whatever pals you had when you first came here, you're never seen with 'em now."

"All that was seven years ago," Michael said. "If you landed in San Francisco with two dollars in your pocket where would it last longest?"

"South of Market, of course. Well, and you can go two ways from there," Sullivan said soberly. "A lot of young fellows start that way with what you might call odd jobs here and there. Nothing really criminal, they'd say, and they had to eat. Hell! I hope my son never gets thrown out on the world like that. He's a good kid but he's had things soft." He looked curiously at the white triangle in Michael's hair "How old are you? I've often wondered."

"Thirty. I came here ten years ago—as I supposed you had found out for yourself. Well, as you say, I've known some queer people but—"

"But whose business is it? Well, what were we talking about? Oh: Howard's trying to make some money. Well, I said to Hunt, you'll never make a jury believe he's a fortune hunter. Maybe he wanted to get rid of the Farley girl."

"She wasn't pregnant, was she?"

"No. I told Hunt, just an ordinary affair with no serious consequences don't amount to so much nowadays. And we can't even prove they had an affair. He knew her; met her and Miss Sheridan at a cocktail party about a year ago. So what?"

"But a guy came forward to say he met Howard by the park at eleven twenty-five. Asked him the time. But Howard always said he went by the park only didn't cut through it. Hunt wants to arraign him tomorrow and ask for the case to be continued while he hunts up more witnesses. The D.A. likes Miss Nolan's testimony. Well, even if she would talk the hind leg off a donkey she looks so damned respectable I suppose she'll go over big with a jury.

"There wasn't anything important in her purse—but here's something." Sullivan took a sparkling bracelet and a pair of clips from his pocket. "I found these in her bureau and I was right: they're worth about five hundred bucks together. Question is: who gave them to her?"

When Michael appeared to be giving the question serious consideration Sullivan studied him thoughtfully: blunt, ugly profile, the thin-lipped mouth at once sensitive and arrogant. For some time he had been missing something in this discussion that had been present in former ones. Something was lacking in Michael's approach to this problem. It was—Sullivan searched for a word—impersonality.

That was why this discussion had been disappointing. He'd counted on Michael for speculations that might be fanciful but sometimes turned out to be helpful. He acted like a man who had preconceived notions or some unadmitted knowledge.

"A man named John Dozier, who is Mrs. Callendar's uncle, lived here before I did," Michael said abruptly. "I offer him for your consideration. I've been told he is well to do and attractive."

"Oh. Yes, I've heard about him." Sullivan weighed the bracelet and clips in his hand. "Maybe he fits the picture; the kind of person I had in mind when I found out these cost money. Of course she may have bought these herself but— Have you anything else to offer for my consideration? If not, I'll be going."

CHAPTER TEN
"POOR BLIND MOLE"

Gustavus Adolphus Lindholm lowered the flame under his Sunday dinner—veal stew, to be later enhanced by dumplings—and went to answer the bell. Standing at the foot of the stairs from the basement to the ground floor, the light from the open door at their top made him blink. Then he saw that it was the new tenant and said:

"You was wanting somet'ing? I come right up," because the new tenant looked like a gentleman who might be free with his money. His kind, that spoke short and quick to you, often were, in a careless, absent-minded way.

"I'll come down," Michael said. "Do you live back here? I smell something."

"Is stew. You come in kitchen? It will be burning."

Gus led the way across the basement, past the heating plant to the room where he lived. He removed a Swedish newspaper from a straight chair and wiped it off with a dirty tea towel. The new tenant looked as though the smell of the stew—or something—displeased him. Just like Miss Sheridan did when she came down. He glanced at the one small window and the low-watt light globe and murmured:

"'All but blind in his chambered hole . . .'"

Gus smiled patiently. You had to humor the tenants.

"I hadn't understood from talking to you that John Dozier had my apartment before I did."

"You know Mr. Dozier? Was a fine gentleman," Gus said. "Had been all over world. He"—Gus smiled slyly—"was fine gentlemans with ladies too."

"So I've heard. Miss Farley—"

"You know about that? She go up to his apartment once or twice."

"So the mole comes out of his hole sometimes?"

"You mean me?" Gus said, displeased. "This is not hole; is damn fine apartment. I take care of this place ten years: clean halls, put flowers in hall, fix light globes."

"Always at night?"

"You mean, how do I know Miss Farley goes to Mr. Dozier's apartment? I was putting new globe in hall light," Gus said majestically. "She is not staying long."

"Oh, that's nothing to get excited about," Michael said carelessly. "I thought he'd marry her."

Gus made a motion as if he were nudging someone in the ribs. "She will not have him. She come to door and he is—well, not mad. Because he is smiling but kind of—of—"

"Resigned?"

"That was it," Gus agreed. "Like maybe he thought he had made good escapes. He say: 'Well, you're a fool, my dear. You will find out you are not having a chance and I am making you honorable proposals.' He talk funny sometimes. Then he says: 'You are having nerve but that will not be enough, maybe.'"

"And they didn't see the little mousie?"

"Me? Oh, I am on the stairs then," Gus said placidly. "Mrs. Callendar would not have liked it. Not for Miss Farley to be friendly with Mr. Dozier or Mr. Callendar. And Mr. Dozier or Mr. Callendar do not like it much when it is the other one is talking to Miss Farley. Because I do not t'ink they like each other much."

"No? I didn't know that. Because Dozier is devoted to his niece."

"Oh yes," Gus agreed. "He gifs her nice t'ings. Mr. Callendar says this apartment cost too much so I guess he does not have much money. His mother is fussy lady: talk, talk all time and use big words. She is—is what you call clubwomens."

"Dozier has a temper, though," Michael said reflectively. "I suppose you know that?"

"Oh yes, he can get very mad. I put the newspapers before the doors after the boy leaves them on front steps. Mr. Dozier was mad just before he leave and ask do I put anything else under doors." Gus shrugged, scratching at the whitish stubble on his long chin. "But I do not see very well without I wear my glasses and is not fitting my nose any more. So I see nothing under doors and I do not know what he means. Newspapers is too thick to go under. I just toss them by door. Anyway, Mr. Dozier say to forget it."

"Wasn't he ever angry because sometimes the hall lights go out?"

"That is not my fault," Gus said indignantly. "I am keeping good globes in all lights. If someone turns them off at the switch in the lower hall, is not my fault. I cannot stay up all night. I tell you what I t'ink: people want to spoon in hall. Mr. Dozier never complained and he came in late sometimes."

"But you've found the lights off in the morning since Mr. Howard was last here, haven't you?" Michael said.

"Well—yes. But I cannot stay up all night."

"Of course not. We don't get any cleaning service in our apartments, do we?"

"It is not included but I wacuum, wash windows, polish floors. I do it for Miss Julian. She is very foolish lady and not good housekeeper. She is hearing voices."

"She probably hears her brother's frequently."

"He was very drunk today, isn't it? Was never like that before. But Miss Julian she has little thing with legs puts fingers on and writes."

"A ouija board?"

"That is it. Should be married and have kids, then no time for foolishness. Would have husband to fight with about money, not brother. If Mr. Julian is cross sometimes is only because he has indigestions. She is not good cook and talks all time. Miss Nolan follows me around and tells me how to do things better. I would rather work for Mrs. Putnam."

"But isn't she—" Michael tapped his head significantly.

"Is not crazy. Is smart old lady. But does not talk all time like other two. I will be glad to clean your apartment."

"I suppose you wouldn't want to work at night?"

"Oh, I am up late," Gus said. "I keep heat on till ten, drink coffee, read. I will come any time."

"That's fine. And when I'm out," Michael said pleasantly, "and you are keeping an eye on the place— Well, I had better warn you that you cannot open that Chinese chest or the top drawers of the chifforobe. Or if you can you are wasting your time in your present occupation. And I do not like my whisky watered, so if you feel the need of a drink, don't bother to fill up the bottle again. I would like to feel that we understand each other. We do, don't we?"

Gus, recovering, began to discourse upon the dangers of fire and theft in unoccupied apartments but upon the receipt of a dollar bill and an unsympathetic look from Mr. Dundas was forced to agree that they did understand each other— perfectly.

Valerie opened the door, said: "You're early, aren't you?" And then: "But I'm glad you are."

"We can ride," Michael said. "'Why so wan and pale, fond lover?'"

"Oh, reconciliations are wearing even when engineered by Herbert and Geneva with their great tact. And reporters taking pictures—'Raise your skirt a little higher, will you?' I suppose that's one way to earn a living. I'll get my hat."

"Don't you think," Michael said, "that it would be a nice gesture if I came in and met your mother?"

"Since when have you taken to nice gestures? I wanted to ask you, though," Valerie admitted. "She is more or less up and having tea. Michael, please don't—don't snub her."

"I wouldn't think of it," Michael said serenely. "Not even the Albatross. 'The man hath penance done and penance more will do.' Be a good girl and let me in."

Valerie looked back at him doubtfully, leading the way down the hall. If he had been Tommy she would have said he was in a freakish humor or at least in unusually high spirits. But neither mood was one she associated with Michael. With mingled resentment and amusement she watched him bow over Patricia's hand in a manner essentially Latin, sit down beside her, accept a cup of tea and refer with great deference to her "recent ordeal."

This was exactly calculated to win Patricia's approval even if Michael had not been—as she would later tell Geneva—"distinctive looking." And Patricia liked men who picked up her handkerchief or sprang forward to light her cigarette quickly and as if it were a rare privilege to serve her.

When Michael had progressed from this point to that of hinting astonishment that she should have a grown daughter, Patricia's captivation was complete. Her voice became soft and babyishly hesitant. She said pathetically:

"I have lived such a sheltered life, Mr. Dundas, and I was a mere child when I married and so protected by Mr. Sheridan. It's hard for me to advise Valerie. She is so young and headstrong, you know."

"Y-yes," Michael said with every appearance of regret. "Of course, but that is a failing of the very young, don't you think?"

"I," Valerie said briefly, "am going to put on my hat. No, don't bother to get up for me." And was barely able to refrain from further speech when Michael managed, somehow, to look grieved and misunderstood while springing up to open the door for her.

"Poseur!" she said to her reflection in the mirror. "I always suspected it and—well, he's sensitive to hats. I'll show him a hat what *am*," picked out a black felt consisting of one large bow and a stunted crown and snapped its elastic defiantly under her hair.

Going to the closet to get a light coat, she stopped to look at Maxine's clothes. That coat. The entire front was Persian lamb besides its high, upstanding collar. Valerie smoothed the fur thoughtfully. Yes, Maxine had certainly paid more than the seventy dollars she claimed for that.

She considered a hanging row of dresses; decided they were really "fourteen ninety-fives." There was nothing else but the "costume" Charles Julian had paid for: the short coat with its clever sleeves and lining of the same sea-foam green that formed the top of the dress. Valerie wondered to whom she might give that outfit before Geneva decided that with "a little inset here and there" she could manage to wear it. Maxine had been very lovely in it and the wide black hat with the oddly shaped green buckle. . . .

She turned to the dressing table and opened the drawer where Maxine had kept her jewelry. There was a good deal of it: Maxine had had a weakness for costume jewelry. Valerie frowned, missing the rhinestone bracelet and clips. At least she had supposed they were rhinestones, but now she wanted to look at them again. They had been Maxine's favorites so perhaps she had worn them Friday night.

She turned over the bright mass of bracelets, earrings and necklaces, frowned again and singled out a piece that seemed to her incongruous. It was the cheapest sort of bracelet: crude elephants dangling from a brass wire. Schoolgirls wore that sort of thing. They could be bought for twenty-five cents in Chinatown. But Maxine had loathed anything that looked cheap or tawdry.

Valerie put the bracelet in her purse, went back to Patricia's room to find Geneva dispensing freshly baked cookies and probing delicately for information. She was in time to hear Michael say regretfully:

"I am afraid I am a lily of the field, Miss Nolan. Ah, well, early training and being brought up to expect something quite different—"

His look begged Patricia to understand before he gazed wistfully out the window, as if staring at some remote and splendid past. "Well, one does not talk of that," he said bravely. "Or wish for the old regime again though when one reads of Russia today—"

"Oh, my goodness!" Geneva murmured. "Not really!"

"No, no! Not royalty," Michael said hastily.

"Oh, of course we understand about those things. The real princes or—or earls—"

"I never heard of any earls in Russia, Mother," Valerie said, helping herself to cookies.

"Well, whatever it is. The real ones never tell, you know, and I'm sure we'll respect your secret."

"Madam!" Michael bowed over her hand. "It is not secret and your daughter, I am afraid, is skeptical."

"Oh, Valerie! I mean," Patricia said, recapturing her sweetly maternal tone, "she is so practical. Like her father."

"Ah, yes, the American men. Mr. Farley—"

"We-el—Wayne wasn't exactly practical. But he'd traveled a great deal and talked of it so interestingly. I do think travel is so broadening, don't you?"

"Oh, undoubtedly." But Michael stood frowning at the floor until Geneva breathed respectfully:

"Russians—moody—"

"Moody, my eye!" Valerie said. "Are we going or not?"

"I don't see why you do," Patricia said. "It seems to me it would be so much better to stay and—"

"But I promised this friend I would meet him. And it would be good for Miss Valerie to meet him—and you, when you are recovered, Mrs. Farley. He is from Hollywood and I am sure you will find him most interesting."

Michael had his hand under Valerie's arm now and without any appearance of undue haste they still reached the door very quickly. "I will hope that our acquaintancc will bc continued and I will return the young lady at a very early hour. The car's already out in front," he said in his normal voice, shorn of the faintly foreign intonation that had been present while he was talking to Patricia. "Let's go."

"Gladly!" Valerie jerked her arm free. "Chameleon! Oh, you—you lovely liar!"

"I did it all for you, darling. From now on I will be the white-haired boy so far as your mother is concerned. Besides, when people like the Albatross ask impertinent questions they should be grateful for a courteous and interesting lie instead of a bald: 'It's none of your business.'"

"That's what you'd have said to me. And I prefer that. But it should occur even to Mother and Geneva that Dundas is not a Russian name."

"They will decide it is an assumed name and they will be partially right because it is mine only legally. And I distinctly did not say I am Russian. You're very unreasonable. Just what did you want?"

"Well—not for you to make a fool of my mother. But that isn't fair," Valerie admitted. "She's like that and your acting like a—a gigolo doesn't change her. But I shouldn't have talked about her so you knew just how to treat her."

"Your mother is not unique," Michael said dryly. "I wouldn't need your previous description to classify her. After all, my early education took place mainly in a boudoir. Inspector Sullivan came to see me today."

"Oh. But—why?"

"We've talked before about his cases when we've happened to run into each other. He told me a number of things. Some of them, from your point of view, not too pleasant. It seems that Miss

Farley sometimes stopped in at a place called the Black Raven."

As he talked they drove past Automobile Row, down Van Ness, across to Fillmore, and out Marina Boulevard toward Land's End. It was a drive Valerie loved but for once she was not looking at the bay with its Sunday adornment of small sailboats. She failed to glance toward gray Alcatraz or the high red span of the Golden Gate Bridge, so soon to be opened to traffic. They passed through the Presidio, by the cemetery with its soldierly parade of square white stones; came out of dark green cypress into patrician Seacliff. When they reached Land's End Michael stopped the car, ending his summary:

"So you see Sullivan is not satisfied. If his mind were a trifle more elastic he might be a great help to us. I spoke to him about Dozier because we can't investigate the man ourselves."

"I don't see how that can do him any harm. Even if he did give Maxine that jewelry. I imagine he did: I don't know who else could have. But he certainly didn't give her this," Valerie said, producing the bracelet with its dangling elephants.

"He might have," Michael said after regarding it thoughtfully. "As a souvenir of a jaunt into Chinatown. But—he could have afforded a more worthwhile souvenir than that. And I hadn't gathered that Miss Farley was particularly sentimental."

"Of course she wasn't. And she certainly never wore this—wouldn't have been caught dead wearing it."

"Then why— It doesn't fit," Michael muttered. But Valerie was staring at the shimmering bar of sunlight across the water, a golden impalpable bridge to some unseen point where sky and water merged beyond the Golden Gate.

"There are so many things the police can do better than we can," she sighed finally. "I hate to tell about those letters but if no one else does and they keep appearing—"

She sighed again. Michael said unsympathetically:

"You'll blow away. But I imagine the time will come, and rather quickly, when we will have to tell the police about them." He looked at his watch. "I'll have to tell you what our worthy janitor said as we go along. We want to get to the airport early enough to park where we can see the field."

"Why didn't I think to talk to Gus? He must know a lot of things he isn't telling."

"And some that he is. I will repeat his remarks verbatim—minus the accent."

"I thought," Valerie said, "that you were rather good at accents."

"Not Scandinavian." They became a drop of the slow-moving traffic stream in the lanes paralleling the Midway and Esplanade. "We'll turn off in an instant," Michael said, "and go over to the airport via San Mateo. Now, regarding Gus . . ."

CHAPTER ELEVEN
"RATS IN A TRAP"

"You're good at intimating things, aren't you?" Valerie said when he had finished. "Though he is stupid."

"Do you think so? His conversation profited him to the extent of one dollar. And cheap at the price."

"Do you think so?" Valerie said, mimicking him. "I could have told you most of it for nothing. For instance, that Miss Julian plays around with a ouija board. And of course Mr. Julian would consider it all damned foolishness. Gus feels he more or less owns the place. And I suppose all janitors know a good deal about tenants."

"I've yet to see a resident janitor or manager who doesn't. It wasn't so much what Gus told me as the fact that *he* told it that's important. Though certainly the conversation he overheard between Miss Farley and Dozier is—suggestive. Does the Albatross talk freely to everyone?"

"Oh yes: delivery boys, grocery clerks, streetcar conductors—anyone. She'd talk to Gus, if that's what you mean. Or rather, she would advise him and ask him questions. Miss Julian would simply talk. Why were you interested in learning Wayne had traveled? That was before Maxine was born."

"Was it? But a great many people in our apartment house appear to have traveled. And as you report Sara Putnam to have said, it's queer how Americans, traveling, run into each other. And Mrs. Putnam said Miss Julian was once given a trip to Europe."

"So was Winona Callendar. And Geneva was there. But what of it? It doesn't make sense. Nothing does. Michael, is there anything I can do for Tommy, except to get him a good lawyer?"

"Not now. Later. Do you remember the ditty Julian started to sing? The one called 'Twenty-one Years?' He never reached the second verse—'So go beg the gov'nor, upon your sweet soul,'" Michael sang, "'If you can't get a pardon, try an' get a parole . . .'"

"There are times," Valerie said stiffly, "when your sense of humor is slightly misplaced."

"What would Mr. Howard say?"

"Well—he might think it was funny too. Men are so—"

"If it is a question of paying a lawyer that is souring your sweet disposition, I'll take your IOU against your expectations when you come of age. Which I would do for few men and almost no woman. And I'll see if I can get Morris Hirsch for you. If he can't convince a jury Howard has been crucified to make the police a Roman holiday, no one can."

"Oh, will you? I'm sorry I was cross."

"But you are so much more interesting when you forget you're a well-bred product of Miss Head's school."

"Do you think so? Were you really in radio or was that just another interesting flight of fancy?"

"I was, some seven years ago, one of these cowboys who never saw a cow," Michael said with unusual patience. "In a joint on Market and we did broadcast for a quarter of an hour. Twice a week I did an impersonation of Maurice Chevalier."

"Your mouth's not right. I wish I had heard it."

"I sounded more like Chevalier than he does himself. I'd heard him in Paris. But before people began to imitate Vallee I'd put aside my chaps along with my mustache."

"Mustache?" Valerie considered him thoughtfully. "What would you look like with a mustache?"

"Like—to use the common term—a wop. Would you mind being quiet for a while? If you can't sit and think, just sit."

When they had left San Mateo behind and were passing Bay Meadows, Valerie said meekly:

"May I speak? I suppose we can get out to see the plane come in and if we find ourselves near the Callendars—"

"Exactly. We must find ourselves near the Callendars."

"Then I will welcome Mr. Dozier and be girlishly charming and introduce you to him. What then?"

"I will be charming too," Michael said sardonically. "Perhaps he'll come up and see what I've done to his old home. I don't believe," he added as he snaked the car into the one narrow space left before the wire fence, "that they are here yet."

"I don't see their car. What a disappointing place," Valerie said. "I've never been here before."

"It's an eyesore, besides being the windiest place in a windy city."

A flat brown field stretched away to a dike that hid the bay from their sight. Dry weeds bent low in the cold wind that rattled the car windows and shook its top. The shabby wooden clubhouse with a glassed-in porch facing the field had not yet been abandoned for the new concrete structure back of it. Half-a-dozen people sat on the porch now; as many walked back and forth, holding tightly to hats against the wind or leaning on the wire fence that kept them from the field.

A huge aluminum silver plane had just been emptied of passengers and the field attendants were wheeling away the canvas gangplank. A hostess, small, brunette, piquantly pretty in bright green suit and yellow blouse, scurried through the gate and into the clubhouse. Valerie looked at her admiringly.

"Why didn't I take up nursing and get to be a hostess? Why haven't I gone anywhere by plane?" she said in a defrauded tone. "See that woman with the two little boys? They're so excited. And that little blonde. She's probably a bride—"

She broke off to smile at the Callendars with what she felt to be suspicious cordiality and put down a window to hear Grant's:

"Well, Valerie, what are you doing here? I wouldn't have thought—I mean—"

"She can't be expected to go into seclusion," Winona said. "We're meeting Uncle John."

"Oh, how nice," Valerie said with sweet, girlish enthusiasm. Her reward was the fugitive twitching of Michael's lips before he said soberly:

"I thought a ride would be good for her. A friend of mine may be on this plane though I doubt it. Valerie, I don't believe I know—"

"Oh, I'm sorry. Winona, this is our new tenant, Mr. Dundas. Mr. and Mrs. Callendar. Is Mr. Dozier going to be with you long?"

"We don't know. Funny, his flying up."

"It isn't," Winona said flatly. "When Uncle John wants to get somewhere in a hurry he usually does. I doubt if he stays long. We can't make him comfortable. Our apartment is just like yours, Mr. Dundas, except that we haven't a view."

"It is?" said Mr. Dundas, politely interested. "I wondered. It is a back apartment, then?"

"Yes. By the way, we're having a few people in Wednesday night. I wonder if you'd like to come."

Michael said promptly that he would be delighted and Mr. Callendar, looking rather sulky, said that it was too cold to stand outside any longer and hadn't they better get in the car? Winona, still smiling at Michael, nodded absently. But someone shouted: "Here it comes!" and with the rest of the waiters the Callendars crowded to the fence.

The winged speck grew to a puppet plane hung by invisible wires against a background of darkening clouds. A soft voice at Valerie's elbow complained:

"It just doesn't seem to move at all, does it?" And with a shy smile the small yellow-haired girl added: "But I'm impatient. And I can't help being nervous. Even if he does save a whole night this way, I wish he'd taken the train. All those accidents this winter . . ."

"Oh, but that was in bad weather or flying over the mountains. They're as good as here," Valerie said. "Listen."

The wind blew the roar of the motors toward them and a stray shaft of sunlight knifed through the clouds and glinted on silver wings. The ship grew to life-size, flying low over the field, turning and soaring out toward the bay. Valerie's neighbor made a little sound of distress and disappointment.

"Why didn't they land?"

"I think he means to land on the East-West runway," Michael said. "He'll bank to the right out there and that will bring him back in the right direction."

Out beyond the dike, over the water, one of the silver wings dipped as the plane began its circle. One minute it was there; the next, swiftly as a falling feather, it was gone. There was nothing before their eyes but the flat dry field and the dike that hid the bay. And in their ears the sound of water flattening and surging up under a crashing impact.

The fog was massed like battle smoke along the northern hills as they drove through the stark ugliness of south San Francisco. Valerie shivered and pulled her coat over her shoulders. She wished that she could draw a curtain in her mind, shutting out the memory of faces and sounds: the sobbing groan that shook the crowd before the fence; the high senseless screaming of the girl behind her.

That woman with the thin sweet face, standing so still with a child's hand clutched in each of hers. The handsome boy in the clubhouse saying: "There's just the two of us and Dad was flying up because tomorrow's my birthday."

"Why tear yourself to pieces?" Michael said suddenly. But his swarthy face was still pale and he said under his breath: "*Ayúdales Dios. Son caídos en una ratonera.*"

"Rats in a trap? Isn't there any chance at all?"

"The plane was several miles out over the water. Even a strong swimmer won't have much chance. If they'd ever prepared for such an emergency!" Michael said angrily. "But you saw they hadn't. They'll search all night when they get lights and equipment."

"I wonder if it was right for us to leave? But the Callendars did. He said he would come back but there's nothing he can do."

Valerie closed her eyes, seeing again the blank look of shock on Winona's face. Later, in Grant's arms, she had wept, her arms tight about his neck.

"Now there's no one. Don't let me talk to you like I do sometimes," she had said. "Don't ever leave me after we quarrel. You might not come back."

"I suppose," Valerie said, "she would feel that way."

"Mrs. Callendar?"

"Yes. Seeing those other women. That little blonde girl you carried to the clubhouse when she fainted had only been married six months. I wouldn't have left her if it hadn't turned out she'd come with friends. I can't forget her."

"It happens every day, Valerie—death. 'All follow this and come to dust . . .'"

"But not like this! They were home; the pilot might have landed. But he didn't; he went out there again and—what happened? No one has any idea."

"They may never be certain what happened. Some of them may be saved."

"You don't really think that."

"No. You haven't said: why, of all possible planes, did John Dozier have to take that one?"

"I've thought it."

"Naturally. He may have known something of importance and he took that plane. You'd be less

than human if you didn't ask why he couldn't
have taken another. Well, perhaps his number was
up and it wouldn't have mattered what he did or
didn't do."

"Oh, Michael, you don't believe that?"

"Why not? Round and round the little wheel
goes. Make your bets, gentlemen. If by morning
we know there are no survivors, we can make up
our minds never to learn, from Dozier, at least."

"Don't! But Tommy's life is important too," Valerie said in justification. "And Maxine may have
confided in Mr. Dozier. I think he wrote to her."

"Why didn't you say so before?"

"It just occurred to me he might have. I remember Geneva's bringing the mail in one day
when we were eating breakfast and saying: 'My
goodness, Maxine, who's writing to you from Los
Angeles?' And of course Maxine was furious and
made some insulting answer. But Geneva always
gets the mail."

"And Maxine destroyed letters? Remarkable
woman."

"She didn't write to many people. I suppose
the letters she did get weren't worth keeping. And
what do we do now?"

"There's something you might do," Michael
said, turning off Mission Street into Dolores. "But
you won't."

"Why? What is it?"

"Talk to Mrs. Callendar—tonight."

"Oh, I couldn't. Not tonight, when she—"

Michael shrugged. "No, nice little girls don't do things like that. But tonight, while she's still upset and might tell you something, is your best bet."

"I suppose she does have some idea why Mr. Dozier wanted to get here so quickly. But—oh, I can't. You can—"

"There's no reason why I shouldn't make polite inquiries but I have no excuse for asking questions about a man I never saw. So, since you insist on respecting her grief—"

"You, apparently, respect nothing," Valerie said coldly. "Unless you don't think she is grieved?"

"I'm not at all certain she will be—permanently. Shocked, certainly. Who wouldn't be? But my impression of Mrs. Callendar is that she cares deeply for only two people."

"Herself and Grant? I'm—I'm afraid I have to agree with you. And of course she will inherit—"

"Yes, I suppose she will."

"Michael, you ran right through a stop sign! What on earth are you thinking about?"

"That, though it will not suit your sense of the fitness of things, I am hungry," Michael said, turning down Market. "Also, about the wording of that wire of Dozier's. If you don't care to eat steak at John's, will you watch me do it?"

"I'm hungry too," Valerie discovered. "But, Michael, there was nothing peculiar about that wire."

"Don't you think so? Not even taken in conjunction with the Callendars' conversation?"

Valerie frowned. "Well, of course they didn't know anyone was listening."

"I imagine they said very little they wouldn't say to friends, if not the police. Simply because they didn't realize its importance."

"But how—"

"I believe," Michael said thoughtfully, "that I will have the very special porterhouse, with shoestring potatoes."

CHAPTER TWELVE
A PICK-ME-UP FOR CHARLIE

Miss Julian had her head out a front window as they parked before the apartment house and was hauling up the extra a newspaper vendor had just tied to a string. She peered at them nearsightedly and then said in a deafening whisper:

"Oh, good evening. I suppose you've heard. Isn't it just too terrible? That poor Mr. Dozier. Such a good-looking man. And Winona is just simply— But I mustn't keep you standing there and I don't want to disturb poor Charlie."

A voice from beyond the window yelped: "For God's sake bring me that ice water or do I have to get it myself!"

"Oh, he's awake again and I thought he was asleep. And he feels so terrible that—I hate to ask you, Mr. Dundas, but you did say—"

"I'll be right up," Michael promised. Valerie murmured:

"Is this where I take a bow and exit gracefully?"

"Why should you? She'll be glad to talk to you."

Miss Julian, still shedding ostrich feathers, met them at the door.

"So nice of you and really, I don't know—I feel absolutely exhausted. And I was with Winona but she seems to want to be alone and Geneva is with her. Only Mr. Callendar asked me to go in because he was going back to the airport, so— What would you do, Mr. Dundas? For Charlie, I mean."

"Where is your kitchen? Did you try coffee?"

"Oh yes, but he—he swore at it."

Michael looked at the pale liquid in the coffee-pot and remarked gently:

"I said strong coffee. This slightly resembles anemic tea. Valerie, suppose you see what you can produce. Have you any Worcestershire sauce?"

"Why, whatever— Charlie likes it on his steak though he says I always cook steak too— But I don't know exactly where—" Miss Julian looked helplessly at the kitchen cupboards. "I put it away somewhere."

"In here?" Michael opened the door of a cupboard built up to the ceiling. "On this top shelf, perhaps? May I stand on a chair?"

"Oh no! It's not on that shelf! I—I just keep odds and ends up there. You know Gus comes in to clean and he does pry into things except when it just looks like empty jars. But the Worcestershire sauce wouldn't be there. In this cooler, I think. Will this do? I'm afraid it's rather old."

"That's all right," Michael said, taking the small dusty bottle. "Now, an egg."

"Egg?"

"Yes. A small whitish object usually associated with a hen. In other words, an egg."

"Oh—oh yes." Miss Julian blinked at him uncertainly, apparently not resenting the marked absence of his morning's "excess of chivalry toward a helpless maiden lady." She opened the frigidaire, releasing an odor at once rancid and sour.

"There should be one. Oh, dear, these leftovers. But you never know when you might use— These potatoes: I'm afraid they're not—not quite—"

"I should say," Michael drawled, "that they are—quite. It was an egg we wanted."

"Oh yes. I don't see— Oh, dear! there's Charlie again. Wanting his ice water and I forgot to fill the ice trays so I'm afraid it isn't so very— You just help yourself," said Miss Julian, seizing a pitcher of water in which one shrunken ice cub floated lonesomely and scurrying away in the direction of her brother's irate bellow.

Instantly Michael opened the door of the tall cupboard again, picked Valerie up before she guessed his intention and set her on his shoulder.

"Take a quick look at that top shelf. Can you see over the empty fruit jars?"

"Yes, but, Michael, I don't want to—"

"Unless you close your eyes you can't help seeing. We haven't all day and I'm not Atlas—and you're not precisely emaciated. Well?"

"A ouija board," Valerie whispered. "And a bottle of hair dye and—and some rat poison. And an old candy box that might have anything in it."

"Could you— No, you couldn't," Michael decided, letting her slip through his arms to the floor. He extracted an egg from a remote corner of the frigidaire and was breaking it into a glass when Miss Julian returned with an undepleted pitcher of water.

"He doesn't want it and— Did you find what you wanted, Mr. Dundas?"

Michael looked at the collection of small bottles he had dug out of the cooler. "I think this will do. There; give him that."

"Oh, but it looks so awful," Miss Julian quavered. "Will it be good for him? I don't see how it—"

"Experience has proven that it will. Tell him to swallow it in one gulp. It isn't something you sip daintily."

"Oh, but tabasco and— Well, I'll try, but— Do you have to go? I'll be right back."

"Yes, we do," Valerie said, turning out the flame under the coffeepot. "That's ready to drink and very strong. Good night. No, we'll let ourselves out."

"Don't say it, not here," Michael whispered.

"I suppose I'd better not," Valerie agreed as the Callendars' front door opened and Geneva backed into the hall, still talking.

"Well, dear, if you want to be alone, I'll go. But you mustn't brood because things like this do happen. It's the age we're living in. It must simply be God's will and— Oh, you mustn't take it like that," she said to some gesture of Winona's, visible only to her. "And he probably never knew what happened." As the door suddenly closed with an unmistakable slam she said: "Well!" and turned to face Valerie and Michael.

"Oh! Well, I didn't hear you. The poor girl is simply distracted and doesn't want anyone with her though she shouldn't be alone. She— Oh, Mr. Dundas, your friend!"

"No, no, we have that to be thankful for," Michael said quickly. "It was not certain he would come but"—he shrugged—"you may imagine my anxiety until I knew—"

He winced imperceptibly as Valerie deliberately kicked him and then went on smoothly: "But it happens he has a so-important engagement that keeps him in Hollywood."

"Well, I certainly am glad of that. Just think of all those poor souls, wondering and waiting."

"Ghoul!" Valerie muttered.

"What is it, dear? Are you coming down now? Mother will want to hear all about it, you know."

"She'll have to wait," Valerie said, starting up the stairs. "Michael and I have something to discuss."

"You little fiend," Michael said admiringly, switching on the lights in his living room. "You've crippled me permanently. And why?"

"Oh, you make me mad when you put on that Russian grand-duke act! Have you no pity for foolish women?"

"No. Nor fools of any sex."

"Oh. Well, that's definite enough. But, Michael, Miss Julian simply can't have been writing those letters. She's too vague and absent minded and—yes, foolish."

"Doesn't it strike you she's just a bit too vague? She was fairly terse when she objected to my investigating that cupboard."

"And when she asked me for that money," Valerie recalled. "She was worse than usual tonight. It did seem she might almost be overdoing it though she's had an upsetting day. Maybe she's found it's the easiest way to slide through life and isn't just trying to—to—"

"Establish a character against a possible police investigation? You're right, of course," Michael said. "It's the Albatross who seems to enjoy death and disaster. But that candy box of Miss Julian's could hold a rubber stamp or two."

"So could any box in any apartment. I had one of those sets when I was a kid. And I never thought of it until now. Rubber letters, an ink pad, tweezers to pick the letters up with and put them in the stamp. I haven't any idea if it was ever destroyed. Tomorrow I'll look in our hall closets. They are full of things that never get thrown away. I'm going to bed. And please don't consider burgling the Putnams' apartment or the Julians' to try to find a stamping outfit. Or ours either."

"If you put on the night latch you'll be quite safe."

Michael walked to the door with her. Sara Putnam was just crossing the hall with a small hairy dog on a leash.

"This damn poodle has to go for a walk—or else," she said bitterly. "It's acted all day like it was possessed of seventy devils. Lily sent word she has a misery in her back and I've had everything to do. I think I'll tie a large stone to this and toss it in the bay."

"Is it any particular breed?" Michael said politely.

"It's not a dog; it's an abomination. Has it ever struck you, Valerie, how much it looks like Grandma? And just as full of cute tricks. Oh, well." Sara stooped and picked the dog up, tucking it headfirst under her arm. "Hell! if you won't walk, you won't. But there's one thing you might as well make up your mind to do for yourself—and right away."

"She appears," Michael said thoughtfully, "to be a trifle overwrought. I think I'll ask Mrs. Callendar if she's heard from her husband."

"Well, I suppose there's no reason why you shouldn't, since we were out there. But I won't."

"No, of course not," Michael said with suspicious affability. "Your scruples do you great credit . . . I hope we haven't disturbed you, Mrs. Callendar? We wondered if you had heard from your husband."

"He telephoned. No news. Won't you come in? No, I mean it. I want company if I can choose my own. Come in and have a drink."

Pouring out whisky she added: "I don't know why I'm not tight. Walking the floor and waiting. They haven't even found the plane, Grant says. It's like the thing had vanished into thin air. I told him to come back—and I wish he would! The Bayshore highway is so crowded Sunday nights and he drives like a fool. I— Valerie, I forgot you don't drink. Sensible of you. I wish we'd never started."

She stopped, smiling apologetically. "I'm sorry; rattling on like this. Do you want ginger ale?"

"I'll take it straight," Michael said. "But do you think you'd better?"

"Oh, one more won't hurt. After all— You heard Grant say it was odd John should travel by air. And it was though I wouldn't admit it because I thought John would want to talk to me privately. He wouldn't have confided in Grant. Did you know, Valerie, or ever suspect, how well Uncle John knew Maxine?"

"Not until just lately."

"Well, I don't know, myself, how intimate they were. John politely told me to mind my own business. And of course he had a right to," Winona admitted. "But I hated to see her make a fool of him."

"I got the impression your uncle wouldn't easily be made a fool of."

"Well, that's so. Of course you are probably thinking that naturally I didn't want them to marry; that no one likes to see a well-to-do uncle marry a young woman. If the police knew about her and John that would probably occur to them. But, after all, he moved away and left her here and that was the end of it."

"Do you think he may have heard about Maxine?"

"He must have. Over the radio, probably. Because he wired us so we got it Saturday night and the wire was filed in Los Angeles at six o'clock. Well, perhaps by that time it was in their papers down there but I don't think they play up our murders very much. But I can't think of any other reason for his coming unless it was business. I suppose he had something to say to the police. Or he might have thought I'd be suspected—or Grant."

She picked up the glass she had filled for Valerie and drank from it. Michael, lazily relaxed in his chair, seemed to be gazing with respectful appreciation at his whisky. But to Valerie his attitude was deliberately provocative; as if he had said: "This is your chance. Only a fool would let it slip by." She said slowly:

"Had Mr. Dozier known anyone here before he came here to live?"

"Mr. Julian. John was with the Pacific Importing Company and he had some business with Julian. He told John about this place when Grant and I were looking for an apartment. And John liked that top apartment so well he took it for himself."

"Then he might have known Mr. Julian better than— Why did he say Mrs. Putnam was crazy?"

"I didn't know he did," Winona said. "Or that he ever saw her. I've only seen her once in two years myself. And it took a fire to get her out of her hole."

"Fire? Oh, you mean when Miss Julian dropped a lighted match in a wastepaper basket? I wasn't in—"

"You missed something. Seems she just went around wondering if she didn't smell smoke until finally some curtains caught. Honestly, that woman should be confined. I was in bed with a filthy cold and first thing I knew the firemen were here and I had to dash out as was. There was old lady Putnam with that dog under her arm. From the way Mr. Julian stared at her it must have been the first time he'd seen her. I wouldn't blame John for saying she was crazy, just from her looks."

"I thought she might have known your uncle. She'd traveled a great deal."

"And so had he? But there are lots of things I don't know about John," Winona said, finishing the drink Valerie hadn't taken. "My father died a long time ago and I was passed around from one boarding school to another. I was finishing near San Diego when he came back here to live five years ago. Before that he'd always traveled for his firm. He came to see me and took quite a fancy to me."

She looked contemplatively at the nearly empty whisky bottle on the tray table; shook her head and pushed it away.

"I'd better not. Well, I was terribly fond of John. He sent me to Europe and then I lived with him two years before I married Grant. But except for these last four years I haven't any idea what he may or may not have done. But how did we get started on this? And why?"

"It's—it's these poison-pen letters," Valerie said. "We've been trying to figure out who is writing them and we thought to find out any connections between people here might help."

"We?"

"Michael knows Herbert and we've all discussed the case against Tommy, but I didn't want to tell Herbert about the letters."

Winona nodded. "He'd dash to the police, you thought? Well, that's the way I felt about it at first: that I didn't want any publicity. And I imagined we weren't the only ones who were getting them so if no one else wanted to talk— But if I get any more of the things, I'm taking them to the police. Will you back me up?"

"Yes, I will. Because it can't go on forever."

"Of course we'll all be under suspicion but that can't be helped. I think it's a draw between Miss Julian, Mrs. Putnam and Geneva. If John got any letters before he left he didn't show them to me. He couldn't have had very many or he'd have raised a fine row about it. He didn't take things lying down. And he's never mentioned them in his letters and of course I haven't either."

She started up as a key grated in the lock. "That's Grant. . . . Darling, I thought you'd never come. If I hadn't had someone to talk to— You don't need to tell me; they haven't found anything, have they?"

Grant shook his head, patting her shoulder. He rubbed his bloodshot eyes.

"That wind out there— No; they're still look-ing. Searchlights and boats and things, but it's like looking for something in a well. Just the water and— For God's sake, give me a drink."

CHAPTER THIRTEEN
A DOG WHIMPERS

Valerie sat up in bed, murmuring: "Those potatoes at John's were too salty," and groped for the water bottle on the table beside her. From its weight she knew it was empty and lay down again, half dazed with sleep that had been too long in coming. Because Geneva had insisted on "tucking a poor tired girlie into bed", which meant she sat on that bed for fifteen minutes discussing what she called the "terrible tragedy" at the airport.

It was after midnight when she took herself away. And Valerie had laid awake in the dark and thought of Tommy. Because already it was Monday and their day of grace was gone; the day in which she had so confidently expected something would happen to make the police see they must release Tommy.

And something had happened: a plane, for no good reason, had crashed in the bay. Perhaps John Dozier would not have been able to help them. But that intervening of outside forces—malevolently, she was tempted to say—shook her confidence.

Waking at some unknown hour of early morning, all vitality was at low ebb. She seemed for a dizzy moment to have no relation to her surroundings. The black shapes of dressing table and desk were fantastic and unfamiliar. Even her own flesh seemed insubstantial and impermanent. As it was. What had Michael said? "'All follow this and come to dust.'" She and Tommy, "golden lads and lasses . . ."

Valerie sat up; switched on the light. It was good to see her own face and tousled hair in the mirror across the room. And Tommy grinning at her reassuringly in his photograph. She could hear him saying: "You and your poetry! I'm not going to die before my time. When you're dead you're a long time dead." She looked irresolutely at the empty water jug; got up and put on robe and slippers.

Because her bedroom was toward the front of the apartment she had to pass the front door to get to the kitchen at the back. And, passing it, she remembered Michael's: "If you put on the night latch you'll be quite safe."

She stopped, fumbling in the darkness for the small bolt, to make certain Geneva hadn't forgotten to turn it. Her foot slid over something small and slick, lying close to the door. She picked it up quickly; felt the sharp edges of an envelope under her fingers and, not stopping for thought, opened the door and stepped into the hall.

The hall lights were out; not only in the lower hall but throughout the house. The switch that controlled them was near the front door but she was uncertain of its exact location. And as she stood there she thought she heard someone moving in the hall above. Or perhaps on the stairs. In their curving they formed an oblong and down that oblong space noises often echoed clearly.

But the soft pad of feet on thick old carpets, if she had heard it, ceased abruptly. Valerie put the envelope in her pocket, clutching it like a charm against evil, and started up the stairs. She reached the second floor and found it black and silent.

Listening again, with a hand on the stairway's curved banister, she heard no sound from above. She passed her hand foolishly over her eyes, feeling the darkness thick against them. Then, still gripping the banister, she crept on toward the top floor.

She had nearly reached it and stopped for an instant because she felt, strangely, that absence of light was affecting her as would lack of air. She put her face down against her arm, gasping a little. Before she could move a strong hand came over her mouth and an arm gripped her waist. She tried to twist away and the hand relaxed suddenly. Michael's voice said, close to her ear:

"I might have known it would be you. This is just a movie, after all. Since you're here, come on up."

He must, Valerie thought as he guided her sure-footedly up the stairs, be able to see in the dark. Inside his apartment he gave her a disgusted look, walked over and closed the Chinese chest by the window and the door into his bedroom.

"Don't you know that only fools and heroines of mystery stories wander around in the dark?"

"Well, I'm both, I should think," Valerie said meekly. "How did you know it was me?"

"The skin you love to touch. And Mrs. Callendar would be more of an armful than you."

"You said I am not precisely emaciated."

"My dear, this isn't the time or place for me to pay compliments to your figure. You no doubt are aware it's very satisfactory. What brought you out at this hour"—he glanced toward a small French clock—"of three in the morning?"

Valerie told him, taking the envelope from her pocket and opening it. "NOW YOU DONT HAVE TO WORRY ABOUT YOUR SISTER TAKING YOUR LOVER AWAY FROM YOU JUST WHETHER THEYLL HANG HIM OR NOT. Isn't that sweet?

Did you get one?"

"No. You thought this had just been put under the door?"

"I didn't think at all. I simply stepped into the hall. Were you on the second floor before you caught me?"

"No, I was just going to bed."

"At three o'clock?"

"It's not your concern when I go to bed, Valerie. I might remind you that I've had very little time these last two days to do my own work."

Valerie glanced around the room. "I don't see any signs of labor."

"Oh, I have just returned from robbing a house. The spoils are hidden in that chest," Michael said unpleasantly. "I am a combination Raffles, Saint and Lone Wolf with just a dash of Arsene Lupin. I repeat: I was going to bed, mixed myself a drink and stepped onto the back porch to dispose of some garbage. I—well, come out and hear for yourself."

Because the apartment house was an old-fashioned one there were back porches off the kitchens. That is, one fairly large porch shared, on second and third floors, by the tenants of two apartments. On either side of the service stairway were two large garbage cans. Michael, stepping to one of these, said:

"Do you hear it?"

In the light that streamed onto the porch through the door he had left open Valerie could see the door of the Putnams' kitchen. And hear, on its other side, the faint, unceasing whimper of a small dog. The whining grew to a tiny yelp, died away for an instant, began again to the accompaniment of claws scratching on woodwork.

"Well, I suppose he wants out," Valerie said uneasily. "I thought he slept in Mrs. Putnam's room. I wonder why she or Sara doesn't quiet him. Not that it matters; but—"

"You asked me what made me uneasy. That did. I opened the front door, found the hall dark and decided to investigate. I'll admit that alarmed me."

"The hall's being dark? Well, naturally, it would. It did me."

"But I should have realized, after what Gus told me— Valerie, how long ago was that fire in Miss Julian's apartment?"

"Why—let me think. Only about two weeks ago," Valerie said. "It happened fairly late in the afternoon because, as I told you, I wasn't in. Geneva would remember the exact day. Why? Are you thinking that Mrs. Putnam told me she was afraid of fire? But—but that wasn't anything serious."

"It brought her out of her apartment, along with everyone else here. Well," Michael said abruptly, "it couldn't have been I you heard a few minutes ago. I didn't reach the second floor before I heard you."

"I may not have heard anyone. I suppose this door is locked?" Valerie said, putting her hand on the knob.

"Do you suppose I wouldn't make sure?"

"You didn't make very sure—or someone's unlocked it since then!"

The door swung open and the long-haired dog frisked joyfully about their feet, barking shrilly. Michael said perfunctorily:

"Shut up, will you?" found the lights and switched them on.

The dog trotted to a corner, found a well-worn bone and proudly laid it at Valerie's feet. When she disdained that offering, he dived under the stove and brought out three bits of pulpy paper. Michael stooped quickly to pick them up.

"I have an idea we'll want these."

"Yes, but where is Sara? Why doesn't she wake up?"

"I wonder," Michael said, his eyes on an empty quart bottle that had held whisky. "You'd better stay here."

Valerie let him go, considering argument a waste of time. Then, pushing the dog away and closing the door on him, she followed Michael. In the Putnams' apartment the living room and one bedroom looked down on the street. Mrs. Putnam occupied the front bedroom at the end of the long hall. Sara's smaller room was nearer to the kitchen.

Its door was open and Valerie heard, as Michael stopped in front of it, Sara's heavy breathing. For an instant he stood there, waiting, but Sara only groaned in her sleep and moved restlessly. Valerie, forgetting she was there in disobedience of his orders, crept to his side and put her hand in his. She whispered:

"It isn't natural for her to sleep so soundly. If you'd turn on the bedroom light—"

Michael looked at her absently. "She's probably been sleeping too long." He went on, toward the end of the hall. Valerie followed him, not wanting to now, with sick apprehension for what lay on the other side of that door. . . .

But you would not have known, except for the rigid openness of her eyes, that Mrs. Putnam was dead. She might have been sleeping, slack-mouthed, in her chair, huddled into a filthy shapeless bathrobe. The damp red blotch spreading down its front merged imperceptibly into the fuzzy red flannel. But the lights caught a dull gleam of cop-per: the square handle of a knife driven in to its hilt.

There were plants everywhere: in small pots and large pots, in wrought-iron ferneries and red-and-white coffee cans. The top of an old walnut desk was covered with them and on the windowsill an enormous fern extended dry feathery fingers toward the carpet and brooded over a family of smaller plants on either side. The room smelled of damp and decaying leaves, cigarette smoke and, indefinitely, of drugs.

That much Valerie saw before she leaned back against the wall and closed her eyes. Michael turned instantly, said:

"Satisfied? You would come." But he moved so that she could not see Mrs. Putnam's chair. "Go on; get out. I'm coming too."

"Then you're not going to—to look for—"

"Clues? No." Michael joined her in the hall and closed the door to Sara's bedroom. "You and I are not going to be popular with Jim Sullivan. It's better not to disturb anything until he gets here. And while we're on the subject—"

He hesitated, then: "You go home and forget you've been here," he said. "In fact, forget our activities together from the beginning."

"And what will you tell Mr. Sullivan if I do?"

"I'll think of something," Michael said casually.

"No." Valerie sat down on the telephone stool and planted her feet firmly on the floor. "How could you account for being mixed up in this if you left me out of it? No! I won't argue with you. And don't spoil things. You've treated me—well, almost like a man. It's made me pretty mad some-times but I imagine it's really a compliment."

"You'll never know how much of one," Michael muttered. He looked at her appraisingly. Her chin came up under his scrutiny and her hazel eyes met his challengingly. At last he smiled—for once with no hint of mockery—and reached for the telephone.

"You're quite right, of course. So much for my tardy impulse to protect a poor weak woman. Look up Sullivan in the directory, will you? He lives on Marina Boulevard."

"Are you going to call him? I didn't think—"

"Of course it isn't the prescribed manner of reporting a murder," Michael snapped. "But why complicate things by littering the place up with radio-car and precinct men? It will be difficult enough to explain to Sullivan. And they might send us the wrong man from the Homicide Squad and we'd cool our heels in jail while they tried to understand what it's all about."

"Oh. Well, his number is Fillmore 0100. He'll be sound asleep."

"With the telephone by his ear," Michael said, dialing. "Policemen and firemen— Sullivan? This is Michael Dundas. I think you should come over here right away. Mrs. Putnam has been murdered and . . ."

He grimaced, muffling the telephone against his chest. "No, of course it isn't the right way to do things," he said when he was able. "But I think you might be glad if you took charge at once. . . . Irregular? Well, does that matter? . . . Certainly I think it ties in with Miss Farley's death or I wouldn't be calling you. . . . No, we won't touch anything. . . . Oh yes, Miss Sheridan is here to . . ."

He put down the telephone. "He is coming over at once. His language was not fit for your young ears. Would you rather sit here?"

"Shouldn't we wake Sara? She must be drugged."

"I think we'd better not. Sullivan is apt to believe only what he sees with his own eyes."

"Well, it will take some explaining. Even if she is drugged. Could anyone have done that purposely?"

"Who but her grandmother? Do you know if that knife belonged to Mrs. Putnam?"

"No, I don't. But if it did her murder wasn't planned ahead," Valerie said. "I've never seen any knives like that in any of the other apartments. And Mrs. Putnam has so much junk in that room."

"I wish," Michael said almost wistfully, "that I dared look through that desk of hers. Perhaps if you kept watch and warned me— No, I'd better not. Mr. Sullivan can move very swiftly when he wants to. That reminds me: you'd better be prepared for certain omissions in my story to him."

"How we knew Mr. Dozier was coming here?"

"That and Brother Charlie's canceled check. I'll tell him about that if I have to but I don't think tonight would be the perfect moment. That large fern in the window looks as if it hadn't been watered often enough."

"They do die, you know," Valerie said. "Too much steam heat. Does it matter?"

"Not now. I wish I'd never seen that room or had it described to me. That," Michael said, as the doorbell snarled at them, "will be Mr. Sullivan in a bad temper."

CHAPTER FOURTEEN
"SHE WAS GOING TO DIE"

He opened the door, carefully, with the tips of his fingers. "Won't you come in?"

"So good of you. I brought a few of the boys along with me. Hope you don't mind," Sullivan said.

A few of the boys were no less than five, "a mere skeleton force," Michael murmured. "Straight ahead, gentlemen. The door on the left. We'll wait here if you don't mind. You see, we've been there."

The five looked at him with a marked lack of sympathy or amusement and thundered down the hall with Sullivan bringing up the rear. But after a very few minutes he came back to Valerie and Michael, closing the bedroom door behind him.

"Now, what have you two been up to? Is there anywhere else we can talk? That's a living room there, hunh? What about this door here? Where's the old lady's granddaughter?"

"We wanted you to see that for yourself," Michael said. "Not that you would doubt our word, of course. Miss Putnam is in bed, asleep."

"With all this racket?" Sullivan yanked the door open. "Well, damned if she isn't. Unless she's faking. Hey! Hey, miss!"

The bed springs creaked. Sara said thickly: "What—wha's a matter? Grandma? I'm coming." And then, more clearly: "Who—who the devil are you?"

"Police. Look, miss—how about you trying to wake up? There's been a little accident."

"Accident? Oh," Sara said as if speaking from a not unpleasant dream, "you mean someone's killed my grandmother?"

"I'm afraid so. See here, did you expect—"

"Oh, go away, will you? My head feels funny and tight."

"Does it?" Sullivan said mildly. "You just wait a minute." He turned his head, bellowing: "Doc!" and when the small red-haired police surgeon appeared, frowning at the interruption, told him: "I want you to look at this girl in here—right now. It'll only take a minute and"—he looked at the doctor significantly—"it can't wait. We've—uh—got to talk to her."

"And be certain she isn't putting on an act," Sara said. "Come in, Doctor . . ."

"Can't I do anything for her?" asked Valerie.

"Not right now, Miss Sheridan. I want to talk to you two. Come into this living room. Now," Sullivan said, settling himself solidly into the room's largest chair, "you talk!"

When Michael was nearly done Mr. Sullivan said explosively, "Jesus H. Christ! I'm sorry, miss. My pal! I should have known you were holding out on me yesterday."

"Inspector, that was my fault. Michael said he thought we'd have to tell you about those letters. At first I was afraid you'd frighten whoever was writing them into destroying all the evidence," Valerie said defiantly. "And while I didn't mind showing you mine, there were others."

"Look, this isn't the first time I've come up against smart youngsters who hold out on the police. They always want to avoid publicity. And," Sullivan said, grinning, "they always think they could handle things a little more delicately than I would. I've come up against this kind of letter writing before and, generally speaking, no one ever wants it made public. We try to see that innocent people don't suffer too much in such cases. But we'd started doing a hundred things that take a lot of time and don't get you anywhere in a hurry—things you two couldn't do."

"If you'll get me a small thimble, I'll crawl under it," Michael said. "Now you have only to add that you probably would have saved Mrs. Putnam's life."

"Probably," Sullivan said complacently.

"But how?" Valerie asked. "She was the most inactive person in the building. How did she get her information?"

"You're jumping at conclusions. You don't know, yet, that she was killed because she wrote those letters. She may 've been killed because she found out *who* was doing it."

"Yes. But," Michael said, "six will get you ten you find a stamping outfit cached in that largest fern."

"Hunh? Well, if you knew that—"

"But I didn't. I didn't see her room until a few minutes ago. Naturally then I noticed that large fern doesn't seem to have been watered. And I've wondered, all along—as you would have, Inspector—where the letter writer hid her tools."

"Sure. But there are lots of places to hide things."

"Are there, when two and three people share an apartment? But I hadn't seen Mrs. Putnam's room so I didn't know that it fairly teems with excellent hiding places."

"Well, it does," Sullivan admitted. "It don't seem ever to have been put in order. You didn't know that, of course. And the janitor didn't tell you so?"

"I've told you exactly what he told me," Michael said wearily. "Including his remark that Miss Nolan and Miss Julian talk all the time and that Mrs. Putnam didn't. Well, I was very stupid. I should have guessed that the eagerness with which he defended her meant she probably made it worth his while to say nothing about her to the other tenants—while telling her a great deal about them."

"Oh? That's an amateur's way of figuring things out. Imagination and no facts. But you may be right. The janitor certainly showed he knows plenty about everybody if you think Mrs. Putnam got most of her information from him."

"She had a maid, but I imagine the woman is very ignorant," Michael said. "She can't read, at least. Oh, Valerie told me Mrs. Putnam lived in her bedroom and Miss Putnam is away in the afternoons. So I should have seen too that Mrs. Putnam had plenty of opportunity for uninterrupted letter writing. Have I abased myself sufficiently?"

"Maybe. I'll want to talk to the janitor and the maid. And Miss Putnam." Sullivan looked at Valerie reproachfully. "The thing that needed explanation was both of them chasing around at an ungodly hour of night when you stayed here. But you amateurs want to do things the hard way. Well, it looks like we want to talk to Dozier."

"Don't you read the newspapers, Inspector?" Michael asked gently. "Mr. Dozier was flying up from Los Angeles tonight."

"What? Not *that* plane? Holy mother! Well, it happens. Once I was chasing an important witness and a hit-and-runner got him before I did. Well, there may be something in his letters or papers he left in L.A. And his niece should know."

"She says she doesn't but you'll want to talk to her yourself. After I talked to Gus, Miss Sheridan and I went out to the airport."

"What for?"

"The ride. Peculiar coincidence, wasn't it?" Michael said blandly. "That's how we knew Dozier was coming up. When we got back we talked to Miss Julian for a while. As I told you, her brother was thoroughly and unusually soused this morning. And since it hasn't yet been proved to your satisfaction that Mrs. Putnam did write those letters, you might like to investigate the top shelf of Miss Julian's tallest cupboard. Valerie had better tell you why she came up here."

"Oh, so that was it," Sullivan said when Valerie had finished her story. "Let's see the letter. Umm! Where's the rest you say you kept?"

"In my apartment," Michael said. "Do you want them now?"

Valerie started to speak, thought better of it and stared fixedly at the toe of her slipper to avoid Sullivan's eyes. She had considered for an instant reminding Michael that he had also kept Maxine's sketch of the cavalier with the featureless face. But he hadn't mentioned its existence to Sullivan and she suspected the omission had been deliberate.

"I'll get them pretty soon," Sullivan said. "I got to see what the boys are doing. You wait here; I'll be back."

"Well, he might have said a lot more than he did," Valerie remarked. "And it was all true. And my fault, really."

"Now that you have realized that, forget it," Michael said ungratefully. "And don't relax prematurely. That paternal manner is one of his best weapons."

"Oh. Do you suppose he'll let Tommy go now?"

"Women and elephants."

"Never forget? Why should I? Oh, I know there's been another murder."

"And, you think, probably a good thing?"

"I didn't say that."

"But it is, you know. It was the next logical step and about the only thing that would help us to advance quickly."

"Michael—I don't pretend to think Mrs. Putnam is any loss to the world. Sara will be happier
now she's dead. But if you'd been certain she was
going to be killed, would you have—"

"Stood aside and let it happen? I suppose not.
We keep cripples, idiots and degenerates alive,
you know. It would have been a temptation. It's
rather late, isn't it, to begin worrying about my
lack of humanitarian instinct?"

"If you do lack it. It occurs to me you do protest too much," Valerie said and had the pleasure
of seeing him flush darkly. "But is Mrs. Putnam's
death going to help us learn the truth? If Maxine
was blackmailing her, now we'll never know."

"I doubt if your stepsister was blackmailing
Mrs. Putnam. If she'd put the screws on someone
else then it wasn't Mrs. Putnam who killed her.
Well, that may clarify things—eventually. But
Mr. Sullivan did make one pertinent remark: that
amateurs always want to do things the hard way.
Suppose we wait and let him—"

Valerie said: "Sh-h!" but Michael went on without bothering to lower his voice—"let him cast
the clear light of his intelligence on this problem
before we take it up again. And never be too apol-
ogetic toward the police except when dealing with
traffic cops."

"Listen to him and he'll land you in jail," Sullivan said. "Sit down, Miss Putnam. Now, where shall I put you two? Because I don't want you mixing with the other tenants."

"If it's my feelings you're trying to spare, I'd just as leave have an audience," Sara said. "Anyway, I'll bet Mr. Dundas would like to hear this. Hasn't he been detecting or whatever you call it on his own?"

"What makes you think that?" Sullivan grinned rather maliciously at Michael.

"Oh, I just thought he might be." Sara brushed back her damp hair. Her skin, always sallow, had a greenish tint under the strong central light. "I feel like hell. I suppose you know I was swacked? I got the idea from Charlie Julian. There was an emergency bottle of Double A in the kitchen so I emptied it."

"You hadn't ought to do things like that," Sullivan said mildly. "Why did you?"

"Lily Washington couldn't come so I had Grandma on my hands all day. Her and the dog and— Well, I was worn out by night. I—just felt like getting pie-eyed. I didn't want to stay awake though I knew I should."

"So your grandma wouldn't get in mischief?"

"No use denying it. I've been expecting hell to break loose any time because of those letters."

"When did you find out she was writing them?"

"At first I didn't suspect her," Sara said. "There were two for her, you see. Of course that's a precaution anyone would take. But I thought she took her pills and settled down and slept the night through, so how could she be putting letters under doors?"

"Oh—you knew other people were getting them?"

"Why waste time by asking that—and looking cute?" Sara snapped. "Of course I supposed the epidemic was general. Nobody confided in me and I didn't go snooping around doors. But about two weeks ago I found a little hoard of sleeping tablets in Grandma's bed. Lily wouldn't have talked if she'd found a—a rat in the bed. And she could shut herself up for hours while I was away and Lily wouldn't know what she was doing.

"Grandma had her buffaloed," Sara added bitterly. "Lily thinks I abused her. It was the same with the janitor. I know she was a perfectly foul specimen but would you believe it she was quite a heartbreaker once?"

"So I've heard," Sullivan said.

"Well, she kept enough of that damned charm to still put it over on people. I'll bet she fooled Valerie the other night. When I found those tablets she hadn't taken I tried to stay awake. I didn't have much luck. I'm a sound sleeper and she was too smart for me. I never caught her outside the apartment; not even that night you were here, Valerie.

"I woke up then and thought I'd see if she was safely in her little beddie. She wasn't. So I went out into the halls and wasted a lot of time looking for her."

"Were the lights off that night?" Michael asked.

"Lights? Of course they were. I suppose she'd go straight downstairs so she could turn them off and then come back up in the dark. I didn't catch her last night. She may have sneaked into the basement and up the back stairs. I didn't think to see if the kitchen door was unlocked before I went out. Then I had a brainstorm, went into her room and found a nice little printing outfit."

Sullivan looked at Michael. "The things were hidden in that fern, all right. She must have bought three or four outfits so she had plenty of letters to work with. Well, Miss Putnam, hadn't you looked for the things before?"

"I'd tried to but look at the junk there was in it. I didn't notice for a long time that she'd stopped watering that big fern. And if anybody disturbed anything she had a fit. I mean that literally. And the doctor said we must give her her own way as long as possible."

"Doctor? Then she was sick?"

"Do you think feeding her dope was my idea?" Sara drawled. "She was going to die and much more unpleasantly than she has. Along with a lot of other things she had cancer. You can see Doctor Rudd about it. His reputation's beyond suspicion, I think.

"The point was, she didn't want to die. She seemed to feel she'd had a bum deal from life. I guess she wanted to hit out at anything that was handy. Anyway, I remembered the last time she went downtown, and the first time she'd gone for months, was two or three days after she had Rudd's verdict. I suppose she got those stamps and started out to have fun."

"You oughtn't to talk like that," Sullivan said. "It don't sound nice. Look: did Miss Farley ever come to see your grandma?"

"Not that I know of."

"Well, what time did you get home Friday afternoon?"

"About six. I had to referee some tennis matches. But Lily was here and would answer the doorbell."

"I've got to talk to that maid," Sullivan repeated. "Well, of course you don't know if your grandma slept Friday night or—"

"For once, I can. Because that night I literally poked her medicine down her throat," Sara said grimly.

"Why?"

"Why? Because she needed to sleep and—and I had to."

"Oh yeah? Again? Look here, Miss . . . Well, don't knock the door down! Come in!"

CHAPTER FIFTEEN
THE GOSPEL ACCORDING TO GUS

A long blue arm shoved Gustavus Adolphus Lindholm into the room. The voice belonging to the arm said: "Here he is, Inspector."

Gus, thrust into the bright light of publicity in dirty trousers drawn over a blue-piped nightshirt, scrubbed at his pale hair and blinked pale sleep-reddened eyes.

"I was sleeping like always and the cop he comes—"

"Well, what do you know about this?" Sullivan was reaching a state of mind where he wanted to browbeat someone and Gus was tempting material. "What have you been doing?"

"I was sleeping. Like always." Gus's accent grew perceptibly thicker. "Ay haf turned off the heat—"

"Never mind that. Did you know someone was writing anonymous letters to people here? Poison-pen letters? Oh hell! Letters that said pretty raw things about people and weren't signed but just put under the doors."

"No, I do not know about letters like that. I tell Mr. Dundas that Mr. Dozier ask me—"

"Yeah, I know. Well, what did you think Mrs. Putnam wanted to know about the other tenants for?"

"She is old and has no one to talk to. Tenants they always want to know about each other. Is funny but is so," Gus said philosophically.

"And you tell 'em?"

"I am pleasant but I am not talking too much."

"Except to Grandma?" Sara suggested. "I've heard you once or twice. And she paid you for it, didn't she, Winchell?"

"Is not good you call names," Gus said darkly. "I am nice to her so she give me presents. Is not nice to leave sick old ladies alone late at night. Like you do Friday."

"And where," Sara said coolly, "were you hiding out?"

"I turn off heat at ten o'clock." Gus addressed himself pointedly to Sullivan. "But I do not go to bed any night till eleven, twelve o'clock. Sometimes I come out, look to see everyt'ing all right. Why not? I see you go out Friday."

"What time?" Sullivan asked.

"Oh, it would be after eleven. I do not see her come back. After that I am in my room."

"I was walking," Sara said. "There's no law against that."

"And today when I bring back dog after I haf walked with him I hear this—this lady and the grandma fighting somet'ing fierce."

"Oh, you did? I suppose you weren't going to mention that, Miss Putnam?"

"Well, you really wouldn't expect me to, would you? Yes, we did quarrel. Most of the day, in fact."

"The grandma," Gus remarked, "say you wish she was dead and you say: yes, and why not? And she say she will take her time to die. And you say: yes, you are sure she will. Then she say when you have her money will you get a husband then? She don't fink so. And maybe you won't be getting it. Maybe she will leave it to—to—"

"A home for aged and infirm poodles," Sara said. "I've been hearing that threat for years."

"Yeah? That all, Gus?"

"There was somet'ing about a man," Gus said, rubbing his chin. "But I do not hear that very good."

"I said it was too bad I couldn't entertain my friends in my own home," Sara said. "That was what started it. I had an engagement I couldn't keep when Lily didn't show up. I wanted to invite my—friend here, instead, but she wouldn't hear of it."

"Your friend being Gregory Lutz? Oh, I turned him up as one of Maxine Farley's friends. And you know him too. I didn't think that was important then," Sullivan said. "Did you get letters mentioning him? I thought so. And that made you suspect your grandmother was writing them?"

"Yes. How did you know?"

"Because Miss Nolan didn't give me his name. Well, if she didn't know he knew Miss Farley or that he knew you too, who else in the building would know it?"

"No one. He's never been here but once. So of course Grandma was the only one who knew I'd seen him since that first time. Like a fool I—I mentioned him to her."

"And she didn't let you forget it?"

"What do you think? Oh, go to hell!" Sara's head went down on her arm. "I don't care what you think. I wish you'd had to live with her just one month and had it cast up to you all the time that you were ugly and unattractive and would like to get married and probably never would. Go on, laugh! It's so damned funny!"

Sullivan looked distinctly uncomfortable. He was used to dealing with women who wept prettily or hysterically but this girl was crying as painfully as a man. Valerie looked indignantly from him to Gus, started to get up and sat back in her chair again. Michael was already offering Sara a large clean handkerchief, saying softly:

"*Vamos, vamos, no llores!* Consider what a great girl you are. Consider what o'clock it is. Consider anything, only don't cry."

Sara raised her head, defenses up again. "All right. I do it very badly, anyway. Go on, Inspector."

"Well—uh—I suppose your grandmother thought it was safe to write you letters like that because you wouldn't give her away?"

"I don't know what she thought. Sometimes it's seemed to me she couldn't be quite right lately. It's funny to remember she was good to me when I was a little girl. But she never mentioned the letters to me after I let her know I knew she hadn't been sleeping nights."

"Did you think she would tonight?"

"I hoped so. She was smart about that. She'd pretend to swallow the tablets and really slip them down in her chair. But I was past caring what she did or didn't do."

"Did you tell her you were going to finish up that whisky?"

"Why—yes, I did. I—I yelled it at her. Do you suppose she doped the stuff?"

"We'll see about that. The Doc says you had the whisky all right but he wouldn't be surprised if you didn't have some stuff from a bottle in her bedroom too. She had a chance to get at the whisky?"

"Of course. I got it down before I took that damn dog walking. She had something in a bottle before the doctor gave her those tablets and—I did feel funny. I'm a pretty good drinker and that bottle wasn't nearly full. I tossed it down; there wasn't any ginger ale—"

"Did you lock the kitchen door before you went to bed?"

"Of course. I'm sure because I shut the door in there. Grandma didn't want the dog in her room though that was the only place he'd be quiet and sleep the night through. But he'd chewed up one of her slippers and was being punished for it. Did you find the door unlocked? Maybe I fixed it like that so I wouldn't be suspected."

"But someone did put a letter under our door sometime after midnight," Valerie said.

"And she didn't leave one for me?"

"No," Sullivan said. "And not for anybody else. But there were three in her pocket. Did she have a chance to write any today?"

"I suppose so. I had the housework today and I kept away from her as much as I could."

"Well, I'm guessing she went downstairs, turned off the lights and left one letter there. But something happened to keep her from delivering the others. She met someone or someone came to meet her. She must have brought 'em in here. Even if she left the front door unlatched so someone could slip in, they wouldn't know you were going to be dead to the world and so they wouldn't risk surprising her here. Or she may even have met someone on the first floor and brought 'em up here. She knew it was safe; that you'd sleep. Would she do that?"

"She wasn't timid," Sara said.

"And don't you think she might want to be amused?" Michael asked.

"Amused? That's a funny word."

"It's a very good word, Inspector. Yes, I think she might have wanted to be amused," Sara said. "See someone squirming on a pin, you know."

"And was she fond enough of money that she could have been bought off?" Michael said.

"She was— Wait a minute! Maybe I didn't dream it, after all. When I did wake up it seemed to me I'd been trying for hours to. And that I'd heard Grandma laugh and say: 'But I don't want money.'"

"What else?"

"That was all, Inspector. Honestly. Well, Grandma was fond of money, of course. But since she knew she wasn't going to have the use of it much longer I think she'd have preferred to—gloat."

Gus, with a sudden cavernous yawn, moved from one foot to another and Sullivan turned on him.

"You! I'd forgotten you! I suppose you don't know what it's all about anyway."

"Just a minute," Michael said. "Since you're a night owl, Gus, I suppose you knew that Miss Farley sometimes went out late at night?"

Gus nodded solemnly. "I see her acting like she is not wanting anyone should know. Come outdoor very quiet and look around to see if anyone is there. And one night she and Mr. Callendar go off together when Mrs. Callendar is not home."

"I suppose you were at the top of the basement stairs with the door ajar, preparatory to coming out of your hole? Did you happen to see Miss Sheridan get home very late one night—or early one morning?"

"With her young man? No, I do not see that."

"But it was at an hour when Mrs. Putnam might very well have seen me herself if she happened to be up," Valerie said.

"Yes, of course. And what is your opinion of Miss Nolan and Mrs. Farley, Gus?"

"Miss Nolan she is bossy lady. Should have husband. I t'ink she do not like Miss Farley. One time I am washing windows outside I hear them talking in room and Miss Farley she is not polite. I do not know what about. Mrs. Farley I am not seeing much."

"Well, then, what did Mrs. Putnam say about her, if anything?"

"She say she is painted doll and lazy. And not want her daughter to marry; wants to keep her money."

"That's enough," Michael said hastily as Valerie flushed. But Gus continued placidly:

"Mrs. Farley do not like Miss Farley either. They haf quarrel Friday after lunch. I am working in garden and Mrs. Farley's windows are open. I hear Mrs. Farley say somet'ing about 'sneaking out nights' and 'got to behave yourself.' Miss Farley do not speak loud but she laugh and I hear her say Mr. Dozier's name."

"I don't call that quarreling!" Valerie said quickly.

"Is not what she say; is sound of her voice. She does not usually have windows up," Gus said regretfully. "But that is very warm day."

"Well, what's the use of it all?" Sullivan said.

"You haven't read our collection of letters yet, Inspector. Miss Putnam did not actually see her grandmother write or distribute them and that stamping outfit could have been planted as you very well know." Sullivan nodded, smiling briefly. "So I wondered if Mrs. Putnam did have enough facts to have written them. It seems she did, with what she got from Gus. A few facts and a great deal of malice were all that was needed. And I suppose you told her all you knew?"

"I talk mit her," Gus said sullenly.

"Well, that's no crime," Sullivan conceded. "Did she make it worth your while?"

"I am poor man."

"Yeah; the kind that retires with a wad at sixty. Well, you beat it. Now, let's see. Do you want to stay here tonight, Miss Putnam? There 'll be cops around."

"She can stay with me," Valerie said.

"All right, then. But I want you three isolated for a while longer. Till I get through with the rest of this gang who 're probably howling their heads off by now. You go over to Michael's place. I'll come over pretty soon and pick up those letters. I 'll put a cop in the hall so you'll—uh—be safe."

"You two go on," Sara said. "I'll get some things together. You can send one of your watchdogs to my room with me if you want to. I suppose you've already helped yourself to the letters I kept?"

"We've attended to things," Sullivan said complacently. "You go on. I got to get to work."

Michael, looking cautiously into the hall, said: "The marines have landed. They're keeping people in their own apartments. And here's our official escort."

"Should we ask him in?" Valerie whispered, looking back at the square blue figure.

"He doesn't look to me as if he'd be a cheerful little playmate," said Michael, not whispering. He opened the door, walked into his living room and over to the windows, looking thoughtfully down at the Chinese chest. "I'll wager that's one lock they didn't force."

"Oh, do you think they searched this place?"

"Why wouldn't they? I can't help a reluctant admiration for Sullivan's refusal to bow his head under the bludgeonings of chance. Because he does have to begin again and get through a staggering amount of detail."

"Things we couldn't ever do. Yes, we were idiots," Valerie said, sitting down. "Will he tell us anything he learns?"

"What does that matter to you if he lets Howard go?"

"But it does! I want to know the truth and—
Michael, how can you be so abominably rude
sometimes and so nice to people at others—as you
were to Sara?"

"Nice? That word used to mean something. As
used by Jane Austen, for example. Now it means
nothing so women use it constantly. At that, it's
better than divine, darling, precious."

"It won't work; not any more," Valerie said,
smiling. "Your way of avoiding an unwelcome
topic by being insulting or merely talkative. You
were nice to her. Why?"

"Oh," Michael said reluctantly, "I didn't want
her to give herself away and then regret it. I don't
mean facts regarding her grandmother's death—
if she knows any she hasn't told. But I know—I
think she must have spent years acquiring that be-
damned-to-you manner. It's her defense: let her
keep it."

"How well you understand her," Valerie said.
"You— Well, never mind. I wonder if she was really walking Friday night. I can't help thinking
wherever she went, making certain first her grandmother would sleep, had something to do with
Gregory Lutz. And— Michael, we haven't looked
at those pieces of paper that dog was chewing on."

"Haven't we? Well—"

"I don't believe you meant to show them to me if I'd forgotten. But they are—yes, they are letters."

"They were," Michael said, studying the three fragments of paper he had spread out on a table. "Dear little Fido did a fairly good job on them."

On each of the tattered scraps a word or two in the familiar black-purple lettering were still decipherable—MAN WHO, CRAZY AS A LOON and FIRE.

"There's no way of telling whether there were three letters, two or only one," Valerie said. "They certainly give plenty of scope for imagination. You remember what Mrs. Putnam said to me about insanity? She may have been hinting Geneva or Miss Julian might be insane. But if she was mentally unbalanced herself—"

"I don't think she was. Only ill and embittered—and malicious."

"Wc-el. Of course she may have been putting on an act for my benefit."

"Undoubtedly. But I think she also said one or two things to you that she meant you to remember if she were killed."

"Oh. Well, I suppose she must have known she might be. And chose to risk it. And I was the only outsider she saw. She did evidently know a great deal about Miss Julian. At least she knew she'd

been in love once and her family didn't approve
and shipped her off to Europe. But I've heard of
ultrarespectable families doing that to hide the
fact that one of their cherished daughters was going to have a baby."

"'The Old Maid?'" Michael said. "However, it's
been done. Well, Mrs. Callendar also had a Euro-
pean trip."

"Phooey!" Valerie said inelegantly. "It's different now. Twenty-five years ago girls didn't just
trot off to Europe and think nothing of it. I have
heard Miss Julian speak as if they were rather hard
up when she was a girl. Oh well, speculations like
that are a waste of time. But you asked me about
that fire and there's the word on one of those
scraps. What do you—"

"I don't. And I would be eternally grateful if
you would stop babbling for two minutes," Michael said.

"Now you sound perfectly natural. I think,"
Valerie said, catching sight of herself in the mirror over the mantel, "that I'd like to wash my face
before Inspector Sullivan pops up again."

"She washes her face! How—nice. The bathroom's off the bedroom. No, wait a minute." Michael disappeared into the bedroom, returned in a
few minutes and said without apology: "All right
now; go ahead."

CHAPTER SIXTEEN
RETURNED TO CIRCULATION

Coming out of the bathroom Valerie heard Sara talking in the living room. She thought: now we can go to bed—if we're ever turned loose and if Geneva will let us, after that. I wonder if they are worried about me. And why don't I feel a little more concern over the possibility that they might be?

She picked up Michael's comb, remembered the dictum that a comb is as personal a possession as a toothbrush, and smoothed her hair back with her hands. The bedroom was womanishly neat and completely austere. There was nothing but the Hepplewhite suite and two pictures.

Valerie looked at one—a reproduction of Daumier's wraithlike Quixote riding his bony nag toward the black bulk of a dead horse—and shivered. Then, looking at the other picture, she laughed. For it, though chastely black and white, was one of Meta Pluckenbaum's pensive and fluffy kittens.

Having shivered, she sneezed, searched her pocket for a handkerchief and called:

"Michael, may I borrow a handkerchief?"

"Go ahead." His voice, she thought, sounded as if he had not really heard what she said. But she opened the top drawer of the dresser, took a handkerchief from a neat pile and then, guiltily, drew the drawer out as far as possible.

She had seen the edge of a photograph toward the back of the drawer and in an instant she was looking at it: the picture of a woman dark and exotically beautiful. A black gown fitted her body slimly and tightly to the knees where it flared into an extravagant mass of ruffles caught up in front to show one small foot and slender ankle. Underneath was written: *A mi querido Miguel—Eternamente.*

Valerie closed the drawer hastily and went back to the living room, displaying the handkerchief ostentatiously. But Sara was saying:

"Today that dog chewed a slipper, a bone, a handkerchief and a part of a newspaper. If he was chewing on some other paper, I didn't notice it. I do remember that while I was getting dinner he came scooting out of Grandma's room into the dinette. Maybe he had something in his mouth then. Spaghetti's the only thing I cook well and I was too busy to notice him."

"But if he grabbed things to chew on," Valerie said, "how could she keep him around when she was writing those letters?"

"When they were shut up together in her room she could catch him or have Lily do it. Lily wouldn't know what it was all about. I did think it was queer, her taking on so about his chewing one of her slippers. Usually she didn't care."

"And he was always quiet at night?" Michael said.

"As long as he was in her room he slept the night through. Well," Sara said with a fleeting grin, "until early morning. Then he had to be conducted to the back porch."

"Did he ever run away?"

"Out of our apartment? Not that I know of. He might have, though. I think," Sara said, "I'll offer him to Miss Julian. She calls him a dear little doggie. She can have him. I don't think I'd even care to take him to jail with me."

"Oh Sara, you don't think—" Valerie began.

"I certainly do, and so do you. You know perfectly well I could have killed Grandma and if you'd ever been around us you'd wonder why I didn't do it a long time ago."

"I have often wondered why more people don't kill because of pure hate."

"I didn't quite hate Grandma, though. That was the trouble; it would have been easier if I could have. I suppose your idea was that whoever killed Maxine was the person who wrote the letters and that she knew it and was blackmailing them. But I can swear Grandma didn't kill her. Anyway, you'd still have to find out who killed Grandma though that wouldn't affect you much, Valerie."

"How do you know Mr. Sullivan doesn't suspect me?"

"Well, you don't. I don't trust him a cent when he acts like butter wouldn't melt in his mouth."

"A very sensible frame of mind. You two watch your step. He can at least detain you on some excuse if he thinks it wise. His strength is as the strength of ten but not because his heart is guaranteed pure," Michael said. "He married the daughter of a perennial supervisor."

"Well, he'll have to take my story and like it," Sara said. "I've told him everything—almost. And I think I hear flat feet in the hall. . . ."

"Well," Sullivan said genially, "you two girls can go to bed. I talked to your cousin, Miss Sheridan."

"And my mother?"

"She was a little—upset. The doctor said it was—uh—nerves. Anyway, she didn't have anything to tell us."

"And Geneva?"

"Oh, she talked plenty. But her bedroom and your mother's are at the back. And yours is nearer the front."

"You know that. I suppose you're wondering why I didn't wake anyone? Well, I was very quiet."

"I'll bet you were, knowing Miss Nolan. She admits she sleeps lightly and she did think she heard someone in your hall. Do you *know* she was in her room when you left your apartment?"

"No. Because I didn't have to pass her door before I got to the front door. But, Inspector, I heard someone on the second floor," Valerie said.

"Sure about that?"

"Well—almost certain."

"Almost isn't good enough. You may have, but on the other hand why was that back door unlocked if someone didn't use the back stairs? It may just have been a smart trick, of course. Done to make us think Miss Putnam purposely unlocked it to point to an outsider."

"Then why wouldn't I leave the front door unlocked?"

"Because it would be safer for someone from another apartment to use the back way," Sullivan said. "But your grandmother was distributing letters."

"Maybe I caught her outside and brought her back."

"I thought of that too. You don't have to remind me. But what I started to say, Miss Sheridan: you can't eliminate Miss Nolan just because you think you heard someone on the second floor but never met up with 'em. Even if she didn't use the back way she could probably have avoided you in the dark by keeping quiet till you came on up here with Michael. Not that I have anything against her.

"You can't tell to a minute or hour when a person was killed." Sullivan made this statement as if it was something he had said many, many times before. "Of course she hadn't been dead long when we got here. If you allow twenty minutes one way or the other, you could have heard the murderer, Miss Sheridan, but he also could have sneaked home a few minutes before you ever got up.

"You might be interested to know Miss Nolan says she didn't know about those letters till yesterday morning. Then she found one under the door. It said"—Sullivan closed his eyes; recited—"so SHES DEAD AND WONT TAKE ANY MORE MEN AWAY FROM YOU ISNT IT FUNNY SHE DIED FRIDAY AND YOU QUARRELED WITH HER THAT SAME DAY. Well, Miss Nolan knew it was meant for your mother. She hadn't showed it to anyone. Why that crack about 'take any more men away from you?'"

"I haven't any idea."

"She has, of course," Michael said. "And I see no reason why I shouldn't—guess. Mrs. Farley, as you've seen, is very good looking and is—shall we say young in spirit?"

For an instant Valerie hated him. But in all fairness she had to admit he did not seem amused and if his words were sarcastic his intonation was not. He looked, besides, unutterably weary as he went on carefully:

"A fact which Mrs. Putnam knew and exaggerated."

"Maybe." Sullivan was unimpressed. "But Dozier was an attractive man of about your mother's age, Miss Sheridan. Only, according to Gus, he wanted to marry Miss Farley."

"And she refused him," Michael said. "I wonder why?"

"I suppose he was too old for her. For that matter, I suppose he's about Miss Nolan's age too." And, as Sara snorted disgustedly, Sullivan added: "I've seen odder things than that. I guess Miss Nolan is human. Well, let it go. . . . Miss Nolan did mention that while you usually get the paper, Miss Sheridan, she gets the mail."

"Yes. I bring in the paper while she's getting breakfast. She never reads it and neither does Mother. She prefers the pink afternoon scandal sheets. But Geneva always goes and gets the mail as soon as she thinks it's in the box: about eight-thirty to nine."

"So if there were any anonymous letters put in your box she'd get them first. Dangerous game, fooling with mailboxes. Well, I guess that's all, if you'll give me those letters, Michael. I'll see you sometime tomorrow."

Michael got the letters from the secretary, gave them to Sullivan and opened the door for Valerie and Sara. He had, as he stood waiting for them to pass, an expression so remote and withdrawn that Valerie felt a sudden unreasonable desire to make him aware of her again. She said:

"I'm disappointed, Michael. You didn't notice the hat I wore this evening and I put it on for your especial benefit."

His answering smile was swift as light. "Notice it! *Válgame Dios!* Can you ignore the Coit tower?"

"What," said Sullivan, bewildered but patriotic, "is wrong with Coit tower?"

"It looks as if it had been begotten by Incinerator out of Silo. And it cannot be ignored. Neither could Valerie's hat. But after due thought," Michael said, "I have decided that if you'll turn it all the way around and wear the back in front it won't look half bad. Try it some time. Good night."

"Would you mind," Tommy said, "shifting to my other knee? This one's numb. No, I don't want you to get up. Gosh," he kissed her for perhaps the twentieth time, "it's good to get out of that lousy jail."

"Tommy, was it?"

"I never actually caught anything but I was very suspicious. Oh, it wasn't so bad, baby. But I had my gloomy minutes. And have you had yourself a time!" He looked at her admiringly then severely. "You'd got no business chasing around like that. Say, tell me about Dundas. I don't know if I'm going to like him or not."

"And I don't know if he's going to like you," Valerie said pertly. "Not that it really matters. Well—yes, it does. Because I do want you to like each other."

"Yeah, but what does he get out of this?"

"I knew you'd say that. I think he wanted to pay off an old score against Inspector Sullivan. Only I guess the police can usually get along without help. But I was so furious when they arrested you I didn't think very highly of them. And if Michael hadn't directed my energy into other channels I'd probably have bitten Mother or Geneva."

"Give both of 'em a bite for me." Tommy cocked an ear toward the door. "Jeez, you can fairly feel this place reeking with icy disapproval. Mamma not reconciled?"

"We made up once but now she's hurt about last night."

"Hurt?"

"Well, I suppose it was a shock to have a policeman announce Mrs. Putnam had been killed and I was being held upstairs. And when I got back I had Sara with me and we were both too tired to answer questions. Tommy, I used to be a nice little girl."

Tommy tightened his arm about her waist. "You still are."

"No, I was really fairly thoughtful of Mother and Geneva. And lately they just don't seem to matter."

"Well, do they?" Tommy said absently. "Maybe he's in love with you."

"Michael?" Valerie laughed. "You flatter me. You should have heard some of the things he's said to me."

"Oh, yeah! Well, he won't say—"

"Anything while you're around. Yes, darling, you could lick him. You're several inches taller and much handsomer." Tommy looked greatly mollified though he still flexed his muscles experimentally. "But if I described him to you you'd think he must look like one of these suave movie gangsters. And I don't know why he doesn't," Valerie said reflectively. "He's dark and slim enough but he's not perfectly tailored. At least I've never noticed what he's wearing. And he has too much chin and his eyes are too blue—"

"Did I ask what he looks like? That's a woman for you."

"Are you jealous?" Valerie asked hopefully. "I like to see you scowl. Well, you're so matter of fact, my love, that I'm sticking to facts. And I don't know any about Michael except what he looks like. He's old."

"Oh, then—"

"Not in years. When he really smiles he looks about twenty-five though I imagine he's older. But—but I have a feeling it's been years since he was really young."

"Oh, I've known fellows like that," Tommy said. "Maybe some woman soured him on life."

"I—I wouldn't be surprised. That is—it happens, doesn't it? Tommy, I didn't know if they'd let you go."

"Well, I was surprised when they did. The papers didn't really tell anything. At least, now you've given me the lowdown I see they didn't. And they had that plane crash to cover."

"Yes." Valerie was silent for an instant, remembering the flat wind-swept field and the crowd

along its fence. This morning they had hoisted
the mangled plane out of the water, found only its
pilots and hostess inside, drowned. And the mute
testimony of unfastened seat belts, and in the mud
two swimmers who had never reached shore. Neither of them was John Dozier; he was one of four
swept away by the tide.

"Well, I'm sorry you had to be there," Tommy
said.

"Forget it. Anyway, they turned me loose. But
I don't know . . ."

He dumped her unceremoniously off his knee
and began walking up and down the black-and-
white room.

"This guy Hunt is a regular sourpuss. He said:
'Don't think we're forgetting you, Howard.' He
can't get that gun out of his mind."

"Well—think, Tommy! Can't you remember?"

"My good gosh, woman! I've thought till I'm
black in the face. I can see the thing in a top
drawer, mixed in with handkerchiefs and stuff."

"But perhaps that's where it was."

"Then what became of it? If someone stole it
to cast suspicion on me why didn't they leave it in
a nice prominent place? Anyway, you know how
I am about my things. And something you never
use but see around all the time— I've carried it

on fishing and hunting trips but never used it and always put it back in the bureau. At least I thought I did. I'm going to ask several guys about it though you'd think if they knew anything they'd have told it by now. Look: I want to meet Dundas. Let's go up there and," Tommy said, grinning, "let him put his mind to work on it."

"Well," Valerie said doubtfully, "if he's awake."

Michael was not only awake but entertaining Mr. Julian. The latter smiled at Valerie, a shame-faced smile that was still a little complacent. He said:

"Well, Miss Valerie, Em says I should apologize to everybody for making a spectacle of myself."

"The hair of the dog that bit you?" Valerie said, pointing toward the highball at his elbow. "If Miss Julian could see—"

"She can't. Anyway," Julian said, lifting the glass and staring at it reflectively, "while I do apologize if I said anything I shouldn't, I'm darn glad I did it. For forty years I've been practically a teetotaler. Just to set a good example to a lot of young fellows working for me that didn't care whether C. B. Julian took a drink or didn't take a drink.

"Well!" Mr. Julian drank defiantly and wiped his scraggy mustache. "Understand, I don't recommend anyone getting like I was yesterday. But it's wonderful how happy you are for a while. Anyway, have I ever got any credit for being temperate? I have not. All I get credit for is a bad temper. I don't deny it. Only thing is, Em's cooking and her—her blanketyblank rambling would make anybody bad tempered. So they let you out, young fellow?"

"They returned me to circulation," Tommy said cheerfully. "The bad penny. Sort of a damaged penny. I've got a record."

"That will be forgotten by the time the prison pallor has disappeared," Michael said dryly. He held out his hand. "Since it doesn't occur to Valerie that she might introduce us, will you have a drink?"

Tommy looked down at him with frank curiosity; finally grinned fraternally. "Sure thing. I have an idea we're going to get along all right."

"Why not?" Michael rescued his hand, shook it experimentally and remarked: "This is not a nut you are trying to crack, you know. Help yourself. Valerie, will you—"

"Oh, she doesn't drink," Tommy said, busy with whisky and seltzer.

Michael looked at her with an odd smile. "Oh, doesn't she?"

"And a good thing. I'm old-fashioned. Only"— Julian chuckled—"funny thing about Em. That prune wine she says is so harmless has quite a kick. See here, Miss Valerie, what's she said about me that makes you look at me like you expected me to bite?"

"Why, she—nothing at all. But I've heard you snap at her myself."

"Do you blame me?"

"Well—no."

"She's an awful good woman, Em is. And an awful homely one. And flighty—my Lord! I'm nothing to look at myself. But that," Mr. Julian said shyly, "don't keep me from liking pretty things. You've seen that place of ours and you know how it looks. I like this room. It's restful. Not too much in it."

He let Michael take his glass and fill it again. "It was because I liked to look at your sister that I— Well, I was going to tell Dundas about that. Because I don't know whether to tell the police. If they find out for themselves it's better I should tell 'em first," Julian said shrewdly. "And there's no reason you two shouldn't know. I guess Miss Valerie's put you wise to everything, Howard?"

"She's been talking hours," Tommy said. "Crammed me full of facts about letters."

"Oh, them. I wasn't thinking so much about them. I never took them very serious. Well, I was going to tell you about me and Miss Maxine. . . ."

CHAPTER SEVENTEEN
OLD HOME WEEK

Julian half emptied his glass, set it on a table and leaned forward, hands planted on his knees. In that position, with his short thick body and long arms, he looked like a frog ready to jump at an instant's notice.

"There wasn't anything between us, strictly speaking, miss. I never asked her out; why should she go with me? But she'd pass the time of day with me and laugh and joke. Well, I liked it. We took a walk or two in the park together when we just happened to meet."

"Happened?" Tommy muttered.

"Sure, I know what you mean. Maybe she was playing me for a sucker but I'm no fool. She was so young and pretty and didn't have much money and I've got nothing to spend mine for. I never wanted to marry her. You can laugh, but the idea of buying a young thing like her don't seem decent to me."

Tommy raised his glass, hiding a grin. Michael looked at the fat little man, his blue eyes friendly.

"So you gave her money and asked nothing for it?"

"You never saw her, did you? Well, if you had you'd know just looking at her was worth something. I gave her a check one time when she was talking about how she wished she had—well, had as much money—"

"As I have?" Valerie said.

"You can't blame her for that. Both of you young and living together. I gave her a check to buy something pretty. She was dressed in it once to show me. Seemed like a hundred and fifty was pretty steep for one outfit but it looked swell on her. It— I don't know. It had class. I never regretted it even if it is the kind of fool thing you wouldn't expect me to do. I'd have given her cash if I'd had it but I didn't, so I wrote a check before I changed my mind."

"She didn't tell me about it, of course. But she did always speak very nicely of you." Valerie's reward for this barefaced lie was Mr. Julian's grateful and shining smile.

"Did she? I felt bad when I heard about her. Why couldn't it have been someone like me or Em, I thought. Not," he said to Tommy, "that I ever believed you did it. Why, anybody that knows you and Miss Valerie— For all I've said about Miss Maxine I saw her faults."

"You didn't give her a bangle bracelet, did you?" Michael asked.

"A bang— What's that?"

"A thing that doesn't seem to fit into this jig-saw. A wire with elephants dangling from it. You can buy them in Chinatown."

"We never went to Chinatown. I was going to say: it don't matter about that check. I got it back the first of this month and I'm carrying it on me."

Valerie glanced quickly at Michael but he was gazing at a framed Audubon print with an expression politely and impersonally interested. Mr. Julian went on:

"I got a letter asking did I think any young woman would marry me for anything but my money. I suppose Em let on she was worried and it got around and back to Mrs. Putnam. Em would even ramble on to her. But if I show that to the police they'll want to know what it means. If I don't they'll probably hear some gossip anyway."

"I'm afraid they will," Michael agreed.

"Well, I guess I'd better give 'em that letter too. I gave them two others. I didn't like to because they warned me against Em. She's the only one thinks I'm such a wonder with the ladies. I'd always take care of her. I don't like to see money

VIRGINIA RATH

wasted the way she does; that's all. She can't resist a bargain, even if it's nothing she'll ever use.

"Anyway," Mr. Julian said candidly, "I'm short tempered with her because she gets on my nerves. The other letter I gave Sullivan I got Sunday morning. I found it in the box when I went out for a walk. It said wasn't it a relief to Em that Miss Farley was dead and where had we been Friday night. Well, that kind of upset me so I just went on to the nearest beer parlor and got drunk."

Tommy whistled. "And you gave that letter to Sullivan?"

"Not safe not to, young feller. Other people had 'em that morning. Em did, for one. Anyway, the police 'll be checking up on us for Friday night now. But I guess it's safe for me to keep still about that check."

"I think it is," Michael said. "Sullivan isn't apt to find out about that. But—if you don't mind—where were you Friday night?"

"That's the trouble. For years I've played cards and that's left Em alone. Lately she's been running out of money a lot quicker than she should. Finally she lets it slip she's been out on Haight Street nights. Now, we don't know anyone out there and Em's timid anyway. Always afraid she'll get insulted or held up.

"So Friday I pretended to go out only I hung around here till she came out. She took the Sacramento cable out to Fillmore and did I have a time keeping her from seeing me? Lucky she's nearsighted. She transferred to Fillmore and got off at Haight. There was a Haight car waiting and she ran for it. But a woman dropped her purse in front of me and by the time I got around her the car was gone. Those fellows on that Market Street railway don't wait for anyone. So I still don't know where Em went."

"Why don't you ask her?" Tommy said.

"I did. She just talked a lot of stuff about faith and hope and I didn't understand and if it was a comfort to her and Mother had told her to look after me. You know how she goes on. The truth is that Mother told me to look after Em."

"What time did she leave here?" Michael said.

"A little after eight. When I missed the car there was no use looking for her."

"Which way did she go?"

"Down toward Market, not out toward the beach. I came back to Sacramento and Fillmore and walked home from there. Stopped for some coffee at a lunch counter there. Em's coffee is dishwater. That was good stuff you made last night, miss. But Em beat me home. And she don't know what time I got in but she does know I didn't play cards that night."

"Faith and hope—and Haight Street. And a ouija board." Michael walked over to the windows and stood drumming his fingers on the pane. "That's queer. Does she go out other times, not at night?"

"I don't pay much attention. Women," Mr. Julian stated, "are always gadding. They fill in their time better than men. Don't you ever retire too early. Year and a half ago I thought I'd worked hard all my life so I'd stop and enjoy myself. I don't. Can't even sleep good any more."

"I don't believe I know what your business was."

"I was a grocer. There's fancy names for it, but when you come right down to it I was still in the wholesale grocery business."

"Then perhaps you'd met Mr. Dozier before you came here?"

"Sure. He worked for the Pacific Importing Company. Say, that was too bad, wasn't it? About him being on that plane? He was a nice fellow though I didn't know him except in a business way. I did recommend this place to him and the young Callendars. I saw more of him the last two years or so I was in business after they brought him back to the office here. Then they moved all but a branch to L.A. so he went down there."

"He'd traveled a great deal, hadn't he?" Valerie said. "And so had Mrs. Putnam. wondered if he might have known her."

"I guess his kind of traveling wasn't hers."

"No, I suppose not. Did Miss Julian know Mrs. Putnam before you all lived here? She mentioned Miss Julian's having been to Europe."

"She and my mother knew each other to call on. I hadn't seen her for years. Not since I was a young sprout and she was a woman in her thirties. I wouldn't have known her. She used to be a beautiful woman. Well, I guess she was close to seventy. But what," Julian said abruptly to Tommy, "about you, young feller?"

"Me? Well, there's still that gun. Look, did you know I had a gun?"

"Me?" Julian looked blank. "How would I know? I've seen you around here but we never talked much, did we?"

"N-no. Well, Sara knew I had one."

Michael turned away from the window. "Where is Sara?"

"She went downtown," Valerie said. "Mrs. Putnam's lawyer wanted to see her. And Mr. Sullivan talked to her again and there was something about her making a statement, whatever that means."

"I hope you never know!" Tommy said.

"Well, he talked to her alone."

"And you didn't listen. But you can ask Geneva—"

"Tommy, please be still! I wanted to go with her but she wouldn't let me. I suppose you and she were talking sports?"

"When I mentioned the gun? Must 've been. We always do. Well, forget it. I don't suppose I've got a job."

"They fire you?" Julian asked.

"Not yet. I'm going down there pretty soon and they'll probably suggest a vacation till things are cleared up."

"Oh, but that—that isn't fair!"

Mr. Julian looked at Valerie admiringly. "Look here, don't you worry about it. You resign: that's dignified. In a week or so I'll give you a letter to our manager."

"Gosh, there is a Santa Claus, after all. I'm not much good at office jobs though. I get restless sitting at a desk all day. I guess I should have been a farmer or something."

"We can farm," Valerie said. "I'd like to live down near Santa Clara or— No; we won't argue here. I think Michael wants to ask you something."

"Who besides Sara knew you had a gun?"

"Well, Callendar did. We were talking one night at a party they had. He said he had one: not the same as mine though. Geneva knew I did too. Remember we were talking one night about that epidemic of robberies around here, Val? A lot of places on Sutter and some nearer had been robbed and Geneva said she was nervous. I said I'd lend 'em my gun but she and your mother said: oh, they'd be scared to shoot it."

"I don't remember."

"I guess you were putting on your hat. If it didn't take you so long I wouldn't get arrested," Tommy said facetiously. "That gives me time to talk to your folks and quarrel with 'em. Like Maxine. But this other time Miss Julian was there too. And that accounts for everyone."

"Sullivan will check on that, of course," Michael said. "Even though Mrs. Putnam was not shot. I don't believe that gun is important."

"You would if it was yours. That guy Hunt isn't going to forget it. Oh well, what the hell?"

Michael grinned. "'Then sware Lord Thomas Howard: 'Fore God, I am no coward . . .'"

Tommy said: "Hunh!" but Michael had gone to answer the doorbell. "It's only me," Sara said dispiritedly. "Or us," she added as Winona Callendar appeared at the top of the stairs. "Are you coming here too? I wasn't up to coping with Geneva."

"Why didn't you tell her to mind her own business?" Winona said.

"I wasn't up to that either."

"That bad?" Michael said, smiling. "Come in."

Winona hesitated and then followed Sara into the living room. "Misery loves company and Grant had to go downtown. Tommy, I'm glad to see you back."

"Glad to be back," Tommy said, giving her his chair. "And say, I didn't really know him but—"

"My uncle? Let's not talk about that. Only I hope the others who were out there at the airport didn't have to deal with policemen wanting alibis. Mr. Dundas, here's your cigarette case. You forgot it last night."

Valerie looked at Michael with lips disapprovingly pursed. He murmured: "If women drop handkerchiefs can't men drop cigarette cases?" and Sara grinned.

"I know you wonder what my status is," she said. "I'm still at large though I've seen the inside of the D.A.'s office. I went with Sullivan to see Lily Washington. Lily would have none of me. Give me a drink, will you? A stiff one."

Michael, handing her a glass, said: "Then Lily wouldn't talk?"

"I'll bet she talked plenty after I left her with Sullivan. As it was, she told me she always thought I'd manage to get rid of Grandma sooner or later. Well, I'm going to leave this place here to the police," Sara said with a suggestion of repressed violence. "I hope I never—smell it again. Can I stay one more night with you, Valerie?"

"As long as you want."

"I'll go to a hotel then."

"I wonder," Winona said, politely conversational, "when the hotel strike will be over."

Mr. Julian delivered himself of a few well-chosen remarks regarding the insufferable impertinence of any employee who dared to strike against a benevolent and all-wise employer and Michael's eyebrows suggested he did not share Mr. Julian's sentiments.

"They abolished Negro slavery," he drawled. "It usually takes violence of some sort or degree to change anything."

"Then they shouldn't change things," Mr. Julian said firmly. "You don't," he added, "look to me like you'd ever worked hard."

His eyes were, rather scornfully, on Michael's slender long-fingered hands. In his turn Michael regarded them thoughtfully, as if they belonged to someone else.

"I am not," he said finally, "entirely a theorist. I have worked in a lumber mill and a garage, driven fussy old ladies with fussy Pekes who want to get places in a hurry without any danger to themselves and be damned to the pedestrian. I have also washed dishes in an open-all-night café, tried my hand at waiting on tables and been fired."

"Because you insulted a customer?" Valerie said quickly. If he wanted to go on, he would. If he had momentarily forgotten to whom he was speaking she had at least recalled their presence to him.

The question, the first that had occurred to her, proved an effective stopper. Michael said: "Exactly," smiled at Mr. Julian and added: "I don't like to be suspected of being merely a parlor pink, you see."

"Well, I think I'll go downtown and resign," Tommy said. "I never liked that job anyway. The manager always had it in for me. Little guy with a big forehead who'd yell murder if you stepped on his toes."

He stopped beside Valerie to whisper: "Look, baby, ask Dundas to have dinner with us tonight. I've got some money. It 'd be nicer to be alone but maybe we do owe him something." He patted her shoulder, grinned at Winona and opened the front door. "I'll be seeing you all. Oh—hello."

"Here," Sara muttered, "is the rest of the gang. What is this: old home week?"

Michael went to the door to admit Geneva and Miss Julian. "Valerie, I think you're elected to sit on the floor or that chest . . . Yes, I'll see you later, Howard."

"Oh, but I'm not coming in," Miss Julian said, doing just that. "It's only that lunch is all ready, Charlie, so I just came— Such a nice chop and the mashed potatoes. But they're all dried up and I'm afraid the chop's too brown and I don't know why the sauce for the cauliflower looks so lumpy."

"Oh, I'll tell you what to do about that," Geneva said. "Use your broiler and time the chop and it won't be too brown. First cut off all the fat because if there is too much grease—"

"But the lamb we're getting now is so— I'm sure meat is high enough that we ought to get— And of course too much isn't good for you. A vegetable diet, some people say, and don't cook anything."

"If there is too much grease it will catch fire," Geneva said firmly. "You know that. Five minutes on each side should be about right for a chop. And to keep mashed potatoes from drying out—"

"But you couldn't eat potatoes raw," Miss Julian said. "And baked potatoes are much easier but they just won't get done in time."

"Put them in a pan over hot water and cover them," said Geneva. "And I never can believe it's healthy to eat the skins," said Miss Julian. "And to keep your cream sauce from being lumpy you must be sure to mix the flour and butter well," said Geneva. "Because even if you wash them well,

I'm sure you can't get all the dirt out of them," said Miss Julian.

Michael suddenly put his elbows on the mantelpiece, his head in his hands and laughed until tears stood in his eyes. Valerie, after one contrite look toward Miss Julian, laughed with him. Geneva, slightly baffled, drew herself up.

"Well, I'm sure I like a joke just as well as anyone. In fact I always say you just can't get along in this funny old world of ours if you haven't a sense of humor. But for all of you to be up here, drinking and carrying on and Maxine not even buried yet, does seem lacking proper respect to the dead."

Michael, raising his head, drawled: "'Ah! welladay! What evil looks had I from old and young!'" And then, with a convincing appearance of repentance: "Don't pay any attention to us, Miss Nolan. We are a trifle overwrought. We—we are dancing with tears in our eyes."

"We-el," Geneva said doubtfully. "But Valerie knows better. And I should think"—she frowned at the glass Mr. Julian had tried unsuccessfully to hide behind an ash tray—"that after what had happened yesterday some people would have learned a lesson."

"Oh, fire engines!" Valerie said gratefully, standing up to look out the window. "Are they coming this way? I love fire engines!"

"They're going down toward Sutter," Michael said, coming over to her. He muttered: "Don't overdo the girlish enthusiasm. Let Julian insult her again if he has enough nerve." Then, still looking out the window, he said:

"Personally, I can't work up any great enthusiasm for fire engines. I'm afraid of fire."

Valerie swallowed hard and took what she considered to be her cue. "Lots of people are. Like your grandmother, Sara."

Sara, having just added something more—a great deal more—than a dash of whisky to her glass, drank half of it and blinked at Valerie.

"Grandma? Afraid of fire? She wasn't. She wasn't afraid of anything that I know of. Except maybe dying in a hospital."

"But"—Michael's foot touched hers warningly and Valerie finished lamely—"it was just an idea I had."

"Your grandmother's dear little doggie; what will become of him?" Miss Julian said. "Such a lively little fellow and so affectionate."

"Is that what you call it? I'll make you a present of him," Sara said, brooding over her glass.

"Oh, would you? I would just love— But Charlie—"

"Don't act like I beat you," Mr. Julian snapped, getting up. "You can have a dog if you want. Not that I'd call that a dog. But we've got enough junk around the place that a little more won't matter."

"And I'm sure Brother will become very fond of the little thing," Geneva said to Miss Julian. "If you are careful to train him not to annoy him. Valerie, lunch has been ready for hours. And you need to eat, Sara. I'm sure you shouldn't drink on an empty stomach. You need to keep up your strength."

Sara slammed her glass down on the table. "Oh, all right. Though why—"

"And Mrs. Farley would just love to have you come down to tea, Mr. Dundas," Geneva went on. "I suppose you had breakfast very late, being up all hours?"

"On the contrary, I had it very early. I also had the pleasure of seeing the inside of the district attorney's office," Michael said. "And since I have no telephone and I must get in touch with an old friend this afternoon, besides going down to the wholesale district, I will have to drive to both places. But if I get back early enough I will stop in for tea."

CHAPTER EIGHTEEN
"WHY WAS SHE KILLED LAST NIGHT?"

Inspector Sullivan propped his feet up on an adjacent chair, sought comfort in a tall glass Michael handed him and went on talking.

The thing must have begun—though he couldn't know that at first, he remarked resentfully—when Mrs. Putnam had begun to write anonymous letters to the people in this building about three months ago. It was a fact that at about that time she had bought several rubber stamping sets. Her appearance was unusual enough for a clerk at Wobber's to be certain that he remembered her and her purchases.

"So, although you couldn't know that, if you or Miss Sheridan had bothered to confide in me Saturday, we'd have known right away Mrs. Putnam was your letter writer. I suppose you figured she wouldn't buy the things or not at a place like Wobber's."

"Wouldn't you expect her to be more careful? However," Michael said, "if we hadn't decided to, as you so touchingly put it, confide in you by Monday, I'd have investigated that angle myself."

"Oh, you would? And how do you think you— Oh, never mind," Sullivan said disgustedly.

Mrs. Putnam, he continued, wrote her letters and those who received them made no complaint. During this time Maxine Farley was cultivating Dozier, Callendar and Julian and perhaps some unknown man. She was also constantly seeing Tommy Howard. Therefore, when the girl was killed—in view of her admitted wish to "do well for herself", her attraction for men, the late and apparently secret appointments she kept at times—in view of all that, Sullivan said belligerently, it was no wonder her death appeared a "crime of passion."

However, he'd always recognized the possibility that Howard had not killed her. Or that she'd been killed not by a man, but by some woman who had reason to hate her. Sara Putnam, Miss Julian, Mrs. Callendar might all come under that category. And possibly Patricia Farley.

But Mrs. Putnam's activities were an immense complication. Because it was also a proved fact that Maxine had been greedy for money. And her remarks to Valerie, Mathilde Jellick and Dozier proved she believed she was, in some way, going to get money. And also that she had blackmail in mind.

But Mrs. Putnam was the letter writer and she could not have killed Maxine. Even if Sara had lied, Dr Rudd doubted that the old woman could have walked to the park and back again without collapsing afterward. And he had seen her on Saturday morning and found her in unusually good health.

So Maxine must have tried to blackmail some other person. Someone whom Mrs. Putnam had been blackmailing "mentally." She was satisfied with her power to make people "squirm." Proof of that, if you accepted Sara's statement again, was Mrs. Putnam's saying to someone: "But I don't want money."

It was perfectly possible that Maxine, trying to discover who was writing the letters, had read some meant for others. They recalled that the letters were not always thrust all the way into their halls: often an edge of white was visible from the outer hall. Perhaps because Mrs. Putnam hadn't cared whether or not others besides the one for whom a letter was intended happened to see it.

"Don't you think she might almost have preferred that?" Michael said. "At least a part of her purpose was to cause people to distrust each other."

"Sure. That's why the Julians didn't confide in each other. Or the young Callendars—for a long time. You don't like to show your brother or wife letters like some of those were. And that's why they couldn't find out right away who was distributing the letters by catching her at it. How could they watch when each one was pretending to the other they'd never had any letters?"

"I see you've thought it out."

Sullivan looked at Michael, quickly and suspiciously. "Well, what's wrong with that?"

"Nothing. It's one way of looking at it. Go on."

"Well, she did put the men's letters in the mailboxes but almost any time something might have gone wrong with her system for keeping them separate."

"And no doubt she knew that her—may I call them 'victims?'—knew that and lived in fear of its happening."

"Yeah. The old— Well, suppose Maxine Farley did get her hands on a letter not meant for her and then put the screws on? None of the letters we've got say anything that's motive for murder or even material for blackmail. We haven't seen the ones that mattered and probably never will. No one has an alibi for Friday night except Miss Sheridan. Howard's in the clear for Mrs. Putnam's death. The rest all slept. These husband and wife alibis are no good. If I could divorce either case from those letters it 'd be plain sailing. I already covered the Farley girl's death from that angle. And the Putnam girl had plenty of reason to kill her grandmother. That n— . . ."

The maid, Lily Washington, though surly and incredibly ignorant, had been eager to describe the constant strife between the Putnam women. Regarding the letters she was vague. Mrs. Putnam had worked in her room while Sara was gone and it wasn't for her, Lily, to ask what she was doing.

But she was quite certain she had never admitted Maxine Farley to the apartment at any time during the last three years. And for three months, except on a day when there had been a small blaze in the Julian apartment, Mrs. Putnam had not been outside, Lily said.

As for Dr Rudd, he confirmed everything Sara had told them regarding Mrs. Putnam's illness and his own treatment of it. But he added that the old woman would probably have lived on for a year or more while claiming Sara did not know this.

"You didn't want to discourage her?" Sullivan had asked.

Rudd, with his best stare of professional disapproval, refused to answer. But he admitted Mrs. Putnam was "difficult." He had advised an operation as a desperate but perhaps merciful measure.

Mrs. Putnam had refused. She disliked hospitals and what she called "butchering people just to prolong their agony."

"But that don't mean she wouldn't tell the girl she was going to live a long time, when they happened to quarrel," Sullivan said. "And sometimes they can't wait for 'em to die. There was a case once . . . Well, never mind. The whisky was doped all right but she could have done that herself. If she's in love with this Lutz she might think he wouldn't wait, and have killed the Farley girl herself to remove competition. I haven't been able to get in touch with him again. He goes off painting and no one knows where he is.

"Here's another thing: Sara Putnam knew about those letters so she knew if her grandmother was killed it would come out about them and we'd start investigating that angle instead of just asking who stood to gain by the old lady's death. Complicating—"

Michael groaned. "You're a bird with a single note. Well, why not forget the letters?"

"I can't," Sullivan said unhappily. "It's possible they hadn't anything to do with either murder. But I don't believe in coincidence."

"What is coincidence? Concurrence? A pattern? But things do fall into patterns. I meet a man and discover he knows someone I knew in Paris.

I say: 'Well, what a coincidence.' But people aren't static; they do move about. And the world doesn't stop before or after someone is killed. The air lines didn't suspend operation because Maxine Farley died."

"Well, that was just bad luck for everyone that took that plane, not just for Dozier."

"Well, would you call it coincidence that I happen to want a living room with a great many windows?"

"So that you came here? I'd call that suspicious if I could connect you in any way with these murders. But I can't. You can't ignore the fact that Miss Farley was interested in those letters and her remarks about expecting to have money soon. Or saying to that hairdresser she hadn't a job but 'just nerve.'"

"That," Michael said slowly, "was by no means all she said to Mathilde Jellick."

"Well, it was all that was important. Unless you're holding out on me again?"

"I told you exactly what Miss Sheridan told me."

"And I confirmed the important parts. Well," Sullivan said, taking some papers from his pocket, "there's no information about Dozier worth telling. I admit I had a wild idea maybe Mrs. Callendar might be his daughter instead of his brother's.

Since he wasn't ever married, that 'd be a small scandal if anyone knew it. But that's out because the girl was born in '14 and Dozier was out of the country for more than a year before that. Well, it was a fool notion but you never can tell.

"Of course I started getting a line on everyone after the Farley girl was killed. They're all perfectly respectable."

"If they weren't, Mrs. Putnam wouldn't have been killed," Michael said.

"If— Oh, I get you. Murder to protect their respectability?"

"Yes. Also, there would be no point in silencing Mrs. Putnam if what she knew was anything you'd be apt to discover in your investigations. Because you'd settle the question of motive if you had any idea what it was she knew."

"That's right. If any of 'em had ever been in the newspapers or had a record, I'd soon know that. Of course there's a kind of surprising number of connections between these folks. Only this is a small place and kind of a nice one, so it's not as odd as if it was a big apartment house."

"What connections?"

"You know Dozier knew Julian and Julian recommended this place to him? And Julian's mother knew Mrs. Putnam years ago. They're both old families here. The Julians were kind of genteel poor till Charlie Julian made his money, but old Putnam was born with it.

"Miss Sheridan comes of a good old family too. I guess her mother's always been flighty but she's never been mixed up in any scandal. This Wayne Farley wasn't worth the powder to shoot him but there's lots like that.

"And it seems Miss Nolan was companion once to a dame Mrs. Putnam knew and she spoke of this place to Sara Putnam. Well, she would and there's no harm in that. But there's nothing definite about that kind of stuff.

"However, here's a letter from Maxine Farley they found in Dozier's apartment in L.A. They wired it up to me. It was the only personal letter he'd kept and the first part don't matter. Just polite stuff. But then she says:

"'I suppose you mean well when you warn me, but I like playing with fire. I've made some progress and with a little luck I'll pull it off. I always get what I want, you know, and I don't care about people's feelings if I do. But I'd better not tell you too much though I don't think you'd ever give me away. You're broad-minded.

"'Only don't think that just because you don't scare everyone is like that. I'd never try any tricks, as you say, with you. At that, you were pretty swell to me. Maybe I'll be seeing you some day if things go right.'

"Then there's a postscript," Sullivan said. "'Geneva would like to know if you write to me and was Patricia burned when you left without saying good-by!'"

Sullivan folded the paper and returned it to his pocket. "Well, there it is. I'd bet Dozier gave her that jewelry. She evidently confided in him: remember what Gus overheard? I guess he warned her blackmail is dangerous but, as she says, he wouldn't give her away. But when he heard about her being killed he decided to come up and—"

"Why didn't he bring that letter with him?"

"What? Oh, I suppose he didn't think it was important. Or overlooked it." But Sullivan's scowl showed that Michael's question had revived doubts he already harbored. Therefore, in a mild way, Mr. Sullivan lost his temper.

"As you so politely told the D.A. this morning, we haven't any right to know what you think. But we've a right to know what you know. You act like you don't agree with my reasoning or I've missed something. Well, what do you know that you aren't telling? Maybe you'd remember better in jail?"

"I'll just get my toothbrush if you don't mind," Michael said without moving. "I believe tooth-brushes are not furnished."

"Damn it, do you think I don't dare pull you in!"

"Inspector, you don't know it and won't care when you do," Michael said gently, "but there is nothing that I dislike more heartily than being yelled at. As a great favor, would you arrest me in a low voice?"

"Oh—" Inspector Sullivan called on several patron saints. "Put you in a cell and you'd never talk. I know, I picked the wrong person to bluff. All right, I admit it. Now, do you give me any help or don't you?"

"You're asking me for help? Inspector, if I knew who killed those two women I'd tell you—I think."

"That's just it—'you think.' You think too much. Have you any real evidence you're holding out?"

"From your viewpoint of what evidencc is, no. Would you mind telling me before we go any farther what the letters Mrs. Putnam didn't deliver said?"

"Well, one said: STILL SNEAKING OUT FRIDAY NIGHTS ARENT YOU. And another: ARE YOU SURE YOUR HUSBAND DIDNT GO TO THE PARK FRIDAY NIGHT OR DID YOU. I suppose the first was for

Miss Julian and the second for Mrs. Callendar. The other was for Miss Putnam. It said: YOUR ARTIST WILL HAVE TO WAIT TILL THE OLD LADY DIES AND YOU GET HER MONEY BUT WILL HE? She'd kept others along those lines. I guess Miss Farley's death was a new subject for Mrs. Putnam so she wanted to use it while it was still fresh. As to Friday nights in general, seems the Julians both go out then and everyone knows it. The Julian woman got kind of hysterical when I asked where she goes. To get some fresh air, she says. I've got to work on that. Julian says he didn't keep his regular date to play cards because he wanted to walk. Phooey! They ought to think of a new one."

"And what did you find in Miss Julian's cupboard?"

"The tall one? Nothing but a lot of empty jars. Did you think she might be writing those letters?"

"At one time I thought it possible."

"Well, she hadn't burned anything in the fireplace lately. Being Monday morning the garbage cans were empty before some dumb cop thought to get at 'em. No fingerprints in the Putnam place that didn't belong there and nothing in her desk to help us. She didn't have any documentary evidence against anybody."

"You can't," Michael said slowly, "blackmail a person who hasn't money." Sullivan snorted disgustedly and got up. "And of course that works two ways."

"What a help you turned out to be. I'm going back to work. Just tedious, unexciting little things, you know." Clumsily, Sullivan mimicked Michael's fastidious enunciation. "Pounding away at people—"

"Of course," Michael said. "You don't like my suggestions so don't blame me later. But I would like to know why Maxine Farley didn't marry Dozier. And I believe his death is rather important. As to Mrs. Putnam's: why was she killed last night? And—"

The doorbell rang and Sullivan opened the door, stared at Sara Putnam and said ungraciously: "Oh, it's you?"

"Have you any objection?"

"Inspector Sullivan," Michael said, "is in a humor to kick a dog. But there's no dog. Come in."

"Well—yes, I will. Valerie is somewhere with Tommy and that Nolan woman drives me nuts. They were expecting you for tea."

Michael glanced at the clock. "Too late. I had other things to do."

"Did you just come up here to sit?" Sullivan asked suspiciously.

"I can stand, if you prefer. If I wanted to discuss things with Mr. Dundas, discussion's free."

"Too free. There's been too much of it."

"You might close the door," Michael suggested. "In front of you or, preferably, behind you."

Sullivan glared at him. Before he had composed a reply sufficiently withering a voice from the hall said:

"Is this Dundas' apartment? They told me Miss Putnam came up here. My name is Lutz. . . ."

CHAPTER NINETEEN
NOT A MAGAZINE COVER

Sullivan said jovially: "Come right in, Mr. Lutz. I've been looking for you."

Lutz glanced at him, unimpressed and uninterested. Mr. Lutz was tall and very thin with a long bony face, long straw-colored hair and gray eyes perpetually squinting as if all the world were a painting whose worth he was estimating.

"I know. They told me. But I came to see Sara. Are you angry with me?"

"Angry?" Color crept into Sara's sallow face but she said casually: "Why should I be?"

"Well, because of Friday night. But we did wait for you for a while. And Nina cooked the spaghetti and it was rotten," Lutz said aggrievedly. "Then someone suggested we go over to Louis's place. They said it was after ten and I thought you weren't coming, after all."

"But you did go, didn't you, Miss Putnam?" Sullivan said.

"I wanted a walk and they don't usually break up so early."

"And you found Lutz wasn't home?"

"He's just told you he wasn't. But that was only half-past eleven."

"I don't know exactly what you're talking about," Lutz said. He put the small square package he was carrying on the floor and draped himself over the arm of a chair.

"If it's Maxine Farley you're still thinking about," he said to Sullivan, "I told you I don't know where I was at midnight. I don't watch clocks. I haven't one. I probably was walking home from Louis's."

"Jesus H. Christ!" Sullivan muttered. "Another one!"

"You've got to walk on Russian Hill. And I like to walk. Anyway, I wasn't in love with Maxine It just occurred to me you thought I might have been. Did you, Sara?"

"I never gave it any thought," Sara said stiffly.

"Well, I didn't suppose you would. You have too much sense." Sara's cheeks flamed red but Lutz went on serenely: "Why should I have been?"

"She didn't have any money?" Sullivan suggested delicately.

"Didn't she? What's that got to do with it? Neither have I. I just met her at the School of Fine Arts and came to a party here once." Mr. Lutz shuddered. "Good food but terrible women. That one with the hair—Miss Nolan, I think it was. And that kittenish mother. God, I hate pink-and-white women that won't get old. I don't see how she produced that daughter."

Sullivan, distinctly harassed, remarked that Maxine Farley had been very beautiful. Mr. Lutz said that some people thought girls on magazine covers beautiful but for his part he considered it was "bones that count. What's underneath. Look at Valerie Sheridan. The line of her chin, her cheekbones. Or Dundas here. You wouldn't call him handsome but he'll age well," Lutz declared. "And Sara—"

"He's about to say I'm nothing but bones," Sara interposed nervously. "He always talks like this, Inspector."

"Well, but if I'd been in love with Maxine Farley, would I have painted her like this?" Lutz tore the wrappings from his package and triumphantly displayed a small portrait. "There!"

"We-el, it looks all right to me," Sullivan said cautiously. "Very pretty, in fact. I'd expected just a kind of skeleton. Bones, you know."

He laughed. Lutz looked at him in patient sorrow and turned to Michael.

"You see?"

"Yes, I think so. It's—clever."

The painted face looked at them, smiling softly, the eyes limpid and dreamy. But about the sen-
suous lips was a suggestion of greed and self-will.
Even Sullivan, as he looked at the portrait again,
felt that perhaps it was not so pretty as he had at
first thought. Michael said:

"Was she looking at you while you worked?"

Lutz chuckled. "You see that? No, she was looking out the window. Good, isn't it? At first glance
it might be a magazine cover. But it isn't. I hav-
en't seen you for a long time, Dundas. You don't
attend classes any more?"

"No. I only wanted the elements of freehand
drawing."

"I thought you showed some talent. Maxine was
the rankest amateur though she could draw."

"What's that?" Sullivan barked. "Did you go to
classes at art school too, Michael?"

"For a short time. Didn't I tell you? It must,"
Michael said without even a decent appearance of
regret, "have slipped my mind."

"Like a lot of other things do! When was this,
Lutz? When Maxine Farley was going?"

"Oh no; that was three or four years ago. And
I came here to talk to Sara." Lutz turned his back
on Sullivan. "I've been thinking maybe you'd
marry me."

"Since you saw this morning's papers?" Sara said bitterly.

"Louis told me your grandmother was killed. Was that why you didn't come yesterday after you phoned him you wanted to see me in the afternoon? He told me and I waited for you."

"I couldn't get there. And I didn't suppose you'd remember even if Louis bothered to tell you."

"Well, when they find out who did it, it's better she's dead," Lutz said calmly. "Because she must have been very unpleasant and now you won't have to look after her. A sense of duty is very inconvenient and unnecessary. I did think maybe I could help you. Only I don't know how because you're very practical and I'm not. You know that.

"But the thing is, something's been missing the last two weeks and I couldn't decide what it was. Then I discovered it was you not coming in to cook and darn socks and trim my hair if I couldn't afford to have it cut. You're so quiet I didn't realize I missed you being quiet around me. So," Lutz concluded, "when I figured that out I came right over and brought the picture just in case you had funny ideas."

Sullivan muttered: "Well, I'll be—" Michael's thick lashes hid his eyes as he looked at the floor. But Sara had forgotten both of them. She said piteously:

"Gregory, don't you know my grandmother had a lot of money? Didn't you always know?"

"Why, no. You work for a small salary and you said you had to take care of her."

"You must have known these apartments aren't cheap!"

"They haven't any elevator or an awning or a doorman," Lutz said. "So why are they? How much money?"

"Grandma? A lot."

"Then," Mr. Lutz said, "I don't know about marrying you. Money makes people soft. I couldn't do good work if I got soft. I'm sorry but I'll have to think things over."

He picked up his portrait of Maxine Farley and ambled toward the door. It closed behind him while Sara sat motionless except for her fingers tearing at her handkerchief. Then Michael said softly, a thread of laughter in his voice:

"Don't be a fool, my dear. It's not an act . . ."

He sat back again as the door slammed and Sara's voice calling "Gregory! Wait!" died away. Sullivan said:

"Well, it takes all kinds of people. No, I won't bother them for a while. I'll be going."

"Have you more than one copy of Maxine Farley's letter to Dozier?"

"Yes, but— Oh, you can have this one," Sullivan decided. "I don't see what harm you can do with it though I suppose I ought to know better."

Valerie, settling herself before the fireplace, said:

"Tommy went home to dress and then we are all going to dinner. I didn't have a chance to ask you with everyone here this afternoon. And, Michael, what should we walk into but Sara and Gregory Lutz embracing in the hall. And afterward Sara told me all about it just like any other girl would. But she's going to have to forget how much money she has because Gregory won't live in luxury. Or anywhere but a studio on Russian Hill or perhaps very cheaply and bohemianally in Paris. Well, love is the queerest thing!"

"Isn't it?" Michael said drearily.

Valerie looked at him quickly and something in his attitude, relaxed yet weary, made her dare to say:

"Michael, we haven't known each other very long but I do feel we're friends. And I'll go on thinking we are whether you like it or not. And I would like to see you happy too."

"Don't be maternal," Michael said rudely. "Unless—do you, by any chance, imagine I am—as

you would put it—suffering from the pangs of un-
requited love?"

"I would not! Say it like that, I mean. Only you
don't appear to think very highly of women. And,"
Valerie said meekly, "I wanted to tell you because
I shouldn't have looked. When I borrowed a handkerchief last night there was a picture—"

"A— *Ave María purísima!* That picture? And
you thought— Well, you've been a good child and
restrained your curiosity nicely—now and then. A
reward for virtue."

Michael got up and, returning from his bedroom with the photograph, tossed it into Valerie's
lap. "I think you didn't look at it very closely."

"But I did."

"At the hair?"

"The— Why," Valerie said, "it looks like there
was a little streak of white like you have."

"There was. Otherwise I don't resemble her,
but that's my mother."

"Was she a dancer?"

"If you call twirling a seductive ruffle to a slow
Argentine tango dancing. She was an Argentinian;
half of one of those dance teams that are forever
appearing and disappearing. A few of them do well
but she didn't need to dance long. She had talents
in other directions. Of course she claimed to be
from an excellent family that had lost everything

in some vague revolution. But she was the world's worst—or best—liar."

"We-el?" Valerie said suggestively.

"Yes, my dear. But I never believe my own lies and she did, if she told the same one often enough."

"She's beautiful," Valerie said, studying the photograph.

"Certainly. The kind of woman who would smother you with kisses one instant and beat you the next."

"Oh. But your father—"

"Yes, my father. His name was Maclean. His father was Scotch and made a sizable fortune in the lumber business in Wisconsin. He's everything suggested to the average person by the word 'Scotch.' But my father yearned after art with a large A, so the old man disowned him in proper style and he took himself and an inheritance from his mother off to Chicago, and there met my mother, and after I was born, in New York, went to Paris, still in pursuit of art. And that's all."

"Oh, but it isn't. Why do you call yourself Dundas if your name is Maclean?"

"That was my childish way of thumbing my nose at my grandfather. When Mother died I was shipped back to him since my father had been dead some time. But I was sixteen, which was a trifle old to be made over according to my grandfather's ideas. We fought each other for four years and then I cleared out. And took my grandmother's maiden name because that's the kind of thing you do at twenty. Eventually I found it convenient to make it mine legally."

Valerie studied the vivacious pictured face and let one question after another go unuttered until Michael smiled reluctantly.

"Your face is a perfect battleground of conflicting emotions. What is it you want to know?"

"Did you always live in Paris and were you practically brought up in a boudoir, as you said once and— Oh, all sorts of things. Why not? I've told you all about myself and I like to know all about people I like."

"You're a sweet child, Valerie. No, where we lived depended on who happened to be paying most of the bills at any particular time."

"After your father died?"

"And before. My father," Michael said with careful cynicism, "had a really artistic ability to close his eyes to anything he didn't want to see. He and Mother were very much in love once but it didn't last. However, he did see I was fairly well educated in a hit-or-miss way. I had one young English tutor who filled in a lot of gaps and I liked him.

But of course he fell in love with Mother. As to being brought up in a boudoir, she liked to have me around when I was older. I will say it never seemed to occur to her to keep me under cover. She was always beautifully sure of herself.

"I spoke English as early and as often as Spanish but always Spanish to her. That's why I revert to it sometimes. And don't let your imagination run away with you. I was not abused or neglected. In fact, I was a thoroughly spoiled and precocious brat!"

"I understand perfectly," Valerie said. "You grew up too soon and— All right, I know you don't like that. And to make matters worse I'll say I suspect you're not half so hard-boiled as you want people to think. And I don't see why you make a secret—"

"In fact, your romantic expectations have been disappointed," Michael said provokingly. "You hoped I was a Russian prince, after all. And who or what I am is my own business and it amuses me to see people fish for information and pretend they aren't." He took the picture from her and put it in the secretary. "You say we are all going to dinner together?"

"Tommy wanted me to ask you. He went down and resigned," Valerie said, "though perhaps they would have been nice about it. But I do think a ranch, Spanish style, with an outdoor grill for barbecues and fruit trees—"

"Farming for a gentleman?"

"Oh, of course. Nobody makes money farming, do they? Tommy has lots of friends down around Stanford. We could have horses. I know he'd like to play polo. Of course I haven't convinced him yet that we can put my money into a place like that. But I will, and then he can see we make our expenses at least. Is it all right about dinner?"

"Of course. And then I think I'll take you two with me. It might interest you and perhaps I should have witnesses . . . That must be Howard now."

He opened the door. Grant Callendar stood in the hall, his soft fair face flushed. The scowl that was meant to be intimidating only made him look like a sulky child. He said:

"I'm going to knock your block off!"

"Then would you mind coming inside to do it?" Michael asked, stepping back into the living room. Grant followed him, assuming the attitude of a prize fighter posing for newspaper pictures.

"And you needn't think you can talk me out of it! Nobody can insult my wife and get away with it! Are you going to stand up and fight like a man or—"

"Must you talk like a second-rate horse opera?" Michael said with a cold distaste that made Mr. Callendar blink momentarily, before he remembered he was a husband defending his wife's fair name.

"I knew you'd try to crawl out of it! Just the same I'm going to beat hell out of you! No one can make a pass at my wife and—"

"Get away with it. A very commendable attitude. But do you see that picture over there?"

"Picture? What the hell's that got to do with it?"

But Grant turned his head to look at the Audubon bluejays. Michael's left arm lashed out quickly, his fist catching Grant on the point of the chin. He went down and lay still, breathing heavily.

Michael said: "*Jesús María y José!*" gripping his left hand in his right. Valerie looked at him with wide-eyed surprise and disapproval.

"You—you hit him when he wasn't looking!"

"Don't be an idiot. If he'd been looking I probably couldn't have hit him at all. Why should I try to fight a man who outweighs me fifty pounds?"

He closed the front door and stalked into the kitchen. Valerie followed and watched him turn on the hot water. "What's that for?" she ventured.

"Did I ever mention that I have what are known as bad hands?" He displayed swelling reddened

knuckles, filled a pan of hot water and plunged his
hand into it. "And my hands happen to be valu-
able to me. I need them in my business. Would
you mind making yourself useful to the extent of
getting me some ice cubes and a drink?"

Valerie emptied a tray of cubes into a dish,
mixed a drink and brought it to him. "Does—does
it hurt?"

"Oh no; boiling water on your skin is always
very pleasant." Michael took his hand out of the
water, shook it experimentally and held it against
the ice. Valerie said charitably:

"Of course you have common sense on your
side."

"But you would admire me if I'd let Mr. Callendar beat hell out of me. Woman, the gentler
sex! 'Not love, but vanity,' quoth he, 'sets love a
task like that.' Never mind, Tommy won't let you
down. Shall we go in and see what Mr. Callendar
has to say for himself?"

CHAPTER TWENTY
FAITH AND HOPE

Mr. Callendar was sitting up, massaging his dimpled chin, looking about the room with lack-luster eyes. Michael picked up a heavy decanter; sat on the arm of a chair, eyeing him speculatively.

"If you're thinking of taking up where we stopped, I'll brain you with this," he promised. "I haven't time to indulge in heroics. But I would like to know what makes you think I insulted your wife. Aside from the fact"—he sniffed critically—"that you have been drinking a very poor grade of brandy."

"How the hell did *you* knock *me* out?" Grant mumbled.

"Treachery and a fairly good straight left. Well?"

"Oh, well, maybe I was wrong." Grant pulled himself to his feet, saw Valerie and flushed pinkly. "I—I didn't notice you. Well, Mother said— You see, Mother said Winona walked out on her this afternoon. And she saw her get a man's cigarette case out of the bureau and she saw her come up here."

"Perhaps there's something to be said for this idea of test-tube babies after all."

"Hunh? Well, then Nona and I were kind of fighting because she treated Mother like that. And Geneva had said to me weren't you attractive and Winona seemed to think so."

"Did Geneva mention that practically everyone in the house was here when Winona was?" Valerie said. "And I was with Michael last night when he left his cigarette case in your apartment."

"Well, why didn't Nona say so? Only I guess I made her mad, listening to Mother. Well, men do like her, you know."

"That's your side of the story."

"You mean— Hell, I wish I never had to hear Maxine's name again. Well, I do! I was just pleasant to her and you know how she was. She liked John Dozier better than me though he was too old for her. Why couldn't he have fallen for someone like—well, like your mother? That would have been more—suitable. Anyway, things are a mess. Those letters and policemen all over the place and people sneaking around."

"Sneaking?" Michael repeated.

"Well, Miss Julian. This morning she came out on the back porch with some kind of box in her hand and sneaked downstairs. I guess to your porch, Valerie. I heard something like the lid of a garbage can banging. The police were around but they hadn't gotten around to the back porches. Well, I'm sick of the whole thing. And I guess I'll go back and make up with Nona."

"I think," Michael said when Grant had gone, "there is a soft, cheesy substance where his backbone should be."

"And where his brains should be?"

"Oh, not quite that bad. And sometimes a strong instinct for self-preservation makes up for lack of intelligence. Valerie, except for saying she is a poor relation, you've told me very little about Geneva Nolan."

"But there's so little to tell. Her mother died when she was about eighteen and her father was a terrible old grouch, Mother says. Maybe that's how Geneva acquired her bright and cheery manner."

"And perhaps that helped to preserve Father's grouch."

"Well, she must have been thirty when he died. Mother is forty-one and Geneva is only a year older though Mother wouldn't care to have me say so. They're second cousins, I think. Geneva used to visit Mother sometimes when they were girls but I think even then she specialized in running errands and admiring other girls' clothes and beaux."

"And after her father died?"

"She was some old man's housekeeper. That was in Sacramento. He married and dispensed with Geneva. But she was with him for a long time. Then she took that old lady to Europe."

"I imagine that's the best way to put it."

"You know she would take charge of any expedition. But I think she must have overreached herself in some way. Because she'd expected to be Mrs. Kelsey's permanent companion but Mrs. Kelsey dispensed with her services."

"What sort of person was this Mrs. Kelsey?"

"I never saw her and Geneva very seldom speaks of her. Pityingly, when she does, but that means nothing, because the woman's dead. But I told you Sara spoke of her as 'foul.' I don't suppose that means anything either. Then Geneva helped us move here and made herself so useful she's never really left. She did take a girl who'd been sick to the seashore."

"The seashore? Where? When?"

"I don't know where. Some quiet place Miss Julian used to go to. When? I'll have to think. The Julians had just moved here and the Putnams hadn't and Mother had just met Wayne but hadn't married him. It was about five years ago; a little less."

"I see. But Miss Nolan came back to you?"

"Oh yes. That was just sort of a vacation. The girl was dying anyway, poor thing. When Mother married Wayne—well, he liked Geneva's cooking. Otherwise he pretty well ignored her but he was much more agreeable about it than Maxine. Besides, Geneva saved the wages of one servant or perhaps two. And of course she was invaluable when he was sick—he had pneumonia—and after he died, so Geneva is a permanent fixture with us. Well?"

"What? Oh, I think I'll wash up before Howard comes if you don't mind," Michael said.

"He's late. But where is it you're taking us? You said you wanted witnesses. . . ."

She sighed and picked up a magazine as the whir of an electric razor in the bathroom discouraged further question. She had time to skim the magazine before Tommy arrived, Tommy with his tie under one ear and his hat on the side of his head. He said in a subdued shout:

"Whoops!" picked her up, kissed her soundly and waltzed her around the room. "And is Hunt burned! Oh—c'mon in, Bill, and tell 'em about it."

Bill Jackson, a thick-necked young man with a prison haircut and a sunburned nose, said: "Hi, Valerie. You see, I just got back—"

"You remember, I told you . . . Mr. Dundas, Mr. Jackson," Tommy said as Michael appeared at the door of the bedroom with a military brush in each hand. "I hope you don't mind us busting in this way. I'm kind of excited."

"But, Tommy, tell us!"

"Baby, I am. You know I spoke about Bill Saturday?"

"I don't. Oh, you did say you expected him to come by. I forgot about that."

"If I didn't have to go to Merced," Mr. Jackson said. "But I did. Took my mother down to my sister's, see? They live on a ranch and don't bother about city papers. Sunday night we heard a broadcast that said they were holding Tommy. Of course that was a surprise but it didn't say anything about a gun, see? Well, we were late getting back today and I didn't get around to reading the papers right away."

"Remember how I started to say something about a satchel? No, I guess we heard the O'Dea coming up the stairs. But I'd started to say the gun might be in a satchel I throw things into when I go on fishing trips or hunting."

"But, Tommy, didn't you look?"

"Sure, I looked. Or the cops did. And there wasn't anything there but socks and a sweater and a half jar of salmon eggs. I couldn't remember if I took the gun along that trip or not. I remembered wondering should I or shouldn't I. I knew I didn't

use it on the trip and couldn't remember even seeing it then. And as I forgot half my flies that time,
or thought I'd packed them when I hadn't, I guess
I could forget other things. But just try to tell old
sourpuss Hunt that! He's got it in for me."

"Every time we move, and we're always moving, we go through the same thing with the trunk
keys," Jackson said. "On account of my mother
knows right where she put 'em and she can just
see 'em there—but they never are. Well, we took
my kid brother with us on that trip, see? And he's
always into everything."

"I never thought about the kid," Tommy said.
"I knew Bill wouldn't meddle with things."

"You don't know Pete," said Pete's brother darkly. "Well, we left him at camp one morning because we'd had our fill of him shying rocks at the
stream, see? When we got back I thought he might
've been up to something. Seems he had him a little target practice off in the woods.

"Then he gets scared, see? Knew I'd tan his
hide if I found out. So he puts the gun away in
the rumble with a bunch of junk, see? Then I was
reading the papers out loud and Pete's no dumb-
bell. So he finally owns up about the gun. I got in
touch with Tom right away and we went down to
see the police and took the kid brother."

"And was Hunt burned?" Tommy repeated. "Because there was the gun with all the shells fired
and not cleaned or anything. He didn't need any
experts to see how it was. He wanted to know
where Bill's car was Friday just in case I'd planted
the gun there, spite of all Pete said."

"And did we needle him?" said Mr. Jackson.
"Because the car was in the garage getting repaired
and that's why I wasn't certain till Saturday morning we were going to get down to Merced, see?"

"Then Hunt wanted to know if I didn't have
another gun. Hell! I only had this one because I
had a job where I had to carry money to the bank.
Sullivan was there," Tommy added. "But he just
said: well, thank God that was one thing he didn't
have to bother with any more."

"And I got to go," Jackson said. "My girl's waiting for me, see? Glad to 've met you, Dundas. Like
to interest you in some insurance sometime. Well,
see you in church. . . ."

Tommy cast himself into a chair and fanned
himself with his hat. Michael hummed: "'There is
no one with endurance, like a man who sells insurance,'" and Tommy finished:

"'He's everybody's best friend.' Well, he certainly is mine! Oh, I'd have asked him if he remembered about the gun. But suppose the kid hadn't
come clean? Well," he said candidly, "it made a

better impression having him think of it himself. Jeez, I'm hungry. I could eat a horse."

"Then let's go to Bit O' Sweden," Valerie said. "You simply can't help eating too much there."

"I'm ready."

"I'm not," Michael said abruptly. "Just a minute." He sat down at the secretary, drew a sheet of paper toward him and began to write. Tommy fidgeted, straightened his tie, cleared his throat.

"Are you going in for letter writing too?" he inquired at last. "Can't it wait?"

Michael frowned, folded the sheet of paper, put it into an envelope and that into his pocket. "I suppose we'd better go. We should finish dinner by eight at the latest."

But when they had reached the ground floor he said suddenly: "You two go on to the car. It's parked outside."

"Why?" Tommy said suspiciously. "We can wait."

"Don't stand there chattering like a monkey! Go—on—to—the—car! I'll be back in a minute. . . ."

"Well, I'll be damned," Tommy muttered, his face very red. Valerie fought a desire to laugh at his look of blank astonishment. "How does he get that way, talking to me like that? And how," Tommy said, grinning reluctantly, "does he expect to get away with it? I could break him in two with one hand."

"Nerve. And—nerves," Valerie said. "Let's go on to the car."

Tommy looked at a small piece of cheese with something approaching dislike but he ate it and triumphantly indicated his empty plate.

"Success," said Michael who had been smoking for the past ten minutes, "at last has crowned our labors."

Tommy groaned. "Why do we do it? Because there's no limit? Well, I'm not the only one."

He watched a party of six circling about the smorgasbord, plates in hand, piling pickled fish atop cheese and cold meats, mixing green and jellied salads with Swedish meat balls, potatoes and a questionable creamed entree; then topping this structure with olives, pickles, spareribs and smoked salmon.

"They'll find out," he prophesied. "But there's no use telling 'em."

Michael, his eyes on the old Swedish clock before a fireplace, said: "You'll have to hurry with your dessert if you don't mind. And I'll take that letter now."

She handed the copy of Maxine's letter to Dozier back to him. "It—it sounds like her. But it only verified what we already knew. I'm surprised Mr. Sullivan let you have it."

"He let me have it because he won't see that Dozier's death is very important."

"But he must realize that if he hadn't been killed there's so much he could have told."

"I didn't mean it in just that way. You missed seeing that portrait of Lutz's."

"You might as well save it, Val," Tommy said, dealing manfully with Swedish apple cake. "This is swell sauce. He wants to be mysterious. Well, it's still a nice mess."

"No," Michael said, "not nice. Not nice people, you know. But human, quite human. However . . ."

Valerie giggled. "How thin your face has grown, Mr. Fortune. Do a Doctor Fell or H.M."

"All the H.M. I know is: 'Burn me, you're a good-lookin' nymph,'" Michael said, smiling at her. "Have you finished? Then let's go. . . ."

"And where," Tommy wanted to know when they were in the car, "are we going? If it's safe to ask?"

"Haight Street."

"Haight—Miss Julian! I should have guessed it," Valerie said. "But, Michael, how do you know where?"

"I don't. But six will get you ten I'm right."

"Well, but how can you—" Tommy began.

"Mr. Sullivan would call it coincidence. And coincidences distress him. But if he knew as much as we do about Miss Julian he would probably guess where on Haight Street she goes."

"Yes, but Sullivan's a cop."

"And I have lived in several of the less desirable rooming houses in this city and, as Mr. Sullivan himself says, have known some queer people."

Tommy said: "Oh!" and was silent until they turned off Market up Haight. Then he muttered with some justice: "Jeez, this is a crummy district."

For Haight, east of the panhandle, is relic of pre-apartment house days: block after block of high narrow flats, gray or bilious brown, with long flights of steps from street to front doors. On one corner was a building not so tall; a reddish structure suggesting both church and social hall. Valerie read the words printed on the tattered canvas stretched across the double doors:

"'Temple of Faith and Hope. We Have a Message for You.' Oh, gosh! 'Faith and Hope!' Are we going in?"

"Yes. The free performance will soon be over," Michael said. "You might like to see it."

"My good gosh!" Tommy said, helping Valerie out of the car. "Mean to tell me the Julian comes to a jernt like this?"

The small vestibule was dimly lighted but no one was in attendance at the doors. Beyond was a cold draughty hall with long splintery benches. The place was dark except for shaded lights focused on a small platform at the front of the room. It bore a table and one chair, occupied by a woman with a broad doughy face quite devoid of expression. But the voice that came from her lips was deeply and startlingly masculine. It said:

"She is here. She is well and happy. Laura is here too. She has a message for Marjorie."

From somewhere near the platform a feminine voice cried: "Laura! Oh, but how . . . My name is Marjorie."

"She wants Marjorie to tell Joe not to grieve," the flat monotone continued. "She is happy: she knows the truth."

"Nicely rehearsed," Michael muttered. "It's the standard come-on."

An indignant voice near them hissed: "Shh-h!" and the medium twisted uneasily in her chair. "I cannot tell you any more. There are others here who have messages for their dear ones but they cannot get through. I must go now."

Her features writhed as someone in the back of the room switched on the lights. A man ascended the platform and raised a white admonitory hand. He was a fat little man whose round blue eyes shed love on his audience. He said in a bland and buttery voice:

"If we have brought help and comfort to you we are—*glad!* For this work we ask nothing but your faith. If some of you wish more personal guidance that can be arranged. We must charge a small fee to carry on the work you have seen tonight. You have seen what Madam Gould"—he bowed toward the medium who smiled wanly—"can do under adverse conditions. In more favorable surroundings her gift is truly startling. That is all, friends. Have faith and hope."

"Good heavens! do they really fall for this?" Valerie whispered. "They look respectable—most of them."

She stared at two women, obviously sisters, decently shabby in well-worn black; at a florid, flashily dressed man who was twisting a loose coat button indecisively, at a young woman in a thin sleazy suit drying her eyes with a crumpled handkerchief. "But how can they—"

"It's crude," Michael agreed. "Even for this kind of thing. But they aren't catering to the wealthy or educated. We might as well go up now."

They were in time to hear a tall gray-haired woman telling the impresario that "it was just wonderful. Because how could anyone know my sister Marjorie was engaged to Joe? He will be so comforted when I give him the message. And I certainly will bring him with me tomorrow. Oh, I do hope she will speak to him. It would be too wonderful."

"It shall be arranged," the fat little man said pontifically. "Perhaps some of our literature at a nominal cost?"

"Oh yes, I'll tell him." The woman backed away, a peculiar glint in her eyes as she caught Michael's sardonic glance. He said, too low for the few persons lingering in the hall to hear him:

"My name is Dundas."

"Oh—oh yes." The man's malevolent smile vanished. "Well, what about these two?"

"They're safe. Where can we talk?"

"Oh—well, there's a room off here. I guess you'd better come too, Dot—uh—Madam Gould. This is the—uh—gentleman Flo spoke about that wants some special—uh—attention. Right this way. . . ."

CHAPTER TWENTY-ONE
CURTAIN—ACT TWO

In a small room off the main hall Madam Gould settled solidly into one of two available chairs and began drawing a tangerine Cupid's bow over the rightful curve of her mouth.

"There's nothing to get jittery about, Doc," she remarked. "Flo said he was a right guy. She knew him at Casey's on Howard Street. When she was working with the Parson's layout over on Fillmore."

"I know. But I didn't bargain for these two." Doc seemed nervously to be estimating the width of Tommy's shoulders. "Where's Mac?"

"Tailing a sucker. And we don't want no strong-arm stuff. I guess we can make a deal. What do you want, Dundas?"

"Some information about a Miss Emma Julian."

"Oh, that dame? How'd you know she was coming here?"

"She talks too much about faith and hope," Michael said wearily. "And she's spending a good deal of money she isn't willing to account for."

"That 'd be on account of this brother? Charlie?"

"Now, Dot? It's in the papers there's been a murder in the place this Julian dame lives at. We don't want to get mixed up in nothing like that."

"Miss Julian's brother doesn't know she has been coming to you for—you call it guidance, don't you?" Michael said nastily. "I think he would have another name for it. I think he might even tell the police all about it if he knew the facts."

"Yeah, I figured it that way," Madam Gould said coolly. "Doc here is a good front and great on the sob stuff but he scares easy. We're overdue for a raid and he's got the heebies. Well, I say: get it while you can. What's in it for us?"

"*Hable el dinero.*" Michael took a billfold from an inside coat pocket. Doc said suspiciously:

"What's that you say?"

"Let money talk. *Y toma si habló*. And it did talk." Tommy whistled involuntarily at the thickness of the roll of bills he handed to the medium. "That's the top price. Let's say it's for 'more personal guidance.' Well?"

Madam Gould put her lipstick into her purse and the bills, calmly, under the rolled top of a stocking.

"Well, this dame started coming here about two months ago. Don't know how she found out about us. You know how we work? Mac tailed her home and next day circulated round the neighborhood and got enough on her for me to get past the first seance.

"After that I find things out from them. She's easy to pump; never knows you are. She took a lot of our lit'rature and she wanted to talk to her mother all the time. Well, I give 'em enough to keep 'em coming."

"Could you possibly be more definite?"

"Sure. First she wants to know is her mother happy. They always do. Then she keeps asking her mother about this Charlie. She don't come right out and say she's scared he'll marry but you can see she is. She wants to know can her mother tell her is he and what should she do about it."

"And you told her?" Michael said.

"Same old line: be patient and have faith. Well, at first I did. But she says her mother's told her to look after this brother. So"—the medium shrugged—"I told her to take care of Charlie. It went over big with her. But then she wants to know what to do. That was a sticker. So I just said, for her mother: you will find a way. And once—"

"When?"

"Friday night. She says: 'But will I be forgiven?'"

"And you said that she would be forgiven?"

"That's the best answer I know. She was upset. So was she about a month ago. The most I could make out of it, from the fool way she talks, was that somebody was a 'bad woman' and it had 'gone farther than she knew.' I suppose she meant than her mother knew."

"And what was your best answer to that?"

"That everything would come out all right," Madam Gould said, insensible to the contempt in Michael's voice. "And that I—her mother—trusted her. She told her mother wicked people were cruel to her. Once she said: 'There's been another one.' I never had a dame quite like her; so indefinite. Mostly they ask pretty definite questions."

"And when she said there had been 'another one' you told her again to be patient?"

"Cute, aren't you?" Madam Gould said humorlessly. "When I said that she sniffled and says she can't stand it. Then she mutters something about 'nervous breakdown once.' Oh yes, there's one other person she asks about. Someone named Wilbur. Wants to know if her mother's seen him and is he happy. She acts like she was afraid her mother and Wilbur wouldn't be on such good terms. But that's all I can tell you."

"You've said too much now. If that dame's mixed up in murder," Doc said, "how you going to be sure this guy ain't going to the cops?"

"I'm not, no matter what Flo said. The cops may come asking questions anyway. If they don't, that dame's scared of her brother. If he complained to the cops they'd raid us. But if this guy spills what I've said to 'em maybe we can make a deal. See?"

Doc brightened. "I never thought about that."

"You never do. And I'm not putting out any more—"

"Just a minute," Michael said. "Has she been to you since last Friday? No? Well, she's in funds again—borrowed—but if I were you I'd refuse her patronage. Because Mr. Julian tailed her last Friday but lost her. Next time he might be more successful."

"I get you," Madam Gould said briefly. "Show 'em out, Doc. . . ."

When they had run down Fillmore at a speed that more than once made Tommy apply imaginary brakes he protested:

"You seem to be in a hurry. Going to call Sullivan—or talk to Julian?"

"I have no telephone." Michael swerved into Sacramento, cutting dangerously in front of an oncoming Fillmore streetcar. Tommy said resignedly:

"Oh well, Stanford hospital's just a couple of blocks up," and Michael took his foot off the accelerator.

"I'm a fool to drive like that. I was thinking. Sullivan will find out about Miss Julian for himself."

"How?" Valerie said.

"He's already interested in her Friday nights. He doesn't neglect such things."

"And Geneva might give him a useful hint. She wonders where Miss Julian goes on Haight Street. I think Mr. Julian will protect her as long as he can."

"Well, I think you ought to tell Julian," Tommy said. "Jeez, what a racket that is. Of course Miss Julian is kind of a lame-brain. Who was this Flo they talked about?"

"She was a stooge in the same sort of racket," Michael said so docilely that Valerie suspected he was thinking of something else. "Like that gray-haired woman you heard identifying herself as Marjorie who had a sister Laura, who had a fiancé, Joe—"

"But she looked so respectable!" Valerie said.

"Of course. And perhaps she was on the level but I doubt it. Flo looked like a schoolteacher, old style. I had the flu at this rooming house— Casey's—and she used to feed me canned soup and eggnogs. I'd heard her speak of the Faith and Hope outfit. They've been at it off and on for years. Several convictions, I think, but they always pop up again and usually in the same neighborhood. Sullivan knows all there is to know about them."

"Well, there's nothing criminal about going in for spiritualism," Tommy said. "But some of the things that dame said don't listen so well."

"But they might turn out to mean just nothing at all. And in that case it would be much better to warn Miss Julian. Or Mr. Julian, if you think she wouldn't believe you. Michael, it was probably some of their literature she had in that box in the cupboard. Because Mr. Julian would make fun of it or want to know where she got it. And she even bothered to get rid of it—"

"Yes," Michael said inattentively. "Valerie, do you think your stepsister would ever have told Miss Julian it was Julian's money that bought that black-and-green suit from Gisele's?"

"Why, yes. If Miss Julian saw it and admired it—as she would—and Maxine happened to be in a—not a very good humor, it might amuse her to see Miss Julian's reaction. And I suppose to her a woman who let a man buy her clothes would be practically a kept woman. Maxine didn't care what she said to people like Miss Julian and Geneva."

"Or anybody," Tommy muttered.

Valerie, looking toward the left where the red tower of KJBS's antenna glowed against the sky, tried briefly to think what words of Michael's had rung a warning gong in her brain. But they were passing the black-green slopes of Lafayette Square's lawns and Tommy said repentantly:

"I didn't like Maxine but I didn't wish her that bad luck. And seeing this place at night—I don't know: it looks spooky, doesn't it?" He squeezed Valerie's hand. "Tired, baby?"

"A little. I do think, Michael, that you should tell Mr. Julian you have that check. If he should miss it he'd be very uneasy. He may have missed it by now. Couldn't you tell him you picked it up in the hall?"

"He wouldn't believe that. But I'll tell him."

Michael stopped the car in front of their apartment house but for an instant he made no movement to get out. He folded his arms on the steering wheel and sat without moving. Tommy looked at Valerie, shrugged and shook his head.

"Don't you feel good?" he said condescendingly.

"*No hay remedio*." Michael sat erect. "Will you come in and have a drink?"

"We-el, I don't mind. I'm still not a welcome visitor as far as Valerie's mother is concerned. So I guess I'll say good night out in the hall. It's kind of public but the air isn't so icy."

They waited while Michael found his key and opened the front door. Inside, Geneva was saying to Charles Julian:

"Why, no, I haven't seen her. Now where do you suppose she could have gone? She shouldn't wander around nights, alone and unprotected. And she's so absent-minded and nearsighted—"

"Yes, yes—I know!" Julian turned quickly. "You—have any of you seen Em?"

"We've been gone since seven," Valerie said. "When—"

"We had dinner about six and I laid down and dropped off to sleep. It isn't like her to go out nights when I'm home." Julian pulled at his scraggy mustache. "She's been upset. The Callendars are out so I can't ask—"

"Oh yes, they've gone to his mother's for dinner I thought they might like some of our cold lamb, being upset and all. Well, and so you got back?" Geneva beamed on Valerie and Michael and, with reservation, on Tommy. "Not that you really should go out just now, dear. Now, Mr. Julian, don't you worry one bit. Sister's probably just stepped out for something and didn't want to spoil your little nap. Mr. Dundas, won't you come in and—"

"Sorry," Michael said. "Not just now."

He was already halfway up one flight of stairs. Geneva began:

"Well! You can't tell when he'll be polite and when—" But Valerie had followed Michael. He was unlocking his own front door before she caught up with him, whispering:

"Michael, what did you do with that letter you wrote? Did you—"

"*Cállese!* Be still—please!"

He picked up the unaddressed envelope lying on the floor of the small entrance hall. There was more than one sheet of paper inside but he scanned them quickly. For an instant his eyes were sick. Then he said:

"So endeth the second act. I'd better call Sullivan. No; there might be time yet. I'll go."

"Where?"

"Over to Sutter. You'll have to stay here."

"Well, I won't!" Valerie said mutinously, catching his arm. "I was in at the beginning and I'm not quitting now."

"I know that." Michael jerked his arm free. "Valerie, it isn't a question of your helping now. I haven't time to argue with you so don't blame me if you don't—like it."

"Like what?" Tommy met them on the ground floor. "Going somewhere? Count me in. But you'd better stay here, Val."

"She won't," Michael said and they went down the front steps together with Geneva's: "But, Valerie, you're surely not going out again? Poor Mother," pursuing them futilely.

Michael turned the car in the middle of the street and headed for Sutter. Tommy clutched the side of the car with one hand, Valerie with the other and muttered, not facetiously:

"Hold your hats, kids, here we go again. What the— Well, here come the cops!"

Somewhere ahead of them the siren of a police car screamed angrily. "That's not for us," Michael said and ran through a red light.

He turned into Sutter. From more than a block away they could see the crowd swarming like flies over tainted meat; the cars that slowed as their occupants stared toward a tall white hotel; police inviting people to "move on there." Michael parked at the nearest corner, in front of a fire hydrant, and again sat very still, looking toward the top of the ornate, old-fashioned building.

"It's—high enough," he said at last and a man, passing them, his expression one of pleased horror, told his companion:

"They say it was a woman. Jumped out of a top window. Like they do: checked in like anyone and then—bam! I faw down and go boom. Guess there wasn't much left of her. Can't see why they do it. . . ."

Valerie put her face against Tommy's shoulder. He said gruffly: "Buzzards! Look, let's get out of here. I don't see why you ever let Valerie come."

"Wait," Michael said. "There's Sullivan's car. They must have called him at once."

"He's seen you," Tommy said uneasily. "He's stopping."

"So," Sullivan said, "you turned up here too? A little late but— Just out riding, I suppose? Mere coincidence?"

Valerie raised her head. "No," she said before Michael could answer, "it wasn't. Mr. Julian told us his sister was missing and we thought—"

"Oh, you did? Well, that's interesting," Sullivan said grimly. "I'll want to talk to you pretty soon, Dundas, so don't bother to go to bed. If it was Miss Julian you were looking for it's damned funny you turned up here. Because it was Mrs. Callendar that jumped out that hotel window."

CHAPTER TWENTY-TWO
"'TWAS A FAMOUS VICTORY"

"After hearing Sullivan's unexpurgated opinion of amateurs in general and me in particular it will be a pleasure to talk to you two," Michael said.

But a little pulse throbbed erratically in his temple and a furrow was deep graven between his black eyebrows. Valerie, while they watched the street and Sullivan's parked car, had said to Tommy:

"I don't see why he doesn't go. And Michael looked exhausted. I don't think he's so terribly strong."

"He's hard as nails," Tommy said. "And I don't mean physically. That guy—Doc—may've watched me. But the dame was the brains of the outfit and she watched Dundas. Well, and he's stronger than you think. Wiry and— But I'll admit fellows like that do keep going on a kind of nervous energy. There was a fellow on the Cal team one year like that."

If Tommy was right then Valerie thought Michael had nearly exhausted his nervous energy. Besides, he wouldn't guess there might be flaws in Michael's armor. Dealing with Madam Gould was one thing; driving Winona to her death— But had he? She said:

"Why did she do it, Michael?"

"Because— Oh, I'll read you her letter. I copied it before Sullivan got here. No salutation, simply:

"'In a few minutes I'm going over to the Yorkshire Hotel and take a room there. This building isn't high enough when you want to make sure.

"'I was afraid of you all along. I don't know why because you must have been guessing. But if you told Sullivan to check on me very carefully— Well, it's only a matter of time until they trace your movements, isn't it? And I don't suppose mine were very well covered.

"'And when he found out what I was doing just after I left school, he'd see I had a motive for murdering Mrs. Putnam. How did you guess about the White Sands Hotel? Of course he'd find someone there who'd identify my picture at least and they'd know she was there too and that I was with a man.

"'But what really matters is that I can't count on Grant. Not even if they couldn't ever prove I killed Mrs. Putnam. I know Grant hasn't any backbone and he's conventional and narrow-minded and jealous and under his mother's thumb. So why should I be so much in love with him? It doesn't make sense. But I am and I'm too tired to run away and finally just be caught.

"'I won't go into details about my "past." It would sound like *True Confessions*. I'd graduated from the convent before John ever came back to California to live. I suppose you checked on that with his firm, when you said you were going down to the wholesale district.

Later it was his idea to say I'd been in Europe before I came here to live with him.

"'I had money enough to have a good time, living in Los Angeles. I was alone and accountable to no one and it seemed rather smart to have an affair with a married man whose wife didn't understand him. We spent a long week end at White Sands. He said it would be "safe." I suppose you'd think it would have been; it was quiet and who'd know we weren't married?

"'But there was quite a fire in the hotel, upstairs. So we all came running out into the halls. When I say Mrs. Putnam was on our floor that night, that explains the whole thing. I was too upset to pay much attention to her and I didn't know her name. And it happened I never saw her here till Miss Julian started her little blaze.

"'That was two weeks ago. In a day or two I began getting letters that told me the old devil had put two and two together and made four.

Of course she knew—or could find out—I'd never been married before.

"'Just to make sure, I watched while Grant was asleep. I saw her go downstairs one night and then the lights went out. I could have caught her but what was the use? I couldn't give her away when she could do the same to me.

"'Finally I wrote to John. He'd gotten me out of that first mess. Read me a fatherly lecture and brought me up here. But he was broad-minded. He always warned me Grant wouldn't be. That was one reason he didn't want us to marry.

"'I thought he could buy her off. I'd heard she was fond of money. Or I thought he might be able to put the fear of God in her. He started as soon as he could and you know what happened.

"'But since I'd inherit his money I decided to deal with her myself. I had to. When I found out she'd managed to get letters to Grant I couldn't risk her letting him in on the secret. And there was always the chance he might get a letter meant for me—first. And she could always tell.

"'I honestly wanted to settle with her peaceably. I watched and met her in our hall when she came back up in the dark. She took me into her apartment and I soon saw why. She was enjoying herself. She refused money and when I threatened her she laughed again. She said she was going to die soon and she didn't care if I did tell. Maybe she'd forgotten the knife on the table. Maybe she didn't care.

"'The only luck I had was that the letters she hadn't delivered were harmless. I suppose she was going to have more fun by making me hope she was through—before she began all over again. So it was safe for me to leave them there.

"'I've heard them talking about the back door being unlocked. I was going out that way but when I peeped out the window I saw a light in your kitchen. So I gave that up and didn't take time to lock the door again. That dog was driving me crazy.

"'Grant has gone to his mother's for dinner. I said I didn't feel like going but he wouldn't disappoint her. He went without me.'

"That's all," Michael said. "Except for a note I gave her when she answered the doorbell before we went to dinner. She very kindly returned it to me."

"Then you did warn her?" Valerie said.

"It's fairly obvious I did. Or so Sullivan says. But I told him I'd mentioned fires in connection with Mrs. Putnam before her this afternoon."

"And you did—with my help. I wondered why."

"Well, you're a good little guesser," Tommy remarked.

"It wasn't guessing," Michael said irritably. "It isn't my fault the facts aren't the kind you present to a jury. I tried to give Sullivan a hint or two but he wouldn't listen."

"Did you?" Valerie said doubtfully. "How?"

"For one thing, I asked him why Mrs. Putnam was killed Sunday night. She had been writing those letters for three months—and nothing happened."

"It takes time for people to reach the breaking point."

"This was not a case of standard blackmail, my dear, where the victim finally refuses to pay or can't pay any longer. If you'd rather kill than have some fact regarding your life known, why wait three months to be safe? Because, Sullivan suggested, it took that long to discover who was writing the letters.

"But while it might be hard to watch as Mrs. Callendar did, if the situation were serious enough for murder, it would have to be managed somehow, if one had no other way of finding out who was writing the letters. You remember Miss Farley's activities."

"What— Oh, I see what you mean," Tommy said.

"Since Maxine found out Mrs. Putnam was writing those letters, so could someone else."

"Yes. Besides, whatever the letter writer knew and was referring to in the letters was certainly something not generally known. So why wouldn't the person who received them be able to guess who in this house could have the special knowledge necessary to write them?

"That suggested that at first the letters were merely malicious. But if Mrs. Putnam knew any damaging facts regarding anyone here but Mrs. Callendar, she knew them before she came here. It was then she'd known the Julians and Miss Nolan. And they knew her, and if they knew she was dangerous why, in the name of common sense, would they choose to live here. And why, if Miss Putnam had such knowledge, would she wait to capitalize on it once she began writing those letters?

"But she and Mrs. Callendar had never seen each other until two weeks ago. So that if it was Mrs. Callendar who killed her, you didn't have to ask why she waited three months to do it.

"That conversation we overheard between the Callendars, Valerie, was really the starting point. It showed Callendar was what she calls him: conventional, narrow-minded, under his mother's thumb. And jealous. I had," Michael said, looking at his reddened knuckles, "further proof of that. Also he has a more than average fear of scandal or publicity.

"Mrs. Callendar also showed—and that was emphasized on Sunday night, I thought—that she was very much in love with her husband. All of which answered the question: what person here had most to fear from blackmail? Call it that; it's the most convenient term.

"Well, Julian may be short tempered but I believe he would stand by his sister. And she has always been dependent on him so it's unlikely there's much about her he doesn't know. As to Miss Nolan, she is independent of any close relationships. Your mother might throw her out if she were involved in scandal but she must know you'd stand by her, Valerie. And there's a much more conclusive argument against either Miss Nolan or Miss Julian's having killed Mrs. Putnam.

"But first, going back to the Callendars' conversation. That night Mrs. Callendar discovered her husband had received letters without her knowledge. I thought she was somewhat alarmed by that and that she sounded him out as to any possibility of his turning the matter over to the police. Then she said: 'You can't chase people in the dark and catch them delivering letters.'

"Any fool might suppose Mrs. Putnam would work in the dark. But no one had reported any peculiar lapse in the lighting system. It was Gus who told me the hall lights had often been turned off.

So it did seem Mrs. Callendar knew Poison Pen's mode of delivery—and who she was. It was then too that she mentioned the fact of Callendar's being a very sound sleeper.

"Then, the wording of that wire: 'Will take evening plane.' If someone begged me to come to him at once I'd probably word my answer in just that way. It was a cautious answer but not quite cautious enough. If Dozier had been coming up on his own initiative I can think of half-a-dozen different phrasings he'd be apt to use. 'Must come up on business,' or—oh, write your own ticket.

"His affection for his niece was generally acknowledged; by her as well as others. She said she wrote to him, so why did he destroy her letters and keep Maxine Farley's? And since he kept it, if he was coming here to give some information regarding her death, why didn't he bring the letter with him?

"In fact, why was it necessary for him to come at all? He could have given his information from Los Angeles until the police decided how important it was. And Mrs. Callendar herself admitted she doubted how much he knew regarding Miss Farley's death at the time he sent that wire.

"She said Dozier came back here to live five years ago; that it was then he came to see her and sent her to Europe. But certain remarks of Julian's gave me the idea he believed Dozier stopped traveling about four years ago, not five. I checked up on that this afternoon."

"How'd you manage that?" Tommy asked.

"I borrowed a press badge from a friend of mine," said Michael. "One of the firm's oldest employees is in charge of the branch office here since they moved the main one to Los Angeles. He was able to tell me Dozier was not in this country at the time Mrs. Callendar claimed he first renewed his acquaintance with her.

"Why did she lie about that unless something happened during that time which she did not want known? A young, pretty and reckless girl on her own. . . . That certainly suggests a more likely field for scandal than anything Miss Julian or Miss Nolan might have done five or twenty-five years ago.

"And someone offered Mrs. Putnam money before killing her. Neither Miss Nolan nor Miss Julian could do that. Nor could Mrs. Callendar until Sunday night. It was always evident that she and Callendar had no money to spare. Do you remember her saying at the airport: 'Now there's no one'? I imagine she was thinking: no one left to help me. So Dozier's death was important. It forced Mrs. Callendar to act for herself and also enabled her to try to buy Mrs. Putnam's silence.

"That ends the facts. As to fancies or association of ideas: When Mrs. Callendar told us under what circumstances she saw Mrs. Putnam, presumably for the first time, I did think of her telling Valerie she was afraid of fire. When we knew she was the letter writer I wondered why she had made that remark. And when Sara said her grandmother was not especially afraid of fire I wondered still more."

"I suppose," Valerie said, "she wanted me to remember in case she was killed. Remember and wonder. She dragged Mr. Dozier's name into the conversation too. I suppose because that was a connection with Winona."

"Only she would know what was in her mind. But I remembered that during at least a part of the time about which Mrs. Callendar chose to lie, Mrs. Putnam was living at a seaside hotel. She left, Sara told you, because they had to do the place over."

"You could have asked Sara why?" Tommy said.

"I didn't care to ask her before everyone. I— well, I hadn't decided, then, whether or not to leave Sullivan to his own devices. But there were those scraps of letters, one of them with the word 'fire', another asking—I supposed—'what man?' Perhaps they were old letters or ones Mrs. Putnam had made for future use. It doesn't matter. I had no chance to speak to Sara privately and I did decide I must tell Sullivan what I thought.

"He would eventually have hit the right trail," Michael added quickly. "Because he would have kept at his investigation of the lives of everyone here for months. But meanwhile, killers so often kill again."

"Wasn't it kind of foolish to warn her?" Tommy asked.

"If I was wrong, my telling her I must ask Sullivan to make inquiries at White Sands would mean nothing to her. If I was right—I thought she would run for it. I didn't care if she did. Or that she might try to remove me from the scene. That would have been proof and a fair duel. Women don't usually know when they're beaten. She did and I should have realized that, considering Callendar's character, she would."

"And where are we now?" Tommy said. "Could she have killed Maxine and just not bothered to say so?"

"You can't blackmail people who haven't money or won't pay. Publish and be damned! said the Duke."

"And why wouldn't she confess?" Valerie said. "It seems certain it wasn't Mrs. Putnam Maxine was going to try to blackmail. So we agreed it was the person who killed Mrs. Putnam that she was blackmailing. But Winona was that person and I'm sure she didn't kill Maxine and—and so the letters had nothing to do with her death!"

"Oh, I think they have their place in it," Michael said.

"But we went chasing out on Haight even if you didn't think Miss Julian killed Mrs. Putnam," Tommy reminded him.

"Why not? The facts we learned there still stand. Hate often grows from fear but sometimes it can stand alone." He pressed his hands hard against his temples.

"Let's leave that for another day, if you don't mind. Let Sullivan handle things now."

"You've got something there," Tommy said, rising. "And after all, she had it coming to her. The way she finished it is kind of upsetting but—"

"'Twas a famous victory,'" said Michael.

CHAPTER TWENTY-THREE
"THAT BLACK-AND-GREEN SUIT"

The afternoon was cool and Patricia was wearing a fur coat; not mink but caracul, because it
was "black and while no one expects you to go in
mourning any more, at a funeral, subdued colors
. . ." And she looked disapprovingly at Valerie's
green wool dress and short matching coat as she
topped her own ensemble with a small black hat
and a frivolous transparent veil.

Watching the mortician tuck Patricia tenderly
into his car, something clicked in Valerie's mind.
Maxine and a mink coat she had hoped to buy
and Michael saying: "But with her coloring—why
mink?" And last night: "Do you think your stepsister would ever have told Miss Julian it was Julian's money that bought that black-and-green suit
from Gisele's?"

She stood still, staring at the white Grecian cre-
matorium. Tommy, a hand on her arm, murmured:
"Are you coming with me?"

"Yes." Patricia, informed of Valerie's decision, sighed resignedly.

"Oh, very well. Though considering what I've just been through, you might show some consideration. It doesn't matter, though." She sank back against the cushions and raised her handkerchief to her eyes.

"Home, driver. I—I feel so faint, Geneva."

"We'll just go right home and have a nice glass of sherry and some crackers and a little lie down. Of course you aren't hungry but you'll feel better if you make yourself eat something. That nasty old faint feeling . . ."

The big black car rolled out of the driveway and Valerie turned toward Bill Jackson's scarred coupé. Tommy had borrowed it "Because," he said, "I'm not going to have anyone think I'm afraid to come but I'm damned if I'll ride with your mother and Geneva."

He said now: "Well, where to? You ought to have a car of your own, Val, since your mother hasn't."

"It would be a nice thing to have. Tommy, I'm—I'm—I haven't that nasty faint feeling but I'm hollow inside."

"Hungry? No? Well, then what—"

"How did Michael know it was a black-and-green suit Maxine bought with Mr. Julian's check?

I never told him what color it was. She wasn't wearing it when she was killed. Michael told us he'd never seen Maxine. Mr. Julian asked him. And she didn't wear that suit Thursday or Friday when he had his first chance to see her in the apartment house."

"Well—I don't know." Tommy frowned, starting the car. "Look, baby, I haven't wanted to make you mad and while I don't think Dundas cares about me I kind of like him."

"Yes?"

"Well, what does he get out of this? He moves to your place on Thursday and Maxine gets killed next night. And you admit he practically forced you to let him take a hand in the game."

"I did think that—at first. But he is an unpredictable person and he did have an old score against Inspector Sullivan."

"And in a way, he did show him up." Tommy turned into Geary Boulevard. "But leaving that out of it, he could have known Maxine. And that business with the check."

"I know," Valerie said. "He—he might almost have known beforehand that Mr. Julian would have it."

"And he doesn't seem to want to tell Sullivan about it. He advised Julian not to tell. Well, that's good advice, I guess, if he wanted to help Julian.

But he doesn't strike me the kind to be so damned helpful to someone he hardly knows. You admit he can lie like nobody's business. And he's part wop, isn't he?"

"Oh, Tommy!" Valerie shook her head despairingly. "Anyone not one hundred per cent Anglo-Saxon is a wop to you. Unless he's a spig or a hunkie."

"Well, what would you call 'em? And that la-de-dah way of talking."

"That," Valerie said coldly, "is simply—provincial. You might as well criticize President Roosevelt's diction. This silly habit of laughing at anyone who won't say 'ordin*airy*' and 'Toosday'—"

"Well," Tommy said sulkily, "that way he has of saying: '*If* you don't *mind*.' Meaning probably you do but he doesn't give a damn."

Valerie smiled reluctantly. "Well—yes, it is a little exasperating."

"And when you get right down to it, you don't know one thing about him."

"But I do!"

"Well, what?"

It was odd that what she remembered most clearly was of how she and Michael had laughed together at Geneva's and Miss Julian's duet; his level, carefully controlled voice describing his mother. And what significance would those things have for Tommy? She shook her head and let him go on:

"I don't set myself up to blame him for anything he may have done. But I still say you don't know anything about him. Where does he get his money? He doesn't seem to work any particular hours."

"He—" Valerie stopped, said quickly: "No, he doesn't." She wouldn't tell Tommy that Michael had been up and dressed at three o'clock in the morning or mention that locked Chinese chest or his saying that he needed his hands in his "business."

"Well? There you are. He just might have known Maxine. Might have bought things for her himself. Well, what are we going to do about it?"

"I'm going to Gisele's. I should think they would remember Maxine and if she ever bought anything else there."

"Good idea. I don't have to go in, do I?"

"You do. You might as well begin now—to be one of the few men who takes an interest in his wife's clothes."

"Well—gosh! You look good in anything you wear."

"You will come with me," Valerie said firmly. "And like it. It will teach you to handle yourself gracefully in a china shop. . . ."

Tommy parked finally in an alley next to the Kohler and Chase building, cheerfully disregarding the "no parking" sign. They walked up Grant Avenue, stopping while he bought Valerie a corsage of pink roses from one of the flower stands.

"What," he said uneasily, settling his tie, "are you going to say to them? Will you have to try on dresses?"

"I don't know."

Valerie turned into Maiden Lane. There, between a bookstore of the shoppe variety and a tearoom self-consciously quaint, was Gisele's. You were apt to overlook the very small name plate on the green door but not the contents of the show windows. In one was a single hat, simple, severe, arrogant in its possession of the elusive quality known as "line." In the other a gown of black taffeta seemed to stand by its own stiffness, its full skirt crawling with painted green-and-gold dragons.

Valerie said: "Oh! I never saw anything quite—"

"I don't like it. It's—funny. Maxine could have worn it maybe. Well—"

A little bell on the door tinkled thinly as they went in. A tall svelte creature swam toward them, eyebrows raised, questioning whether this couple deserved attention. She said:

"Mademoiselle desires?"

Tommy looked about the dimly lighted room, shifted his feet in the velvet carpet and wiped his forehead.

"I desire to see the proprietor," Valerie said bluntly. "Or whoever runs this place. Do you?"

"But no. I am Fanchon. You will come this way, please."

She opened a door at the back of the shop, ushered them into a small office and went to another door. "I will tell Madam Gisele you wish to see her. One meenute."

"We—we might as well sit down," Valerie said.

"I don't like the way places like this smell. Or the kind of hushed attitude like a church or something. And suppose this dame doesn't talk English."

"*Aquí se habla inglés.*"

Tommy, still standing, whirled about. Valerie got to her feet, sank back into her chair again.

"It's all right, Fanny," Michael said. "I knew you'd recognize them."

"O.K., boss. I'll go see how the Barlow dame is getting on. Call me if you need me."

Michael sat down at the battered desk that was littered with sketches, ornaments and samples of fabrics. "I thought you might come, Valerie, if that remark of mine about that suit happened to register. But considering that I designed the thing—"

"Jeez! Do you mean you're—you're Gisele?"

"Yes. Sit down if you don't mind. And," Michael said unpleasantly, "don't let your mouth hang open. Well?"

"I'm—I'm just as surprised as Tommy," Valerie said. "Why not?" She began to laugh. "Oh, Michael—"

"You've been letting your imagination run riot again, haven't you? I'm not the apartment-house thief who's been eluding the police for so long. You two are a nuisance," Michael said with a wintry smile. "But from Howard's expression he sympathizes with my desire not to be generally known as Gisele."

"Well, there's no reason why you shouldn't—I mean: there are men dressmakers—"

"I envy you your consummate tact. However, that's what it amounts to. My father painted bad pictures in the name of art and my mother devoted half her time and thought to her appearance. I suppose it really began the first time I told her what was wrong with a hat that displeased her. Then she dragged me to innumerable dress salons. It isn't what I'd like to do—

"That's not quite true," he corrected himself. "Perhaps, as I suspect Mr. Howard is thinking, there's a feminine streak in me. I admit I have a feeling for line, material and color. But no very friendly one for the women who wear the clothes!"

"Well, what the hell?" Tommy said. "There's money in it."

"Enough. And since I'm apparently not fitted for anything else— Well?"

"The Barlow dame don't like the dress," said Fanny-Fanchon. "Thinks it's too plain. With a fanny like hers—"

"She still wants frill where it would do least good?"

Fanny grinned. "That's it. And a lot of gold—"

"Nerts!" said Michael with unusual inelegance. "Sell her one of those coin necklaces if she must have gold. That dress should take fifteen pounds off her and I'm not going to attach ruffles to that posterior of hers."

"She wants to see Gisele."

"Tell her Gisele is out, ill, dead—anything. Trot out the copyist and tell Mrs. Barlow she's the designer. Tell her to try Zukor's if she wants something girlish."

"I can't do that, boss. But I'll turn a strong light on the mirror so she can contrast my girlish form with hers," Fanny promised. "She'll take the dress."

"If something in her inner being demands release in color show her that thing that looks like Van Gogh at his worst. I'd like to get it out of the shop."

"Trade secrets?" Valerie said. "So that's how it's done?"

"Yes. Where were we? Oh, let's go down to Solari's and have a drink. I haven't had any lunch. . . ."

They sat in a booth near the bar and drank Tom Collinses while at intervals the waiter presented bowls of Solari's own dark brown potato chips, trays of canapés and finally something creamed in a patty shell.

"And all for the price of the drink," Tommy murmured. "This is free lunch what is. But I guess this is all—"

"And you want me to finish too? I didn't see Miss Farley when she bought that suit," Michael said. "I work a great deal at home. And keep my materials under cover. It may be foolish but— Well, I'm in the shop as little as possible. Few of our customers have ever seen me.

"But of course Fanny told me that the suit was gone and spoke admiringly of Miss Farley. I also saw the check. Fanny has a sixth sense that tells her when it's safe to accept that kind."

"And you noticed who'd signed it?" Valerie asked.

"Naturally. It might have bounced."

"Well, didn't it?" Tommy said. "Of course lots of women have bought things from you, but—"

"They are still living? However, that's what happened. Only—I had seen Maxine Farley before I moved to Gough. I know now that I did, in the place Sullivan spoke of: the Black Raven. At the time she was only a very striking girl who suddenly left the booth where she had been and walked out of the place. As I sat down in the booth nearest the door I couldn't see whom she was with. Perhaps no one."

"Maybe some guy picked her up and she walked out on him," Tommy said. "Gosh, that jernt! I was surprised when I ran into her that night. Why do you suppose she—"

"I don't suppose anything," Michael said. "And I have to get to work. A lady with money and—as Fanny describes her—a retreating chin, pines for a hat that will make her look like Marlene Dietrich."

"Whyn't you get in with the movies?" Tommy said. "You'd make a hell of a lot of money down there."

"God forbid, so long as the majority of women stars, on the screen, are dressed like superior prostitutes. Valerie, will you do something without asking questions?"

"We-el—yes."

Michael stared morosely at a woman standing at the bar, dressed in a black suit with hat, gloves, purse and blouse in four distinct and varying shades of brown. Finally he shuddered, tore his eyes from the distressing sight and went on:

"Buy a bottle of invisible ink—you can get it at one of the trick shops—and deface the label so it won't look new. And imagine it's been in your desk for some time. Tonight I'll stop in to—to apologize to your mother for not coming to tea yesterday."

". . . because I feel I must leave here now," Patricia said. "It's been home so long and I'm sentimental about such things but I'm afraid it's spoiled for me now. Im-*a*-gine that Callendar woman! Acting so high hat for so long when she— Not that I would ever judge her. Some women might but I wouldn't. I told Geneva, because she is apt to be a litt-*le* strait-laced: 'There, but for the grace of God and . . .' Well, all the rest of it.

"And I heard poor Mr. Callendar never wants to come back here so that will be two vacancies and one never knows what kind of people will move in. So I thought perhaps a trip of some kind . . .'"

Tommy, sitting beside Valerie at the cleared dining-room table, muttered: "Swell! When does she start?" In the living room Patricia's high child-ish voice continued:

"Because while it is ridiculous for a child Valerie's age to marry I have made up my mind not to stand in her way. And she is so de-*ter*-mined. I have brought her up so simply but now she wants a car which she certainly doesn't need. And that idea of a ranch is simply ridiculous. But I won't argue."

"Not much," Tommy said. "She's going to tolerate me like she did at dinner. Dundas had better watch his step or she'll have him hooked before he knows it."

Valerie frowned. "I wish you wouldn't."

"Well, she rubs me the wrong way. Look, baby, you won't like this either, but has she had control of your money or does she have to give you an accounting?"

"She was named executrix but I've always understood our lawyer really handles things. Of course she'll have to give me an accounting if I insist on it. But—you're remembering one of those letters."

"Well—yes. I'm going before I really put my foot in it," Tommy said. "I'll come by in the morning and we'll go somewhere by ourselves. . . ."

"Not that Valerie ever tells me anything," Patricia was saying, "but she did say you'd been in Europe so perhaps you would help me plan things?

I am so helpless and— Oh, Valerie! So Tommy has gone? Do you think it was polite for him to sit in the dining room with you? Not that I cared, but you will have to polish his manners a little if you want people to have a good impression of him. You don't mind my saying so."

"Not at all," Valerie said, walking to the windows. Michael got up from the black-and-white couch with a movement suggestive of repressed impatience as Geneva came in.

"Well, work's all done. Nasty old dishes won't do themselves." She lowered herself starchily into a slick white chair. "I have the funniest feeling, so much has happened I'm still trying to catch up and— Well, now who could that be? I feel nervous when a doorbell rings because you never can tell any more who—"

"We aren't going to stay," Miss Julian announced. "But even Charlie feels it. So still and— Such a pretty girl and Mr. Callendar such a nice young man— You really can't believe that— Oh, good evening, Mr. Dundas. I didn't see you. I do hope we aren't intruding."

"Good evening," said Mr. Dundas forbiddingly. He walked over to stand beside Valerie at the windows. They looked out at a slim crescent moon hanging with a single bright star above the fog that was slowly girdling the city. He said dreamily:

"'See, a moonbeam, come to take me home . . .'"

Geneva, rustling about the room, rearranging ash trays and tables, advanced on the windows. She glanced out, said:

"Oh, how cute! The moon's got herself a cunning 'ittle baby star," and yanked down the blinds.

At the look on Michael's face Valerie giggled helplessly, despite Geneva's: "Well, my goodness, did I say something?" and Mr. Julian's: "Tell us the joke." Michael turned his back on the windows, murmured:

"Murder is justified, after all. Pretend to be talking."

"Pretend?"

"Say anything. Convenient, their coming in just now. Look as if I'd given you a new and interesting idea."

Patricia, after tardily assuring the Julians that it was "very nice of you to come in," was yawning behind soft ringed fingers. The conversation died. Michael's voice, not too obviously raised, was still very distinct.

"Since you have invisible ink in your desk she may have drawn the face in with that."

"Her—her murderer's face?" Valerie said uncertainly.

"Well, it's odd she didn't fill in the face if she was thinking of the person she was going to meet as she made the sketch. I'll find it though it may take some searching to turn it up. I am always putting things away for safe keeping and forgetting where I put them. I'll find it tomorrow if not tonight. I couldn't get in touch with Sullivan even if I did find it tonight. I have no telephone.

"I was just saying to Valerie that I have no telephone as yet," he added, as if suddenly aware their conversation was not so private as he had supposed. "Bothersome things."

"Well, of course, wrong numbers And I'm sure— I'm always very polite but sometimes they are so rude. Men asking for Katie," Miss Julian said, "and I'm sure I don't know who. Dial wrong; so easy to do. And I'm nearsighted, but to call the grocer and get a hotel— Wouldn't send over coffee last night so I had to go out for it. Not enough for breakfast, and while I think hot water or Postum, Charlie— And I had no idea it would take me so long or that Charlie would be worried—"

"I'm sure," Geneva said firmly, rearranging fuzzy strands of hair over her dun-colored rat, "that you need new glasses. And I can tell you just the man to go to. He will fit you perfectly and he's very reasonable. Then you'll be so much happier. We all put these things off, but I always say health is happiness and we all want to be happy, don't we?"

Said Mr. Julian expressively to the stem of his pipe: "Gol-darned nonsense!"

CHAPTER TWENTY-FOUR
THE LAST LOVER

Valerie had gotten into pajamas, put out the lights and lain down, waiting for Geneva to be done fussing about hall and living room. "Winding up the cat and putting out the clock," Geneva called this process, always with the same look of happy delight in her originality of phrasing.

But she was in the bathroom now, filling the tub for one of her long, steaming hot baths. Valerie got up, put on the house coat that Maxine—how long ago—had said was becoming. It was nearly midnight, an hour since Michael and the Julians had left.

That lapse of time, made necessary by Geneva's activities, worried Valerie. For Michael, having made his reference to Maxine's sketch of the Dark Cavalier, had persistently and skillfully avoided her. For the rest of the evening he sat beside Patricia and so successfully reverted to his role of

exiled Russian that Patricia was charmed and
Valerie exasperated to the point of violence.

But she did not for an instant forget that, speaking of Winona Callendar, he had said: "I thought
she might try to remove me from the scene. That
would have been proof." If he had intended taking
that sort of risk once he would, Valerie thought,
do it again.

There could be no other reason for his reference to that sketch and a bottle of invisible ink
that she had bought only this afternoon. But only
Michael, Tommy and herself knew that that sketch
had been both made and found in the living room.

And since he had given her no opportunity to
talk with him she was going either to share a dangerous vigil or persuade him not to go through
with it. If it was not already too late. . . .

That thought sent her, with cautious haste, out
of the apartment and into the hall. There she hesitated, seeing stairs and halls so brightly lighted. It
might be better if she were not seen. Tommy had
already shown a tendency toward jealousy.

It was easy to slip down into the basement,
from there into the garden and the outside service
door that led to the back stairs. Strange gurglings
from Gus's room suggested that he was sleeping
and there was no light in the Julians' kitchen.
Breathless, she reached the top of the last flight

of narrow steps, felt for and carefully avoided the garbage cans and finally located the door into Michael's kitchen.

Again she hesitated, wondering if he would hear her call or if she must pound on the door, then mechanically tried the knob, felt it turn between her fingers and stepped into the kitchen.

A thread of light filtered into that room from a door nearly but not quite closed. Voices came to her, for an instant indistinguishable. Then Tommy said clearly:

"You may be able to pull the wool over Valerie's eyes but not mine. Your explanations are always too damned pat."

Valerie crept to the door, braced herself against the wall. Her limit of vision was narrow but it included Michael, sunk indolently in a chair before the fireplace and Tommy's back as he sat on the arm of another chair.

"You never explain anything till you have to," he went on. "Which I admit is damned clever."

The words were all but uttered—"You're being a perfect idiot, Tommy"—but Valerie bit them back and remained where she was, thinking: let them have it out. He must be wrong, but let him find it out for himself.

"And the first time," Tommy finished, "believing you is easy but after a while it gets stale."

"And so—what?" Michael said insolently.

"You explained just once too often. After handing out all that tripe about wanting to help Valerie and get back at Sullivan you finally admitted you had seen Maxine at the Black Raven. Only of course you never went there but the once and didn't see who she was with or hear her talk to anybody. Oh no!"

"And the joke of it is, Mr. Howard, that I didn't see who she was with. Because I didn't see her at all and I have never set foot in the Black Raven. But," Michael said softly, "I thought that would bring you here. Because you could not be certain I had not seen her there with you or overheard some conversation you two had."

"Now," Tommy Howard said, "it's my turn to ask: so—what?" He turned so that Valerie saw his profile, his strong tanned hand and the short ugliness of the gun in it.

And still she did not move or speak or put out a hand toward the door. Because of that instinct toward dramatization which few can, even in the most sincere grief, entirely repress, she became an onlooker. She could think with numb amazement: this is exciting. And I am going to hear the truth as he would never tell it to me. Without excuse. . . .

For she knew—she seemed now always to have known—that Tommy would never accept responsibility for his failures or faults. "I'm no good at an office job"—"The boss has it in for me"—"If the guard hadn't been sucked they'd never have scored over me"—"It's the depression: people aren't buying things." That had been part of his endearing boyishness to her. And his voice had not changed: a little sulky, humorously resigned.

"Some guys are lucky. I never was. That kind of thing happens every day."

"A fact," Michael said, "of which I temporarily lost sight in my desire to be clever. It happens every day and with even more likeable men than you. You were tired of her and she wouldn't let you go."

"That's it," Tommy said coolly. "Was I to blame if I thought first it was her I was in love with? She was prettier than Valerie—and a regular wildcat. It didn't last."

"And did your discovery that though her name was Farley she was only a stepdaughter and had no money—"

"That didn't have so much to do with it. I never meant to marry her and I thought she was out for money and wouldn't take it seriously. But women change their minds and she was jealous of Valerie too. She had the nerve to say we weren't suited;

that Valerie would expect too much of me. But she's the kind that grows on you. Sure, I was glad she had some money. We'll be happier that way because I'll never make enough to have a good time."

"No, I don't suppose you will."

"What makes you say that? What's wrong with me?"

"You haven't any guts," Michael said briefly.

"And that from you! I never hit a guy when he wasn't looking. That's a dago trick. Though I must say you don't seem very nervous about—this."

He patted the gun. Michael said:

"Latin-Americans are at their best when facing a firing squad. Also, your definition of guts and mine differs slightly, I imagine. And I fail to see perhaps it's the fault of my mixed ancestry?—the delicate distinction between hitting a man when he isn't looking and shooting a woman who runs to you to be kissed."

"God damn you! You only guessed that—but do you think I like remembering it? I had to do it. She was going to cook my goose with Valerie if I didn't marry her. And she seemed to think it was mostly money that stood in the way of that. She'd about made up her mind old lady Putnam was writing those letters and she was going to shake her down. That was too risky; the old girl mightn't have paid though we didn't know then that she wouldn't have. Anyway, money or no money, I was fed up with Maxine!"

"But you do like money?"

"Why not? Traveling with fellows in college that had a lot and getting used to going places where you spend it. I took a chance. I knew someone might 've heard Maxine tell me I had to meet her that night. But I had to go."

"And you could explain that conversation so plausibly?"

"Sure. I knew I might be arrested but even if I was tried I thought I'd be acquitted. There wasn't any proof of anything between Maxine and me. I could wait for Val to drag those letters into it and for Bill to find my gun."

"I've wondered if you knew where it was."

"Oh, I knew it was missing from that satchel. I figured Bill or the kid knew something about it. But I didn't mention it. I didn't dare use it and even that early Maxine was—"

"Troublesome?" Michael said. "It wasn't so early, obviously. It is still May and people don't go fishing in April. So if Miss Farley had been troublesome at any time she probably was being so when you went on that trip. It would be so easy to buy a gun in some small town from a dealer who considers regulations regarding their sale a nuisance."

"You're a great little figurer, aren't you? I was in a hurry so I didn't realize till afterward I'd gone and got the same make as the one people knew I had. That was bad but it couldn't be helped. And did I pack it to the show with me Friday?"

"You hadn't arranged to meet Miss Farley when you left home. But Sullivan knew you could have left Valerie, gone home and got the gun without your landlady's seeing you and then met Miss Farley. And that night Valerie would have an alibi."

"Well, you don't think I'd let her be mixed up in it!"

"'I'm thinking there ain't many as noble as I is.' If she were suspected, you'd have your trouble for nothing. You did go home as soon as you left Valerie at Miss Orton's."

"That's why I let the O'Dea see me come back in the second time after I spotted her waiting for me when I went back for the gun. I did that so she wouldn't ask how I got in without her seeing me. She knew damn well she wouldn't miss me if I came in the front way. That meant she'd tell I came in late but it worked out better in the long run, didn't it?"

"It fitted your role of a victim of circumstances, taking no precautions because he is innocent."

"Well, I could have let them just find that gun in my room and see it wasn't the right one."

"But you also wanted to be clever."

"Well, didn't they concentrate on looking for it instead of another one? And when it turned up like it did that took the wind out of their sails. And I knew Val would tell about those letters. I couldn't because it was Maxine who told me. I hadn't counted on you. Not," Tommy added, "that it's going to matter. But were you really never in the Black Raven?"

"I never was."

"I guess you wouldn't bother to lie—now. We were never in there but two or three times and the bartender just remembered me once. He was looking at her. Why'd you start out to help Valerie when that meant helping me?"

"I thought anyone in whom she had faith must be innocent."

"Well, why did you change your mind? You might as well tell me: you won't tell anyone else."

"Them as dies will be the lucky ones," Michael drawled. "Would you mind not giving a bad imitation of a movie killer? I'm willing to oblige with the lecture. May I smoke? I assure you the cigarettes are nonexplosive. Try one yourself."

He moved the heavy decanter on the table at his elbow and pushed a box of cigarettes toward Tommy

"We let those letters confuse us," he said. "Miss Farley had certainly gone to the park to meet someone. She'd kept other assignations. The natural question was: with what man?

"One man she'd known suggested she was in love with someone. We paid little attention to that because everyone said she was shrewd, selfish, hard. But even that type of woman does fall in love. And is determined to have what she wants and not the kind to surrender without a struggle.

"That portrait Lutz painted of her was the picture of a woman in love. And at the same time ruthless and greedy. Talking to her hairdresser, Maxine Farley said: 'The first thing you know you fall for some fellow that's got nothing—and there you are.' Also that if you have money you can get anything you want. Speaking of herself and you, Mr. Howard—and thinking of you and Valerie.

"And we should not have disregarded that sketch she made. She made it while she was waiting until she could go to meet you. And she thought of a poem: am the dark cavalier: I am the last lover.' And: 'Death comes at last like a dark cavalier.' Well, you were, weren't you? The last lover

—Death. I imagine she even considered warning Valerie—but didn't.

"And why did she refuse to marry Dozier? Apparently that was the sort of marriage she would be glad to make. He was attractive, well-to-do and she liked him. But she refused him. And sometimes when a woman refuses a man she likes she is willing to tell him that she loves someone else.

"That conversation Gus overheard was ambiguous. Dozier might have been warning her against blackmail but when he said that she was a fool to refuse him and that nerve might not be enough he might have been warning her she didn't have any chance to take you away from Valerie.

"And the same thing is true of the warning he apparently had repeated in his letters. She answered that she always got what she wanted regardless of the feelings of others. And that just because he didn't scare he shouldn't suppose others wouldn't. She might have been referring to you. If she was enough in love with some man to refuse Dozier, who was it? Why not you, Mr. Howard? Your conversation with her Friday night might have meant just what Miss Nolan thought it did. You'd had plenty of time for an affair with her before you became engaged to Valerie.

"And Miss Farley was not credited with being sentimental and she loathed cheap jewelry but she kept a very cheap bangle bracelet that couldn't have anything but sentimental value. The sort of thing you might have given her; not at all the kind of thing she'd get from Dozier or Julian."

"Yeah, you mentioned that thing. And I got it."

"I think I've warned you more than once. I let you see Dozier's letter. You were lucky he died. Since he didn't bring the letter with him I doubt if he'd even heard of Miss Farley's death. But once he was here he could have told the police about you and Miss Farley."

"You're guessing again," Tommy said jeeringly. "I don't know if she told Dozier about us and neither do you."

"Six will get you ten she did. We'll never know that or if she told him of her plans regarding Mrs. Putnam. But she told you, which argued a greater degree of intimacy between you than you'd admitted."

"I told you that."

"You told me last night without knowing you did. You said: 'Since Maxine found out Mrs. Putnam was writing those letters so could someone else.' But, Mr. Howard, we'd agreed that since Mrs. Putnam could not have killed Miss Farley she did not know Mrs. Putnam was the letter writer. Valerie must have told you that since she told you everything. She stated that supposition very clearly only a few minutes after your slip and you let it stand. So you see Mrs. Putnam's letters did have their place in this.

"Because of them we knew Miss Farley was contemplating blackmail and that told us she wanted money. Then—why didn't she marry Dozier? And with that you start around the circle again."

"That's not proof; nothing you've said. But I know Sullivan will keep digging away, just like you said he would have with Winona Callendar. Only you aren't going to tell him that or what I've told you. Oh, I'm not being—dramatic," Tommy said. "Just using my common sense."

Michael's eyebrows went up. "You call that common sense? Is that gun the one you shot Miss Farley with?"

"Sure. There's lots of vacant lots and old flats that never get rented. That's why I didn't get home till twelve-fifteen that night. I went a good long way to hide it. I hadn't counted on meeting that guy near the park but— Well, I went back and got the gun where I'd hid it, tonight. Never mind about that. They won't ever trace it. They'll find you with it in your hand. And you let me in yourself! I suppose you were hoping I'd come?"

"Believe me—I hoped you wouldn't! There was always the possibility that even if you and Miss Farley were to meet in the park someone else knew that and got there first. I even baited another trap tonight but that bait was worthless. I left the back door open and you came by the front."

"Just as safe. Ring your doorbell downstairs outside and you'd be waiting for me up here. No more danger being seen and not half as suspicious as sneaking in at the back if anyone saw me. No one did. And it's plenty late now."

"So you're really going to kill me?" Michael's smile had never been more mocking or his eyes more blue. "'She comes, Mors, the indiscriminate madam! Already I am booted with marble—gauntleted with lead.'"

"You and your God-damned quotations!"

"You don't like them? 'Think fast, Captain, think fast.' There must be powder burns, you know, to make my suicide convincing. Have you ever noticed if I'm right or left handed or perhaps ambidextrous?" He moved the decanter again, pulling the cigarette box toward him. "And are you certain you can arrange my hand about the gun in exactly the right grip?"

"And then," Valerie said, "will you kill me too? I'm sorry to be—to be dramatic, Michael," she added. "But he might have fired quickly. Though you were going to throw that decanter at him, weren't you? He wouldn't know that. And I don't think he'd have had the—the guts to shoot. But he might have done it before he lost his nerve and—I'm sorry. My tongue goes on and on as if it didn't have any connection with me."

"Valerie, it was on your account. I'd have made you happy! Honestly, I—"

"Perhaps you would have for a while. But you very likely would have gotten tired of me. Especially if I failed to admire you all the time. And you'd killed one woman you were tired of so why not another? I imagine Michael thought of that and decided he wouldn't risk it."

"I wouldn't have! Everything would have been all right."

Valerie's eyes dwelt briefly on Tommy's face. "You look just the same," she said thoughtfully. "Like someone I met somewhere and— That's trite, isn't it? I'm— Please don't come any closer to me."

Tommy's hands dropped to his sides. He tossed the gun into a chair. "You win," he said to Michael. "I suppose you had anyway. You made me wonder if I wouldn't bungle the whole thing."

"Did you notice," Michael said, "that my car is parked before the house?" He threw a key toward Tommy and his hand flashed up automatically to catch it. "Take the gun: our story will be that you used it to get the car key from me and make your escape."

"Is that all?"

"Yes. No—for God's sake don't ever let them bring you back here— You at least believe you love her."

"So prove it? Don't worry, I'll never see the inside of a jail again—or a courtroom. Well, I'm on my way. In case Sullivan would like to know I got this gun at a little dump called Red River. No extra charge for the information. . . ."

In the doorway he turned; began: "Valerie, I didn't know it would turn out like this."

But Valerie did not look up. It was Michael who answered him, with something both of understanding and finality in his voice.

"You haven't any time to waste. *Que le vaya bien, amigo!* Good luck."

"The same to you," said Tommy. "And all of it bad."

CHAPTER TWENTY-FIVE
"LIKE A WELL-CONDUCTED DAMSEL"

Patricia, sitting on Valerie's bed, remarked:

"I certainly don't know where you get your secretive nature. Not from me, I'm sure. You might have confided in me. Hiding up there in Mr. Dundas' apartment last night to hear what Tommy would say to him. Well, and working all the time to catch him when you were pretending to be in love with him."

"That story was for the newspapers, Mother."

"You mean it wasn't true? But then why—"

"Michael thought it would make things easier for me and Inspector Sullivan agreed to believe it."

"Then you really did think all the time that Tommy wasn't guilty? Well, you know I warned you. And you wouldn't listen to me but I always saw him for just what he was."

Valerie turned and looked at her mother, seeking something she had never found in her. And now, for all time, she gave up hoping that someday she

would catch the least gleam of sympathy or solic-
itude in Patricia's shallow eyes. She thought: people don't change, not at her age, so why should I
expect her to? and took a yellow dinner dress from
her closet. Patricia sat protestingly erect on the bed.

"Valerie, you aren't going out! The way Mr.
Dundas brought you down last night and made
Geneva put you to bed and then called the police.
Of course *he* couldn't take time to talk. But you've
had all day. I know it upset you when they brought
the news Tommy's—I mean Mr. Dundas'—car had
gone off the Santa Cruz road. But I do think it's
time you were sensible. Only however you really
feel, for you to go out tonight doesn't look just
right."

"Doesn't it?" Valerie settled the brown velvet
flower at her waist, picked up wrap and evening
purse. "I'm sorry you think so, Mother. Good
night. . . ."

The sun had penetrated the fog for only a few
hours that day and the night was cold. Michael
had kindled a fire and was sitting before it without other lights. He turned them on when Valerie
was in the living room, walked away from her and
stood leaning his elbows on the mantelpiece.

"Please," Valerie said, "look at me. You didn't
talk to me at all last night. I can understand that
but— Michael, did you think I'd blame you?"

"No. But perhaps that you wouldn't care to see me again."

"But you're the only one who understands. We're still friends. That's why I'm asking you to take me somewhere to dance tonight. I'm not—not callous." Briefly Valerie's lips quivered. "But let people see me tonight and say: well, this business isn't bothering her. I prefer that. And you understand that too, don't you?"

"Yes. Yes, Charlotte, I do."

"Charlotte?"

"'Charlotte, when she saw her lover, Borne before her on a shutter; Like a well-conducted damsel, Went on cutting bread and butter—'"

"Michael!" But he was not smiling and finally it was Valerie who laughed. "You see, I can," she said. And, stoically: "I'll get over it. Do—do you think he went off the road on purpose?"

"Think he did, for your sake."

"I asked what *you* thought!"

"Valerie—I don't know! Certainly he must have driven recklessly and unconsciously, at least, was not taking any precautions. You know that road to Santa Cruz. At night, if you take your eyes off the white lines that guide you around the curves—"

"It would be easy to go over the bank. In other words, a gamble. Yes, he'd be able to do it that way. You don't mind if we tie up the loose ends, do you?"

"No. There's one that Julian tied. He told me he had been more worried than he would admit about his sister. That she'd had what he called 'an unfortunate love affair' as a girl, gave the man up and then had a very bad nervous breakdown. She has admitted to him that some of the letters she received referred to those facts. And she suspected Mrs. Putnam was writing them but— Well, I was entirely mistaken about her. She is evidently just the helpless maiden lady she seems to be."

"I always thought she was," Valerie said inattentively. "Michael, there is still one thing. You never really answered Tommy when he asked you. Why did you want to help me in the beginning?"

"I hoped you wouldn't ask that. And I'd rather not answer—but I will." He laid his hands lightly on her shoulders. "'She should never have looked at me if she meant I should not love her,'" he said softly. "You looked at me. . . . Hotel strike notwithstanding, we'll find somewhere to dance. And would you mind removing that God-awful flower from your dress? I'll buy you fresh ones and brown doesn't do a thing for that shade of yellow."

COACHWHIP PUBLICATIONS
CoachwhipBooks.com

VIRGINIA RATH

DEATH AT
DAYTON'S FOLLY

COACHWHIP PUBLICATIONS
CoachwhipBooks.com

MURDER ON
THE DAY OF
JUDGMENT

VIRGINIA RATH

COACHWHIP PUBLICATIONS
COACHWHIPBOOKS.COM

VIRGINIA RATH

THE ANGER
OF THE BELLS

COACHWHIP PUBLICATIONS
CoachwhipBooks.com

MURDER

with a theme song

VIRGINIA RATH

COACHWHIP PUBLICATIONS
COACHWHIPBOOKS.COM

DEATH OF A
LUCKY LADY

VIRGINIA RATH

COACHWHIP PUBLICATIONS
CoachwhipBooks.com

ANONYMOUS FOOTSTEPS | JOHN. M. O'CONNOR

COACHWHIP PUBLICATIONS
CoachwhipBooks.com

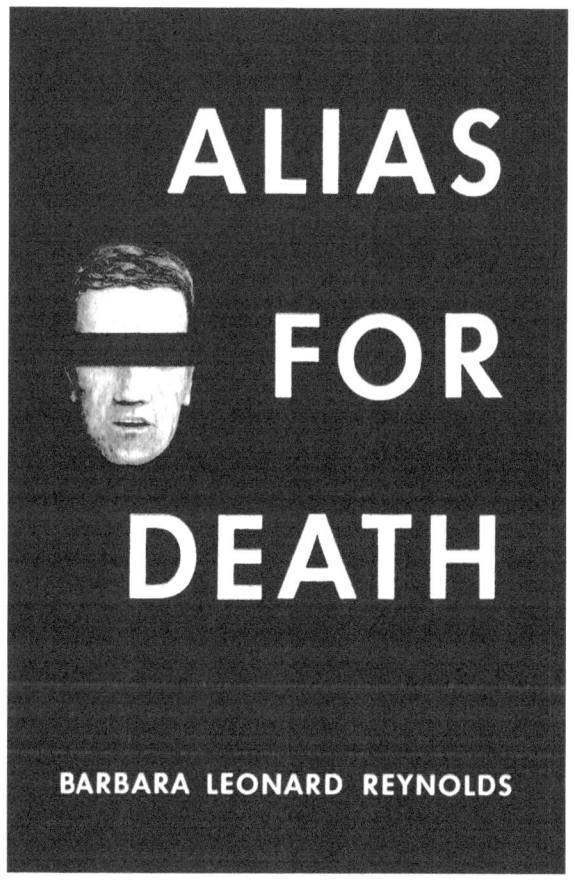

ALIAS FOR DEATH

BARBARA LEONARD REYNOLDS

ANITA BOUTELL

DEATH BRINGS
A STORKE

CRADLED
IN FEAR

COACHWHIP PUBLICATIONS
CoachwhipBooks.com

TWISTS AND TURNS

TALES OF MYSTERY, ADVENTURE,
CRIME, AND HUMOR BY
BERNARD CAPES